BAD GIRLS
NEVER
SAY DIE

Also by Jennifer Mathieu

BAD GIRLS NEVER SAY DIE

JENNIFER MATHIEU

HODDER

HODDER CHILDREN'S BOOKS

First published in Great Britain in 2021 by Hodder and Stoughton
First published in the USA in 2021 by Roaring Brook Press

1 3 5 7 9 10 8 6 4 2

Text copyright © Jennifer Mathieu, 2021

The moral rights of the author have been asserted.

A CIP catalogue record for this book is available from the British Library.

ISBN 978 1 444 96489 9

Typeset in Perpetua by Avon DataSet Ltd,
Arden Court, Alcester, Warwickshire

Printed and bound in Great Britain by Clays Ltd, Elcograf S.p.A.

The paper and board used in this book are made from wood from responsible sources.

Hodder Children's Books
An imprint of Hachette Children's Group
Part of Hodder and Stoughton
Carmelite House
50 Victoria Embankment
London EC4Y 0DZ

An Hachette UK Company
www.hachette.co.uk

www.hachettechildrens.co.uk

For every bad girl – past, present, and future

AUTHOR'S NOTE

Many locations mentioned in this novel are based on real places that exist – or once existed – in my hometown of Houston, including Glenwood Cemetery, Winkler Drive-In, Foley's, Clayton Homes, River Oaks, the Jive Hive, the Shamrock Hotel, the Domed Stadium (better known later as the Astrodome), Playland Park, and others.

The sit-in by students from Texas Southern University at the lunch counter of Mading's Drugs took place on March 5, 1960, and was one of several sit-ins held by students from TSU in the city of Houston in an attempt to challenge segregation. The 1998 documentary *The Strange Demise of Jim Crow* is an excellent resource for learning more about this period in Houston's history. The word *Negro* is used in this novel, as this was common usage in 1964 and the term preferred by civil rights leaders of the time period. With the rise of the Black Power movement in the mid- to late sixties, the term *Black* gained in popularity.

The Gainesville State School for Girls was a real place for female juvenile offenders in the state of Texas. It opened in 1913 and still exists today, although it became an all-male facility in 1988.

While it was my attempt to set this novel as realistically as possible in my beloved Houston, some geographic elements and school names have been changed.

If you or someone you know needs information about sexual assault, please call the National Sexual Assault Hotline operated by RAINN (Rape, Abuse & Incest National Network) at 1-800-656-HOPE. You can also go to rainn.org for more information or to use the online hotline. If you live in the UK or outside of the US, please find further resources and contact details toward the end of this book.

HOUSTON
1964

We're the sort of girls mothers warn their daughters about.

Don't turn out like that trash.

We're the sort teachers whisper about and boys dream about – even the boys who won't give us the time of day in the cafeteria or at a school dance.

Not that we're the sort of girls who go to many school dances.

So what sort are we?

The sort of girls who draw fake moles on our faces with eyeliner pencils we lift from Woolworth's and the sort who laugh too loud when we're not supposed to and the sort who are so bad that some of us have been sent away to places where bad girls go.

Usually we return even worse.

When I was little and wore starched secondhand dresses to elementary school and listened to Miss Carter as she taught us the ABCs, probably no one thought I'd grow up to become a bad girl. But I became one anyway. Being a bad girl can break your heart over and over, and when I think about what happened to me and my friends last fall, sometimes my heart cracks in pieces all over again, and I wonder if I'll find the strength to put it together one more time.

But the truth is if I'd never become a bad girl, I never would have met Diane. And I never would have learned the honest truth that sometimes bad girls are the best friends a girl could ever have.

CHAPTER

1

It's Connie's idea to go to the drive-in. We all say yes, of course. After all, it's Saturday night and she just got home after three months at the state school for girls up in Gainesville. Three months we've spent throwing parties and cutting classes and missing Connie. So the way I see it, she has the right to decide how we spend her first night of freedom. And anyway, when it comes to what we do, Connie's always boss.

'It's so nice to be back in the real world,' she tells us as we share cigarettes by the concession booth. A balding manager with sweat stains all over his white T-shirt comes out more than once to tell us to move along. We ignore him as usual.

'Well, this place is real something, that's for sure,' Juanita answers, tucking her black hair behind her ear and motioning to the weed patches and dirt surrounding us at the Winkler Drive-In. Her words are followed by a sharp laugh. Connie grins back at her, her red lipstick and bottle-blond hair flashing bright under the glare of the lamplights above us and the headlights nearby. I glance back at the screen behind me, not even sure I know what picture this is. I should probably figure it out in case Mama asks too many questions when I get home.

'So it was that bad, huh?' I ask, in awe of Connie, like always.

I tug my black cardigan closer around me. It's cold for Houston in October, and I shiver just a little.

'Real bad,' Connie answers, relishing the chance to spill the details for the tenth time. 'We had to be in bed with the lights off by nine thirty, and they hardly ever let us smoke. But I came off like an angel compared to some of the girls there.'

Now it's Sunny's turn to laugh even louder than Juanita. As she pulls out a compact to check her lipstick, Sunny insists this couldn't be true – Connie is legendary at Eastside High, after all. But then our long-lost leader amuses us with a story about girls who sniffed nail polish remover for a buzz and cut the screens at night to try and sneak out. They got caught and sent to solitary confinement.

'I wasn't going to mess around like that for some lousy buzz off nail polish remover,' says Connie, flashing us a proud smile. 'I just played it cool until I could get home to my girls.'

Her girls. Us. Connie, Sunny, Juanita, and me, Evie, the youngest and the only sophomore in the bunch. In my mind we're four corners of a tiny square, drawn close to protect ourselves from the rest of the world. They're all juniors, and Connie's old enough to be a senior on account of having been held back, but they accept me because I'm the sort of girl who never breaks a promise and never rats out a friend.

'Let's go see who else is around,' Connie decides, and the rest of us troop after her to the back end of the lot, where most of the kids we hang out with park their cars, rusted-out jalopies that are all we can afford. Connie slides up near Sunny, and soon all of us are linked arm in arm. Without Connie around, Juanita, Sunny, and me haven't felt as tight. We still hang out and cut class together, sure, but it's been like a ship without a captain. Not that I've ever been on a ship. Or anywhere a ship would sail to, for that matter.

But now Connie's back, and she leads us with sure steps, her blond curls bobbing like they're as certain of themselves as she is of herself. As we make our way over, my brown eyes take in all the different crowds that gather at Winkler's on a Saturday night – the middle-class kids with their matching sweater sets from Foley's and the no-account hoods with their leather jackets and permanent scowls and the tired moms and dads with their whiny toddlers covered in ice cream stains who just wanted a night out and couldn't find a babysitter.

Only there's one group that sometimes shows up at Winkler's that really bugs me, and that's the crowd from River Oaks High. They could head out to ritzier spots like the Majestic or the Loew's downtown, or they could steal vodka from their daddies' liquor cabinets while their parents are in Europe or at the club, but no. They choose to slum it at

Winkler's, miles away from their mansions and their maids and their mint-condition convertibles.

It's like they do it to remind the rest of us they've got someplace better to be. Like they do it to remind girls like me that we're stuck here while they're just passing through. Or maybe they do it to start fights that they'll never get blamed for because the fuzz believe them over our crowd every single time.

'Check out those tea sippers,' Sunny mutters, reading my mind. She nods toward a crowd of River Oaks girls drinking Cokes and hanging off some sporty boys like they'd collapse into a pile of money without the support. The whole crowd is gathered around two Mustangs parked side by side, one black, one midnight blue. Fancy. It's hard to believe this is some kid's first car at sixteen, and it's nicer than anything I'll probably ever set foot in.

'Why don't they stay in River Oaks where they belong?' Connie says, and loud, too, so she'll be heard.

'Bitch,' one of the boys yells back. It's a sea of khakis and buzz cuts and madras, but it's clear the voice belongs to a blond boy with the build of a football player, all broad shoulders and puffed-out chest. Our gazes lock for just a moment, and he sneers, enjoying himself. I feel a chill I know isn't just from the cool autumn air.

'Drop dead twice,' Connie hollers back at him, not skipping a beat. He scowls at us, and a chorus of angry voices rises up, but not one of the boys makes a move. Not that Connie isn't ready if one does. Juanita and Sunny laugh out loud, but I just want to get away from this snarling pack. We keep moving, and I wonder if I'll ever have half the guts that Connie Treadway has.

We find our crowd of kids by the final row of cars, and soon we're ducking into smoke-filled back seats and taking little sips of Four Roses and Schlitz and trading gossip. I drink enough to make my cheeks flush but not so much the room feels like it's spinning. Mama and Grandma will already be angry at me for taking off tonight without saying where I was going, so the last thing I need is to come home drunk again. Juanita and the girls got me so blitzed on my fifteenth birthday six months ago I could barely walk, and after that I wasn't allowed to leave the house for ages.

Sunny floats away with her sometimes-boyfriend, Ray Swanson, into the back seat of Ray's car, parked in the shadows under some trees. I don't like him, honestly, because he's always acting like Sunny's his property, like his leather jacket or something. But he's probably one of the cutest boys in our crowd, second only to Connie's twin brother, Johnny, who is all dark eyes and lean muscles and cheekbones almost too pretty for a boy. But only just. Sometimes in bed under the covers, I've imagined what it would be like to kiss him, but he would never look at me twice. I'm sure to him, I'm just a kid.

Johnny's here tonight, too. I spotted him the moment we arrived, brooding sullenly by the chain-link fence bordering Winkler's, smoking and staring out over the crowd. His sister is acting the total opposite, quickly making herself the center of the party.

'It's so good to be *home*,' Connie says, over and over again, jumping from group to group, bouncy and grinning, really emphasizing the word *home*. I'm pretty sure she's on her way to getting real loaded, but she deserves to let loose tonight of all nights. For Connie, home is here with all of us. All the kids who make the cops grimace and the teachers nervous.

No one's really watching the picture, and I give up trying to follow the plot. I spy Juanita giggling with a few other girls we know. It's Juanita I'm closest to, really, but sometimes I can't help but wonder if that's only because we're next-door neighbors and she sees me as a younger-cousin type to look out for. When I started tagging along with her about a year ago, right around the time my older sister, Cheryl, left home, Juanita never said I couldn't join in. When it's just her and me, it's all right, but when it's the whole crowd, I worry I don't fit in sometimes. Like I'm really more of a pet or a mascot or one mistake away from being declared not tuff enough. Like if I'm not careful, I might disappear into nothing, leaving only traces of cigarette smoke and Aqua Net.

'I'm gonna go get some popcorn,' I mutter to no one in particular, turning back to the concession booth.

'Get me some, will ya, Evie?' Connie yells to me. 'I'll pay you back later, I swear!'

I smile at Connie's false promise and head off through the crowd. The crisp air hits my lungs and I breathe it in, enjoying the chill against the warmth of the booze. I'm glad that Connie is home at last and everything is back the way it should be. And I'm glad it's a Saturday night and I'm out at Winkler's with the tuffest kids in the neighborhood. The smile stays on my face as I walk off to buy my popcorn, the happy shouts of the others fading behind me.

CHAPTER

2

I approach the concession stand, digging into my pocket for the few coins I got babysitting the Rodriguez kids down the street. Mrs Rodriguez is the only mom in the neighborhood who'll hire me, but that's only because she can't afford to be all that choosy. I might have a reputation for running with the wrong crowd, but I'm good to those Rodriguez kids. I even help Nancy with her homework, which is sort of funny considering I don't really bother with homework of my own.

The thought makes me smile, until I reach the stand, where, of course, a line has formed. The scent of buttery popcorn floats over me, making my mouth water, even though I know Winkler's popcorn always smells better than it tastes.

'Isn't it *wild* that she would dare to show her face here?'

'It really is, Vickie. Some people just don't know when they should stay home.'

The voices startle me out of my popcorn dreams. Girl voices. Judgmental voices. And without even knowing who they belong to, I understand these voices have more than a few coins from a babysitting job in their pockets. Honeyed and smooth, but not too sweet.

Rich voices.

'She looks like hell if you ask me.'

'She really does.'

'Always thought she looked so cute in pink, didn't she?'

For a second I think they're talking about me, but I'm not wearing pink, so they can't be. Then I spot the voices and their target, too. Two girls from the tea-sipper crowd, the River Oaks bunch, are huddled off to the side of the concession stand, sipping sodas and staring down a pale auburn-haired girl in a light pink dress and pink cardigan ahead of me in line. The rich girls spit their poison nice and loud, so everyone hears, but it's clear from what they're saying who the words are really meant for.

Auburn-haired girl turns toward them, her mouth set in a firm line. She keeps her eyes fixed on the ground, but from the way her cheeks are flushing to match the color of her hair, I know she can hear them. They know, too, because they smirk in between every nasty line they toss in her direction.

I light a cigarette and watch. Normally, I wouldn't get involved in some beef between a couple of girls from the right part of town, but then I realize Miss Auburn Hair looks familiar. Her name is Donna or Diane something-or-other, and she started at Eastside High this fall, just a few weeks ago.

11

She doesn't exactly fit in, that's for sure, and her fancy clothes and brand-new school supplies mark her as more of a River Oaks girl than anyone from our neighborhood. She carries herself that way, too. Sort of snooty, I guess. Some of our crowd's even given her a hard time in the cafeteria, bumping into her on purpose, giving her rude looks. That kind of thing. It's just what they do sometimes to kids who think they're better than us. I never have the guts to join in, but I sure wouldn't ever stop them.

Now, watching this girl's eyes start to glass over with tears, I almost feel guilty about that. This girl is already getting it pretty bad from her own crowd as it is.

'She should be ashamed to show her face around here,' the one named Vickie says. 'After everything she did. Look, here comes Betty. She won't even believe it.'

At this a short brunette with apple cheeks appears among her fellow tea sippers, and I hear Miss Auburn gasp in surprise at the sight of her. The brunette takes in what's happening with one quick glance, and I can tell she's trying to bury her first reaction and quick, too. She opens her mouth to say something to Miss Auburn, then snaps it closed almost as fast.

'Let's leave,' insists the brunette, her eyes never straying from this girl in front of me who's on the verge of tears. 'Let's just leave her alone. Anyway, the boys are waiting for us.' The brunette's voice quavers a bit when she says this.

A single tear falls down Miss Auburn's cheek.

'Well, anyway,' says Vickie, turning to go, 'I'm glad she's moved out of our neighborhood and into this trashy one.' She waits a beat, then spits out, 'Because she's trash.'

When my lit cigarette hits Vickie in the arm, sending bright red embers flying, she yelps, then turns and stares me down.

'That was you, wasn't it?' she screams, her face scowled tight. 'You did that on purpose! What is wrong with you?' Her friends' mouths are open wide like fish, their eyes full of shock.

'Why don't the three of you go bother someone else?' I say. 'Or better yet, you can stay put while I get my friends. I'm sure they'd love to meet you.' My kohl-lined eyes don't waver from staring them down, and my mouth forms a sneer I've been practicing in my bedroom mirror since last summer. But my heart is thumping hard.

Still, I'm enough to send those prissy girls racing, and Donna-maybe-Diane turns around totally to face me, gratitude all over her tearstained face. That's how I know she definitely isn't from this neighborhood. The kids I run with would rather die than let anyone see that someone got under their skin that bad.

'Thank you so much,' she says. 'I really appreciate that.' Her voice sounds rich, too, like summer camps and European vacations. But it's softer than Vickie's. Nicer.

'It's nothing,' I say, glancing past her toward the concession stand window, where a man with a pockmarked face is waiting, annoyed, to take an order. 'You're next.' I feel bad for this girl, but she's not exactly the type I could bring back to my group of friends.

'I'm not hungry all of a sudden. But thanks again.' She sniffs, wipes at her face, and slips off into the crowd. Hopefully she's heading home. A girl like that shouldn't be at a place like Winkler's alone if she can't handle a few nasty tea sippers.

I get my popcorn and Connie's, too, plus a Dr Pepper, then head back. Connie devours hers while she continues to hold court, retelling her stories from the state school, adding a little extra to them with each telling. By the time the second picture in the double feature starts, Connie has the whole crowd convinced that she started a prisoner rebellion at Gainesville and they locked up the warden in a broom closet. And she hasn't stopped pulling long swigs off a bottle of Four Roses, either.

'Where's my brother, anyway?' Connie yells. 'He needs to be hearing about everything I've suffered through while he got to stay around here and do whatever he wanted. Boys have it so easy. They never get in trouble as much as girls do.'

'Boys are lucky that way,' says Sunny, who's finally emerged out of the back seat of Ray Swanson's car along with Ray. Her honey-blond hair is mussed and her lipstick is smeared.

'I think girls get lucky, too, sometimes,' says Ray, elbowing Sunny. Sunny rolls her eyes as Dwight Hardaway and Butch

14

Thompson, hanging out nearby, laugh at Ray's remark. I swear, the two of them seem to exist solely to cheer Ray on when he cracks some dumb line.

'Why so quiet, Evie?' Ray says, noticing me. 'Never gotten lucky?'

My cheeks flush just like that poor girl's at the concession stand, and I wish I weren't the center of attention.

'Leave her alone, Ray,' Sunny says, giving him a playful push. 'She's just fifteen.'

Ray says something about how Sunny shouldn't get fresh with him and also that he remembers *her* at fifteen, and there are more screams and laughter. I know I have to come back with something and quick, too. Otherwise they'll just keep going at me.

'Jesus, Ray, we get it,' I say. 'You're a real dynamite in the sack.' And even though it comes out just right and everybody laughs, part of me hopes Grandma doesn't get telegrams from God alerting her to my using the Lord's name in vain. They are awfully close.

I drain my Dr Pepper through the red-and-white straw to a satisfying slurp as Connie starts her one-woman act back up. Then I spot Johnny again, appearing from near the concession stand. He doesn't look any happier than the last time I spotted him skulking near the fence line, but my heart picks up its pace. His big eyes are such a lovely chocolate brown they can only be described as delicious, and he's so tall that if I ever got the chance to kiss him, I'd have to stand on my tiptoes to do it. Not that I'd ever have the chance, of course.

'Hey, Connie, there's that brother of yours,' I say.

Connie squints and spies Johnny, then stumbles for a minute. Someone needs to cut her off and soon.

'There's my brother, all right. He's been acting like a real candy-ass all night. What's he got to be so sulky about, anyway – I'm the one who's been locked up for ages!' She burps and laughs at herself. 'Hey, brother!' she shouts at top volume. 'Come here!'

Johnny looks up and sees his sister, shoves his hands into his pockets, and heads over. A lock of his greased-up, jet-black hair falls into his face as he moves, and he tosses his head to the side until it flips out of his eyes. He's so tuff it's enough to make a girl dizzy.

'Hey, brother!' she yells again as he arrives before giving him a gentle push on the chest with both hands. 'Didja miss me?' She's slurring her words.

'Hey, Connie, maybe you've celebrated enough tonight, huh?' he asks, then glances at me. There are small purple moons underneath his dark eyes, and I wonder why. There's always been something about Johnny that's mysterious. Something that reminds me a little of George, my second-favorite Beatle.

'Hey, Evie, how much did she have to drink anyway?' Johnny asks.

I'm momentarily mute at the fact that he knows my name, then manage to answer, 'I'm not sure. But it seems like a lot.' Not exactly helpful, I realize. I wonder if I'll ever be able to speak to boys.

'Yeah, it seems like a lot,' he echoes, shaking his head. 'Connie, hey. Maybe we should get you home?' His voice is soft and tender.

Connie sticks her tongue out at her brother and crosses her arms defiantly in front of her. A few of the kids nearby laugh at the sight. 'I don't wanna go home!' she says, stomping her foot. 'I wanna stay here. With you and my friends. Even if *you* don't want to hang out because you're so sad and you won't even let me say why!' She draws two fists up to her eyes and mimics a little child's tears, rubbing her hands into her face. Her voice slips into slurry baby talk.

'I'm Johnny,' she starts, 'and I'm a widdle baby who's so *sad* because—'

'Connie!' Johnny interrupts, putting his arm around her and tugging her away. 'Cut it out!'

Connie protests as Johnny walks her off into the darkness, and I spy her stumble a few times before he helps her stand back up.

'Jesus,' says Ray, 'what the hell was that about?'

'Who knows,' says Sunny, and we catch eyes. With Connie and Johnny, anything is possible. The one thing that's certain is that the two of them will always look out for each other with ferocious loyalty. After all, they don't have much of anyone else to look after them. Their mom drinks too much and their dad is sort of rough with them, and that's on a decent day. No wonder Connie ran away.

After Johnny and Connie leave, things grow quiet for a moment, but the party atmosphere picks up again before long, and I realize I have to go to the bathroom. I think about asking Sunny or Juanita to go with me, but suddenly I feel like being alone. Maybe the excitement from earlier in the night is starting to wear off. Or maybe I'm just tired of worrying about saying or doing the wrong thing in front of everyone. I don't tell anyone I'm leaving, and nobody seems to notice.

As my shoes crunch over the gravel and my crowd's voices fall farther into the distance, something unusual happens. The hair on my arms stands up totally straight, and I shiver just a little bit. It's enough that I pause in my steps for the smallest moment. Then a single sentence marches through my mind, demanding attention.

Turn around and go home, Evie.

I frown and keep walking, brushing it aside. I know my mother would call it woman's intuition. The same woman's intuition that told her when I was three years old that my father wasn't coming back from the corner store. The same intuition that told her that her manager at the diner where she used to wait tables was still married even when he swore up and down that he was as single as they come.

18

'Every woman has a little warning system in place,' she's said to me. 'And you have to pay attention to it.'

I love my mother, but I think that's ridiculous. And anyway, if woman's intuition was real, wouldn't she have gotten some warning not to marry my no-account father in the first place? And if a woman's intuition was worth anything, wouldn't being a girl be just a little bit easier instead of harder, like Connie always says it is?

So I just keep walking, wondering why I can't manage to shake off whatever it is that's making me feel so out of sorts.

CHAPTER

3

The Washrooms at Winkler's are in a cinder-block building way at the back of the property line. Far away from everything else, it sits against a sorry-looking chain-link fence that serves as a not-so-secret entrance for teenagers who don't want to pay to get in. Painted a drab gray color and framed by a ring of overgrown weeds, it greets you with a nasty smell several feet before you actually arrive at the twin doors that read GUYS and DOLLS. I approach, wrinkling up my nose, and push the DOLLS door open. Two girls who are a little younger than me are washing their hands. Flannel skirts, matching cardigans. Bright eyes and clean fingernails. They remind me of the girls I used to hang out with, back before I started running with Juanita and the others. Back before I realized what life could be like when you make friends with girls like Connie Treadway. When *these* girls spot me, one of them gasps a little bit, and the two of them hurry on out of there.

After they leave, I mutter, 'I don't bite, you know.' Less so to the girls than to my reflection in the smudged mirror. It wouldn't bother Connie to run off girls like that, but for some reason it doesn't make me feel too hot.

Maybe it's those girls who make me feel prickly. Or maybe Ray's joking around earlier has gotten to me. Maybe it's the realization that a boy like Johnny Treadway will probably never look twice at a girl like me. Whatever the reason, I'm glad the bathroom is empty, and I linger alone, taking a few extra minutes to read the graffiti. Lipstick hearts with initials smeared inside them next to corny doodles and pencil scratchings that say stuff like *Principal Hawkins can get bent*. I wash my hands and straighten myself up in the mirror, and when I push open the door to head outside, the first thing I spot is a boy in khakis and a madras shirt. A River Oaks boy. He's leering and cocksure, standing there against the back fence with a wolfish grin that slices across his all-American face.

A wave of nausea instantly takes hold. My mind skates over my mother's warning, but it's too late for that now. This boy's face promises me nothing good. I know this with certainty, somehow. But I also know with just as much certainty that I don't have an easy way out. In the middle of my panic, I seize on where I've seen this face before. Just an hour or so earlier, when the girls and I walked past him and his crowd. He's the one who called Connie a bitch.

'Hey,' says All-American. I realize he's got a beer bottle in

21

one hand, and he takes a long pull before throwing it casually against the chain-link fence, where it explodes with a smash. 'I recognize you. You told me and my friends to drop dead twice.' Then, with fury laced through it, he spits out, '*Trash*.'

'What do you want?' I manage. I start to move past him and he lurches in front of me, blocking my way.

'I never said anything to you,' I say, hoping I sound tough and bored. 'You're thinking about someone else.' Even though I don't tell him her name, there's a wince of remorse when I mention Connie, but I'm desperate. She and I don't look anything alike. He must be so drunk.

'You don't know what I'm thinking,' he says. His cheeks are ruddy and mottled, his blond buzz cut so sharp I could nick myself on it. 'You probably don't want to know.' He barks out a sick laugh.

Oh God.

My stomach careens and my heart is hammering so hard it hurts. My eyes shoot beyond this boy who won't let me pass, and I spy the concession stand and the field of cars and the giant, luminescent screen where some dumb blond actress is dancing around in a yellow polka-dot bikini. I can hear the occasional laugh and shout. I could count headlights. It's all just a few hundred yards away, but it's like I'm viewing it through a film or a fog.

He laughs again, a soft, low laugh. He's pleased with himself.

What do mean, drunk boys like this want? I know. All girls do. Somewhere along the way, the answer to that question seeps into us until we can't remember a time when we didn't know it.

My stomach twists again. My body goes numb.

'Someone's gonna come by any minute,' I manage, swallowing hard, setting my mouth into a thin line, 'so you might as well let me go.'

'Well, maybe . . .' he drawls, relishing the words, 'maybe I only *need* a minute.'

It all happens so fast. He's behind me, his hands on me, one tight around my torso, the other – calloused and rough – pressed hard against my mouth to muffle any attempt at a scream. I'm being dragged now to the edge of the drive-in's property, well behind the washroom building, to a cluster of overgrown bushes and trees. I can hear my feet kicking up gravel, so I know my body is trying to fight back even as my mind is frozen. I turn my head frantically as much as I can manage, catching a glimpse of the other side of the chain-link fence, where warehouses and a bottling factory sit, big metal husks of buildings that are empty and quiet under the light of the moon.

No one would hear me scream even if I could.

Bam! Suddenly I'm down on the ground, on my back, the result of a violent throw. Pain sears through me as gravel digs into my skull, and white lightning cuts through my vision.

A wave of nausea swells up inside me as this monster pins me down, one knee pressed so hard into my chest I can barely breathe – just enough to take in the stench of cheap beer. He cackles as he starts to unbuckle his belt.

This is all really happening. The words loop over and over in my mind. I squeeze my eyes shut and try my best to squirm out from under him, push him off me, but it's like trying to stop an approaching thunderstorm. Impossible. And each attempt to fight back only pleases him more.

'This is what you get for being cute,' he snarls, his face twisted in rage. He lifts his knee off me at last and as I gasp for air, he grabs me by both shoulders and slams me against the ground again.

Inky darkness starts to swirl in front of my eyes. I realize I'm going to pass out, and the feeling that comes along with that understanding is relief. But then, out of the corner of my consciousness, I hear something.

'What are you doing to her?' a female voice says, but I never get an answer because at that very moment I slide into blackness.

4

Someone is close to me. Shaking me gently.

'Wake up. Please wake up.'

I manage to open my eyes, but it's almost impossible to focus. I see a shadow of a figure next to me in a crouched position. My head is pounding, and my right hand instinctively touches the pulsing pain just above my neck. When I pull it back, my fingers are covered in a warm wetness.

'Oh my God, you're bleeding,' says the figure. 'Here, sit up. Put pressure on it.'

With the help of this hazy stranger, I drag myself into a seated position and obediently fumble for the soft fabric that's being pressed onto the back of my head – someone's sweater?

'That's it,' says the girl's voice. It's shaking ever so slightly. 'Just keep pressing, all right? Do you understand me?'

I blink hard once, then twice. At last, I start to make out just who is huddled next to me.

When my eyes finally focus and my mind catches up with

what I'm seeing, I'm almost certain I have to be dreaming. Because crouching there next to me, her left hand cradling my head like a baby's, is the same girl in pink who I defended earlier at the concession stand.

'I think you should stand up now. All right, Evie?' she says. 'It is Evie, right?'

I manage to nod, then wince.

'My name is Diane,' she tells me.

Not Donna. Diane.

Diane's face is illuminated by the streetlamps surrounding the perimeter of Winkler's, her cherry-red bow lips in stark contrast to her porcelain face. She winces along with me as she helps me up. It's then that I notice a splatter of bright red like an explosion of fireworks on the front of her soft pink dress. My clumsy mind tries to figure out what it could be, but it struggles to accept that my first guess could be true.

'Are you all right?' Diane asks.

It's then that I see him, and I lean forward, the beginnings of a scream starting to explode out of my sandpapered throat.

'Stop,' Diane says, her voice a whisper but still so firm that I have no choice but to listen and shut up. 'Don't make a sound,' she continues, one arm tight around my waist, the other gripping my forearm. 'Listen to me. Don't even look over there again.'

I may be able to muffle a scream, but I can't obey Diane's last command. I gaze back at the crumpled figure, turned face-first into the chain-link fence at the edge of the drive-in's property line. I take in his dust-covered khaki slacks and a rust-colored stain the shape of some unknowable country on a map blooming on the side of his torso. I know, immediately and with certainty, that it's fresh blood. I give silent thanks that I can't see his face.

Somehow, my eyes know to look down at Diane's right hand. Smeared up the wrist and the forearm are streaks of blood. That boy's blood.

'Did you . . . ?' I begin.

Diane nods, her bright green eyes wide and uncertain as if she can't believe what she's seeing, either. She takes a deep breath, then exhales with a shudder.

'Is he . . . dead?' I manage.

Diane nods again, a single, tight nod. She closes her eyes and says, 'I stabbed him. It was so quick. But I'm not sure what would have happened to you if I hadn't done it.' The words she's uttering are as ridiculous as if I were saying something about my debutante ball. But she's saying them anyway.

I shift my focus and look around at the patch of weeds and gravel behind the washroom building. 'No one saw you?'

'No,' she answers, and when I glance back in her direction, her eyes are open, full of fear.

And that's when we both hear the sound of voices coming from the other side of the building, far enough away that we have a chance. But only if we move. Now.

'Under that fence,' I say, ignoring the panic that is trying to paralyze me. 'We have to go.'

She blanches, shakes her head, unwilling. Despite what she's just done, it dawns on me that I'm the one who knows what to do now. I'm the one who's friends with Connie Treadway, I'm the one who understands the dumb-broad voice you have to use when the fuzz ask you questions, I'm the one who knows when it's time to stay and fight and when it's time to run.

And now it's time to run.

The voices on the other side of the cinder-block building are growing closer – I don't even take time to figure out how many and who they might be. All I know is I take Diane by the hand and tug her toward the chain-link fence, near a dip in the dirt that's been worn down by bad boys scuttling through night after night. We are feet away from the body. *The body*. The body that just moments ago was holding me down, threatening me, now lies lifeless in the dirt. I don't even have time to feel any which way about it. All I know is we have to get out of here.

Sliding down on my back causes my head to pulse with pain again, but I try to ignore it. Diane's bloody cardigan still in one hand, I roll under the fence, wincing as the edges of the chain link scratch my arms and back. I roll free onto the other side, into the edges of the bottling factory property.

My heart is thudding so hard it hurts.

'Come on,' I urge, my voice a whisper.

Her face frantic, Diane drops down to the ground and mimics my moves. She's uncertain, and far too prim about it. But she does it, and as soon as she joins me on the other side of the fence, she stands up, breathing heavily.

'Now what?' she whispers, peering back over her shoulder toward Winkler's.

'Now we run like hell,' I say, taking one of her hands in mine. It's stained and sticky with blood, but I give it a squeeze, for her as much as for me. And then, all at once, the only sound in my ears is the steady beat of our shoes on the pavement and our desperate breathing as we run and we run and we run, racing toward a destination we haven't yet named because we have no earthly clue what it is.

CHAPTER

5

We've run straight and hard down Telephone Road for a good two minutes or so before Diane slows to a stop. Then she leans forward and presses her hands into her sides. She needs to catch her breath. I tug her off the main drag down a quiet street lined with houses not far from our neighborhood, and we duck under the branches of an oak tree. There's the sound of someone's television playing through an open window, bursts of studio audience laughter punctuating the night, and it makes me even more jumpy.

'Are you all right?' I ask, the back of my head still throbbing from what that monster did. My mind still swirling with everything that's just happened.

Suddenly Diane drops to her knees, presses her bloody right hand against her mouth in a silent scream.

'What?' I say, my voice just above a whisper. 'What is it?' I drop down next to her. The streetlight illuminates her pale face. Even though it's chilly, her hairline is damp with sweat.

'The blade,' she manages, slowly dropping her hand from her face. 'I left the switchblade.' She stares at me, her expression one of total anguish. My heart sinks. How could I have been so stupid as to not make sure she had it? Me, a girl who should know better.

'We can't go back,' I say, my stomach twisting in panic. 'They've found him by now.' At these words Diane hauls herself up from the ground and runs to the side of the closest house. The sound of retching follows. I don't flinch and I don't judge. Honestly, I feel like I might vomit, too.

But I also know we have to move. 'Diane?' I call out, not too loud in fear some neighbor will hear me.

'Yes,' she calls back from the shadows. Not *yeah* but *yes*. Even in this misery, she's classier than any girl I know.

'We need to keep going,' I say.

She emerges from the darkness. 'My house isn't far from here,' she says. She wipes the sides of her mouth delicately with the tips of her fingers. 'There's no one there, I promise. Do you think that would be safe?'

For a fleeting moment, my mind imagines what my older sister, Cheryl, would say about the situation, even though she'd be too shocked to picture me in it. And I think about my house and Grandma and Mama staying up late and watching television. I can't come up with a better option than to head to Diane's. So we end up at a place on Coyle Street, not far from the high school. A small, squat brick house with a porch full of junk. Old potted plants, cardboard boxes covered in grease stains. A skinny calico cat hisses at us before slipping away into the darkness.

Diane doesn't match this house.

She leads me around back, and we head through a door into the kitchen. I spy a sink full of dirty dishes and countertops stacked high with mail and empty wine bottles.

'Sorry it's such a mess,' she says in a soft voice. Then she stops and looks at me. 'I guess we don't have to be so quiet.'

'There's nobody else here?' I ask, peering over my shoulder, half expecting the fuzz to show up and arrest us right there in Diane's kitchen. I place her bloody cardigan on the counter.

'No,' says Diane, heading to the sink and washing her hands with a bar of soap. She scrubs hard. 'I live here with my aunt,' she continues, 'but she's hardly ever here.'

Diane dries her hands with a dish towel hanging limply from the stove.

And bursts into sobs.

'I knew that boy,' she wails, her face in her hands. I can barely make out what she is saying. 'I knew his name and I knew that boy! Oh God, I thought I would just scare him! I didn't think I would kill him!'

It's all hitting her now, what she's done. I'm not sure if it's hitting me yet.

'How did you know him?' I ask. I take a step toward her,

but I don't know if I should touch her or not. How I wish my girls were here. Especially Connie. She would know what to do. Or at least she'd pretend to.

Diane doesn't answer my question. She just keeps sobbing into her hands, and sometimes the sobs are interrupted by a hiccuping catch of her breath.

'Why don't we sit down, maybe have a glass of water and a smoke?' I ask, my voice tentative, and Diane nods yes, so I reach out and tug her gently by her wrist to the tiny Formica table in the corner of the kitchen. It's just as cluttered as the kitchen counter, but there's a small, filthy ashtray on it littered with a few butts. She sits down, still crying. I find two glasses in one of the cabinets, fill them both with water, and place one in front of her. Until I guzzle mine down, I don't realize how thirsty I was. Finally, I join her at the table.

'Want one?' I ask, offering her my pack of Salems.

'Normally, I wouldn't,' Diane says, sniffling and getting her tears under control, 'but under the circumstances . . .' She plucks a smoke from the pack carefully, like a lady.

We puff away silently for a moment until Diane starts talking. Her voice is soft, gentle. The kind of voice that could put you to sleep if you let it. It's got money in it, too, just like the voices of those girls at Winkler's who were making fun of Diane earlier. But how can Diane have money and live here? What is Diane doing on the east side of town? And how has it happened that I, an east side girl, have had to depend on a girl like Diane to save my life?

'His name is . . . was Preston,' she says, flinching a bit at the past tense. 'Preston Fowler. We went to River Oaks High together. And to junior high and elementary school before that. Our mothers play bridge together at the club sometimes.' She sniffs again, wipes her cheeks with the sleeves of her dress.

'I didn't think you were from around here,' I answer. 'I mean, I had never seen you at school before.'

Diane nods. 'I'm new this year. But I was at River Oaks High before. So that's how I know Preston.'

I wish I had a handkerchief or something to give to Diane to dry her tears, so she doesn't have to get her clothes all covered with snot. Then again, I'm not sure it matters. After all, the blood on her outfit has started to dry into a rust-colored mark. I'll have to make sure Diane knows to destroy it, and the sweater, too. We can't have a trace of evidence anywhere, especially since Diane left the switchblade behind.

No, we can't be tied to even a bit of blood.

Of Preston Fowler's blood.

A chill creeps up my spine.

'Diane, what you did . . .' I search for the words. 'You saved my life.' Despite the glass of water I've just swallowed, my mouth goes dry, and suddenly I'm plummeted back into that moment behind the bathroom. Hands on me. The sound of gravel under my kicking feet. I shut my eyes tight. My head throbs.

34

Why didn't I fight back? Why didn't I find a way to escape? I'm supposed to be tough enough for that, right? My stomach lurches, and I squeeze my eyes even tighter.

'Evie, are you all right?' Diane asks, pulling me out of my thoughts.

At last I nod and open my eyes, crumpling the moment up and pushing it back into the darkest part of my mind, promising myself I'll never think about it again. After all, I'm safe now. He didn't get me. And I have this tea sipper to thank for that.

'I'm fine,' I say. 'You had a lot of guts to help me like that, you know.'

Diane sighs. 'I guess,' she says. 'But that boy. Preston. He was here and now he's . . . not. Because of *me*.' She takes a shaky drag of her Salem.

'No, because of *him*,' I fire back. 'He's the one who made the decision to do what he did. You were only protecting someone.' I don't say *me*. Maybe because it's almost easier to talk about all of this if I think that I wasn't even there to begin with.

'He always got mean when he was drunk,' Diane continues. 'So mean.' She drops her gaze. 'I'm sorry for what he tried to do to you, Evie.'

I shake my head, then jump a bit at the pain it causes. 'Let's not talk about that. And hey, how do you know my name anyway?'

Diane's eyes meet mine. 'We're in the same English class, remember?'

I sort of feel like a creep for not remembering. Then again, even though I go to English class pretty often, I still make it a habit to cut about once a week. And anyway, it's not like Diane and I have ever spoken before tonight.

'Are you older than me?' I ask. She seems like she is. 'Shouldn't you be in junior classes?'

'Yes, but I'm a year behind,' she says. 'It's one of the reasons I moved in with my aunt and came to Eastside. To make up the credits.'

'Why didn't you make up the credits at River Oaks?' I ask.

'It's complicated,' she says. Her eyes go blank, and we sit in the silence together for a moment. Then she stands up, stubs out her smoke, and walks around behind me. 'Let me check the back of your head.'

Suddenly she's a total Girl Scout, her fingers carefully combing through my dark hair. I tense, fighting off the fresh memories of those moments outside the bathroom. As Diane pulls aside a lock of my dark brown hair, I wince.

'I'm sorry,' she says.

'It's all right. How does it look?'

'It's not so bad. It's stopped bleeding, and I think it should heal on its own.'

'Do you have any aspirin? It kind of aches.'

'Of course. I'm sorry I didn't offer you some right away.'

This girl has true company manners.

Diane walks a few steps down the hallway to the bathroom. Without the pressure of my eyes on her, I try another question she might not want to discuss.

'We need to figure out what we're going to do next,' I say, raising my voice just a bit to make sure she can hear me. There's no response. I hear the shutting of a medicine cabinet door. Then Diane walks out with a bottle of aspirin, takes out two, hands them to me, and refills my water. She still doesn't say anything. I swallow the aspirin and try again.

'I mean, what I'm saying is, if the fuzz come looking or asking questions, we need to figure out how we're going to answer them, don't you think?'

I say this with the voice of authority, but the truth is I have no idea what to do. I only know I must know more than Diane. I should have kept myself out of this mess in the first place, so now I suppose I've got to get us out of it, too.

'You're right,' Diane says at last, her voice soft. 'I keep thinking about the switchblade.'

'Can it be connected back to you?' I ask.

There's the longest pause. I hear Diane take a deep breath, exhale shakily. 'I don't think so,' she whispers. Then she eases her way back to her chair. 'And I'm not going to tell you where I got it, either.' Her voice is firm. Her eyes determined.

'I'm not asking where you got it,' I say, holding both hands up in surrender. It's a side of Diane I haven't seen yet. Tough.

Which sounds strange, considering she's covered in a dead boy's blood.

'I think we need to clean ourselves up the best we can and throw these clothes away,' I say. 'Or hide them until we can burn them or something.' Again I think about what Connie or Juanita or Sunny would do in this situation, but I need to admit to myself that I'm in territory even they wouldn't recognize, and I know it.

Diane nods. 'My aunt won't be home until late, if at all,' she begins. 'I could loan you some clothes.'

We end up in Diane's bedroom at the end of the hall. It's like a neat oasis from the rest of the messy, cramped house. A pink chenille bedspread is stretched tight over a twin bed. A tiny brown teddy bear wearing a black bow tie rests in the center of the pillow. There's an oval-shaped fluffy pink rug centered perfectly in the middle of the wooden floor. A little white vanity in the corner is filled with tiny glass bottles and jars and tubes of lipstick, all organized in careful rows like soldiers in some beauty army. A blue teardrop bottle of Evening in Paris perfume stands out. The walls are mostly blank, though, except for a small painting of daisies next to the window above Diane's bed. No photographs. No record player. No stacks of *Seventeen* magazines or pictures of Bobby Rydell or the Beatles tacked up with pushpins.

It's almost creepy.

Diane is combing through the closet and pulls out a

light blue skirt and sweater set that must have cost more than my mother's entire week's pay cleaning rooms at the Shamrock Hotel.

'I'm a little bigger than you,' she says, 'but it should do.'

By bigger she means curvier, but Diane is too polite to say something like that. I think about the way Connie would describe her if she'd had a few drinks and was feeling mean. But Diane doesn't deserve that. I head to the bathroom to change, thinking about the girls who were so nasty to Diane by the concession stand. Were they jealous of Diane's good looks? No, they mentioned something she did. Something so bad she shouldn't have shown her face in public. I wonder what they would say if they knew what she did for me less than an hour ago.

When I come out of the bathroom, Diane is in a mint-green bathrobe and is holding a paper sack. 'I'm going to wash up first, but you can put your clothes in here,' she says. 'I'll hide them in my closet until we figure out where to get rid of them.'

'Don't forget your sweater on the counter,' I remind her. She nods.

I dump my tired blouse and skirt from the secondhand store into the bag, where they land with a thud. I peer down at myself and can't help but grin.

'You look sweet,' says Diane. 'Really sweet.'

'Thanks,' I say, looking up at her. I'm practically swimming in her clothes, but they're comforting somehow.

Diane smiles. 'You can keep them until you fill them out. I've got heaps of clothes.'

Heaps of clothes. She says the words with a shrug in her voice.

I get my smokes from the kitchen table, and Diane walks me to the back door.

'Listen, lay low tomorrow,' I say, trying to sound like I know what I'm doing, for myself as much as for Diane. 'Don't go anywhere. I need to think about this for a little bit, figure out what's safe for us next.' What I mean is that I need to get help from the others.

'All right,' she says. 'If you think that's best.'

Diane's eyes start to water up again, but she gets a grip and takes a deep breath.

'So what about Monday?' she asks. 'Do I go to school?'

I nod. 'Act as normal as you can. Come find me and my friends in the cafeteria and we'll talk more then, okay?' I cringe a little inside at the thought of a tea sipper joining me and my friends, but I'll deal with that later.

'Or I'll find you in English class,' she suggests, raising an eyebrow. 'We have that before lunch.' I get that she's sort of making a joke.

I give her a knowing look. 'Okay, English class. I promise I'll show up.'

And then I surprise myself when I reach out and squeeze

Diane's hands with mine. Hers are soft. The kind of hands, my mother would say, that will never have to work. But those hands did something else tonight. They saved my life.

Diane squeezes back just before I slip out, my head still throbbing, but a little less now.

'Good night, Evie,' her voice calls out. 'Thanks for coming over.'

Thanks for coming over. Jeez, it's like we just spent the evening studying or something. I turn and slip down Coyle Street in the darkness.

6

It's after midnight by the time I make it home, but I can spy the living room light through the front windows. Damn. How will I explain these new clothes?

But I finally catch a lucky break. My mother is asleep on the couch, the *Post* spread over her lap. Grandma must be in bed already. I creep toward my bedroom, but with a creak of the floorboards, my luck runs out.

'Evelyn?' my mother asks. 'Is that you?'

She and my grandmother are the only ones who call me by that name. But I don't have to answer her, because I've already ducked into my bedroom and am slipping out of Diane's borrowed clothes before she can spot me in them.

'Yeah, Mama, it's me. I'll be out in a minute.'

'It's so late, sweetheart.' Her voice is heavy. Sad. And there's a sliver of frustration laced through it.

I keep breaking her heart and I know it. If only I knew how to stop doing it.

I come back out into the living room in my nightgown. My mother is sitting up, yawning. She reaches for her glasses and slides them on, then brushes a few wisps of her dark brown hair out of her pale face. Her glasses make her look older than she is, but then again, it's like everything makes her look older than she is, including her backbreaking job. I sit next to her on the couch.

'Where were you?'

'Just at Winkler's,' I tell her. I draw my knees up to my chin.

'With Juanita from next door, I'm guessing?' she says.

'Yeah, we walked back together,' I say, wondering if Juanita is home yet and whether my mother heard her get home earlier without me. I cross my fingers quickly that my lie will hold, but Mama only sighs and pushes her hair back from her face with both hands.

'I wish you could find some different friends,' she says. But what she really means is that she wishes I wasn't the sort of girl the other mothers in the neighborhood don't like much. What she really means is she wishes I turned out better than I am. Only she can't bring herself to say it. She doesn't want that to be true.

I shift a little with impatience as she talks. My mother has delivered this speech so many times. It annoys me as much as it fills me with guilt.

'Mama, Juanita is my friend. You know that.' What I don't

43

tell her is that as soon as she goes to sleep, I plan on sneaking over to Juanita's, because I need to tell someone what happened tonight. I need to figure out what to do next.

'Fine, we'll talk about it later,' she says, knowing we won't. 'Listen, will you go with Grandma to church tomorrow? She'll want company there, and I have to work.'

The idea of having to play nice at church with Grandma after all that's happened tonight is too much. My face must fall more than I think, because my mother gives me a hurt look.

Like I said, I'm always breaking her heart. But sometimes I really can't bear to. The look does me in this time.

'Fine, I'll do it,' I say. I was really hoping to lay low tomorrow, too, like I instructed Diane to do. Maybe it's not the best idea to leave the house, but I'll manage that in the morning.

'Thank you, Evelyn,' she says with a sigh. 'You know, there are some nice boys at that church. I'm sure you think they're the type you aren't interested in, but they're good boys. The kind that would make a nice boyfriend.' I ignore that last part as she heaves herself off the couch. She's so tired all the time, it seems it takes energy for her to do even the tiniest of things. I imagine her spending all day tomorrow cleaning toilets and hauling dirty sheets for rich people, and my stomach sinks.

I'm such a bad daughter. I know it. Why can't I be like Ginger Blankenship, the straight-A student down the street who's aiming to get a scholarship for college, much to the delight of her parents? Or like Nancy Collins, elected Sweetheart of the football team and Queen of the Winter Whirl Dance? At the very least, why can't I be like my sister, Cheryl, who did the right thing when she had to and got married to a nice boy from the neighborhood, a decent boy who joined the army and who can offer her a safe and secure future?

Because Ginger Blankenship has never spent a starry night on the beach in Galveston for no good reason or sensed the heady rush of too many sips of Four Roses. And because Nancy Collins has never felt the kiss of the wind on her face when she rides in a car going too fast or known the tiny thrill that comes with cutting class and not getting caught.

And because my sister, Cheryl, is now stuck sending me long, sad letters from base housing on Fort Hood in Killeen, complaining about how lonely she is.

There's got to be something more to life, and being with Juanita and Connie and Sunny seems like the closest way to getting it. Even if I'm not sure exactly what it is.

'I'm going to bed,' my mother says, her voice resigned. She doesn't ask me if I'm going to follow. It's enough that I'm home and that I've promised to go with my grandmother to church in the morning. She doesn't push it.

Not long after I hear her light snoring down the hall, I pull on some shoes and my bathrobe and sneak across the patch of grass to Juanita's house. I rap on her bedroom window three

45

times, pause, then rap three more times after that. Our signal.

Just two minutes later I hear Juanita's front door open, and she comes around to the side of the house.

'Oh, thank God,' she says, grabbing me and giving me a quick, tentative hug. Words spill out of her. 'I was waiting up for you! Where did you go? We were frantic! Do you know what happened tonight?' She pulls away, holds me out at arm's length, and stares at me carefully. One eyebrow pops in concern. 'You don't look too hot.'

'Juanita, can we please go sit?' I say, my voice suddenly the weariest it's been all evening. We make our way to her back steps.

In whispers, surrounded by the dark of night and the occasional distant car honk and dog bark, I reveal just what happened at Winkler's and at Diane's afterward, pausing to let her drop a curse word at every shocking moment.

'I can't believe this,' she says, staring at me, then staring out at the backyard, a ratty piece of grass with a clothesline and some sad toys belonging to Juanita's little nieces, who Juanita's mom looks after during the day.

'It's all true,' I say. And finally, at last, I let myself cry.

Juanita and Connie and Sunny and me are careful about when we cry and just who we let see us do it. Partly because we're tough and partly because if we were being honest about things, we'd cry a lot more if we gave in at every opportunity. Connie could cry forever about her lousy home life and Sunny about her creepy stepdad and Juanita about the kids who make nasty remarks about her and her family. If we were honest about things, we'd drop tears every day of our lives. So we have to make sure we don't waste them, I guess.

Tonight, though, I feel I've earned the right to cry.

Juanita puts her hand on my back, lets me sob.

'It's all right, Evie, just cry,' she says, rubbing my back for a good minute or two. I like how she doesn't tell me everything is going to be fine. She knows better than that.

When I finally manage to calm down, it's Juanita's turn to talk. As the tears dry on my face, she explains that not long after Diane and I took off, some kids came back from the washroom building screaming their heads off about a dead boy. The fuzz came, sirens blaring, and most of our crowd took off right away. We know better than to stick around when the cops show. It's not uncommon for fights to break out at Winkler's, but it's common that the kids we hang out with get the blame, no matter who starts it.

'Nobody said anything? Like who they think did it? Nobody spotted us?'

'Nope,' says Juanita with a shake of her head. 'But damn, you should have seen those tea sippers crying. Well, forget them. They shouldn't have been at Winkler's in the first place. And that boy deserved what he got for what he tried to do to you.' She scowls.

I think about Diane saying she knew Preston Fowler since

47

they were kids. I try to imagine him as a little boy, and I can't square that with the monster who attacked me. I squeeze my eyes shut. It's too much to think about.

'Listen, I hate to admit it, but a River Oaks girl saved my life tonight,' I say, finally opening my eyes again. 'Just remember that.'

'Yeah,' says Juanita. 'But she goes to Eastside now, right? How come?'

'She wouldn't say. The place she lives in with her aunt is a real dump. She's hiding something, but I don't know what it is.' I frown, remembering Diane's spotless bedroom in the middle of that cluttered house.

'Well, she's got something more to hide after tonight, that's for sure,' Juanita answers. She presses her lips together in thought. 'You don't think she'd do something stupid and confess, do you?'

The idea had crossed my mind. If tonight sent me into a tailspin, I can't imagine what it must be doing to a girl who has heaps of clothes and such nice manners. It might all end up being too much for her. And anyway, if there was ever a girl who was going to get the fuzz to believe it was all self-defense, it's a pretty rich girl like Diane. Even if she does live on our side of town now.

When I tell Juanita as much, she agrees that I need to get Diane in with our crowd on Monday at school.

'We can figure her out a little more,' says Juanita. 'Get a

48

sense of what sort of risk she is.' There's a calm about Juanita that I can't help but admire. She's acting like this is a regular problem and all we need is a plan. Like this is the same as sneaking out of the house in the middle of the night or lifting smokes from the drugstore or handling a boy who thinks he can get fresh with her just because of what part of town she lives in and what sort of makeup she wears.

But she knows this is different, and so do I.

'I have to take my grandmother to church tomorrow,' I say, resigned. 'I promised my mother. I'm dreading it. I wanted to stay home, just in case.'

Juanita rests an arm around my shoulders and gives me a squeeze. Then she raises her voice an octave or two, makes it real sweet. 'Just say a prayer to God and everything will be just peachy!' Then she winks. Juanita shares as much fondness for church as I do.

'Listen, I don't think the fuzz suspect you had anything to do with this. Why would they? Let's meet up at the park tomorrow morning after you finish being holy. You, me, Sunny, and Connie. You can fill the rest of the girls in on what happened. We'll figure out what to do next.'

I tug my knees up closer to my chest. The night is getting colder. I wish I had my smokes.

Juanita stifles a yawn.

'You need to go to bed,' I say.

'I'll stay out here as long as you need me to, all right?'

I lean toward Juanita, rest my head on her shoulder. I'm so grateful for her. But the truth is, I'm tired, too. Bone-tired.

'Let's go inside,' I say. My voice comes out a whisper.

'If you're sure,' says Juanita. 'But tomorrow. The park. Eleven o'clock. You take Grandma to church, and I'll round up the rest of the girls. Yeah?'

'Yeah,' I say. And Juanita and I sit there for a few more beats, just long enough for me to be thankful again for friends who have my back. After we get up, I shoot Juanita a weary smile before I slip back inside my house.

7

The headline jumps out at us from the front page of the *Post*. Big, bold letters announcing RIVER OAKS YOUTH STABBED BY UNKNOWN ASSAILANT, and underneath that, a smaller headline letting every reader know that Preston Fowler wasn't just any River Oaks boy, but the son of Lamar Fowler, former city councilman, who made a fortune in oil and knows all the best people.

'Damn,' says Connie, drawing out the curse. 'Diane sure did pick an important kid to murder.'

'Jeez, Connie,' Juanita answers, slipping an arm around me, 'do you have to say "murder" like that?'

Juanita's on one side of me on the park bench, Connie on the other, and Sunny is tucked in on the far side of Connie, leaning in as much as she can to see the paper on Connie's lap.

'Well, what do you want me to say?' Connie argues.

'Does it count as murder if someone's trying to protect somebody else?' Sunny asks, wrinkling her brow. 'I mean, isn't that sort of like self-defense?'

'Yeah, but she wasn't defending *herself*, dum-dum,' Connie says, hauling the paper closer to her face to study the article more carefully. I watch her lips move as she reads.

'All right, so it was *Evie*-defense, then,' says Sunny, annoyed.

'So . . .' I manage at last, staring out at the towheaded boys who are playing on the rusted-out playground equipment a few hundred yards away, 'what do we do now?'

Connie lowers the paper into her lap and Sunny snatches it from her, and then Connie lights a cigarette. I realize we're all waiting for Connie to deliver some sort of announcement. Even Sunny, who only grabbed the paper to get back at Connie for her smart remark.

'We don't do anything,' Connie says with a shrug. 'I mean, Evie isn't to blame for anything. She was just in the wrong place at the wrong time when that creep decided to try something. Diane's the one who got herself in a mess. I say Evie should keep her mouth shut tight, because who knows what the cops will say or do if they know she was there when he was killed. They could even try to pin it on her. The fuzz will always blame something on a girl from our neighborhood over some tea sipper.'

My mind flashes on Diane giving me clean clothes from her closet, gripping my hands as I stepped out onto her back porch. I think about her tidy bedroom, her sad eyes.

'But, Connie,' I start, and I realize my voice is shaking. Connie's word has always been law, and now that she's back from the state school, that fact seems more real than ever. 'I explained it all to you. How it all happened. Diane probably saved my life. Or saved me from something terrible at the very least. Isn't that worth something?' I take a deep breath and continue. 'Look, I'm not wild that some rich kid defended me better than I can defend myself. And I'm not saying we become her best friends. But I am saying we owe it to her to at least look out for her.'

I don't normally say more than one or two sentences to Connie at a time, and I definitely don't speak out against her. It's almost like I'm watching someone else, a character in a television program or picture. Like I'm watching someone else be brave enough to speak up. But it's me. And I'm grateful for Juanita's arm still around me, squeezing me tight.

Connie exhales, rolls her eyes, and pops up from the splintering park bench. It's practically impossible for her to sit still for long. She bounces on her heels as she talks.

'Evie, do you remember what happened that time we went downtown to Foley's to look at clothes?' she asks, staring me down. Bounce, bounce, bounce.

I shrug. Connie knows I remember. It was last spring, not long before Connie got sent up to Gainesville. We all thought it would be fun to take the bus and check out the fancy new dresses in pink taffeta and green velveteen that we could never afford to buy and that were too difficult to swipe. When we were trying them on in the fitting room and cracking up over how different we looked, a few high-class girls reported us to the manager, and we were kicked out. Connie made us go back a week later to lift some lipsticks from the makeup counter just to get even.

'That crowd doesn't care about us, so why should we care about them?' she says, her voice firm. 'So let's not do anything. Diane can afford a rich lawyer, I'll bet.' Connie pauses and looks at us carefully. 'And here's another thing. I don't *like* her.' At this final pronouncement, she scowls.

'But, Connie, you don't even know her,' I press, my heart pounding a bit as I push back against our leader, my cheeks pinking up from nerves. I've spoken my mind once, and now it's like I don't want to give in.

Connie eyes me carefully, then opens her mouth like she's about to say something, thinks better of it, and snaps it closed again.

'I know her *type*,' she says finally. 'I know her *kind*.'

She flicks the butt behind her and draws her arms up wide over her head in a deep stretch, ready to move on to the next topic at hand.

Juanita shifts next to me, uncomfortable but quiet. Sunny chews her bottom lip, looks down at the newspaper.

Connie's always the boss. Always in charge. Always.

The sensation of that boy's arms on me, his hand on my

mouth. The sound of my feet kicking up gravel. It all comes back to me, and quick, too. A wave of nausea rolls over me, but I push it down.

'Connie,' I say, picking my words as carefully as I can, my voice shaking a little, 'we gotta help Diane. We just do.' I'm in real new territory here, but I go for it anyway. 'I'm going to help her no matter what you say.'

Juanita stiffens next to me. Connie's eyebrows pop up. Then she frowns, confused.

'Oh, you are, huh?' she says at last. She crosses her arms in front of her and examines me coolly. Her left foot is tapping like a machine gun, *rat-a-tat-tat*.

I shrink back into Juanita, but I don't break eye contact with Connie. I just say, 'Yeah, I am.'

Connie exhales loudly, uncrosses her arms, and lifts her eyes up to the bright blue Houston sky. I can hear the shouts of the little boys on the playground. Finally, she dips her head back and looks at me again. A soft smirk is on her bright red lips.

'All right, fine,' she proclaims at last, and I exhale in relief. 'But this is how we're going to do it. We're nice to this girl tomorrow, I guess. She can sit with us at lunch. We'll talk. But if the fuzz get mixed up in this, I'm putting my foot down. Evie keeps her trap shut.'

I nod, anxious to agree. I don't want to get mixed up with the police, either. And while I'm not entirely sure what happens after lunch on Monday, I know that I can't get caught and Diane can't get caught. She won't be and I won't be, either.

I have to believe this is true.

It's Monday morning, and Mama has already left for work at the Shamrock, but she did pause on her way out the door to gently shake me awake and wish me a good day. I muttered a 'You too,' into my pillow and wished for an extra hour of sleep.

'Good morning, Evelyn,' says my grandmother as I enter the kitchen. She's drinking her coffee with lots of cream and sugar like always. Next to her cup is her weathered daily devotional with the burgundy cover, the words MY UTMOST FOR HIS HIGHEST stamped across the front. She gets up first each morning, slips on a fresh, ironed dress, carefully styles her salt-and-pepper hair, and, while her coffee is brewing, she flips through those onionskin pages, asking God to bless all of us.

This past year or so, I'm pretty sure she's also been asking Him to get a handle on me.

'Good morning,' I say, offering her a smile.

She examines me carefully and sighs loudly. 'I can't see your lovely eyes with all that garbage all over them.'

'Grandma, it's not garbage, it's makeup,' I say, turning away from her to make myself some toast. She exhales again, and it's like I can *hear* her frowning at me.

When I was little and Grandma moved in with us after my dad took off, she and Cheryl and I spent hours making sugar cookies and snuggling on the couch, reading out of my big book of fairy tales. The three of us would sing 'Do Your Ears Hang Low?' over and over in all sorts of funny voices until I laughed myself silly.

She was my sweet grandmother. Now it's like she's my judge and jury, too.

'A lot of the girls wear it, you know,' I say, turning back to face her. I don't want her to be mad at me. I want her to be proud of me, somehow. But like Mama, Grandma thinks girls my age should look presentable. Find the right boy to marry. One who will stick around. They think girls my age should come straight home after school, never leave the house on Saturday, go to church every Sunday, never look at boys, never wear makeup, never smoke, never nothing.

Never have any fun.

My grandmother sighs and shrugs at the mention of other girls. Her lack of a response is the response, I realize.

Almost as if I've chosen the worst possible time to mention other girls, there's a rapping on our front door and Juanita's voice hollers for me from the porch ('*Eeeee-veeee!*'). My grandmother is suspicious of all Mexicans, and she especially doesn't like the Barajas family, because when they go to church at all, they go to a Catholic one, and Mr and Mrs Barajas are always hollering at each other good-naturedly with the windows wide open. What Grandma hears as noise and chaos has always seemed like love to me, and even though it hurts a little to admit to myself, Juanita's house sure does seem a lot warmer than mine has been recently. But Grandma blames Juanita for setting me off on the wrong path, and I've overheard her telling Mama that I'd still be her good sweet granddaughter if only I hadn't taken up with her.

'I have to go to school,' I say, pecking her on the cheek and taking my toast in hand for the walk.

'Have a good day,' she manages.

'You too.'

And I'm out the door and I'm free.

Juanita and I meet up with Connie and Sunny outside Eastside. Kids are milling around on the lawn in front of the big brick building, huddling in their groups, gossiping about the weekend. The sea of faces is made up of white and Mexican kids milling about, killing time until the first bell rings. I spy the smart kids in the Major Works classes crowded together on the school steps, going over notes and quizzing each other. A few jocks are tossing a football, insulting each other's throws.

Some of the pretty girls in the drum and bugle corps are crowded near a large live oak that we usually hang out by. They perform at all the football halftimes, and they've got the shiniest hair and the best figures, and they're some of the most popular girls in the school – even if they are Eastside like us.

But for being a high school drill team, they sure do take themselves seriously. Their officers are notorious for giving out demerits for wearing dark fingernail polish or chewing gum in the halls. One time in the bathroom, Connie asked a corps member who looked down her nose at Connie if the girl could do something with her boyfriend without an officer's permission, and the girl burst into tears and ran out. Connie laughed real loud after that. She'd used some pretty nasty words with the girl, too. But Connie doesn't flinch at anything.

Just like right now, when she walks up to the oak tree and says to the girls, 'Hey, this is our spot. You know that.'

One of the corps members acts like she's staring at a cockroach, but she knows better than to mess with Connie Treadway. They slide off, giving each other knowing glances. Expressions that say, *How does anyone end up like that, anyhow?*

I wonder if any of the cliques are discussing the news about what happened at the drive-in on Saturday. A little voice reminds me that what happened involved me, but I manage to hush that voice as quickly as it comes.

Reading my mind, Sunny says, 'Did anyone see the headlines this morning? My mom and stepdad don't take the paper.' She puts an emphasis on the word *headlines* and raises her eyebrows knowingly, like by saying Preston Fowler's name out loud, somehow the fuzz will come by and arrest us all.

But none of us have seen the headlines, so we don't know

what's going on. Just then, a female voice yelling my name cuts across the lawn.

'Evie! Hey, Evie!'

'Oh, Christ,' Connie mutters, and the four of us turn and spot Diane herself walking – no, running – across the lawn, her hand waving heartily and her hair bouncing with every step. She's wearing a sweet lime-green dress and a chocolate-brown cardigan, and she looks like a teen model from the Sears catalog.

'Here comes Miss America,' Connie continues, but I don't respond. I see Diane's clear eyes, rosy skin, bright white teeth. I try to imagine her pressing a bloody handkerchief to the back of my head, smoking a Salem over her cluttered kitchen table. Even though I know it happened – and it happened to me – I can't conjure up the picture in my head.

Then I try to imagine her stabbing Preston Fowler until he's dead in a heap in the dirt.

I squeeze my eyes closed for a moment, trying to focus on the present, and when I open them there's Diane, standing in front of me. She's a little winded from her sprint across the Eastside lawn.

'Hi,' she says brightly, smiling right at me. Something about it makes me uncomfortable. Is she trying too hard or is this just how she is? 'I know you said maybe we could talk at lunch or in class, but I saw y'all and so . . .' She runs out of steam as her mouth catches up with her eyes, taking in this group of girls who are my friends. My best friends.

I think it's hitting her all at once. The kind of girl I really am. The kind of girls I hang out with.

Bad girls.

Connie gives Diane a sort of bored look verging on outright mean, then shifts her view to pick at a grubby thumbnail. Sunny is studying her, taking in Diane's fancy clothes and peaches-and-cream complexion, and not without some real jealousy. I count on Juanita to be the most decent one and she is, finally offering a, 'Hi, I'm Juanita.' But her voice is hesitant.

'Well, I'm Diane,' Diane says, her voice too loud, her smile so big her gums show. She's nervous all of a sudden. I can tell. She swallows hard and reads my face, making sure she's all right standing here.

'Hey,' I say, at once shy and kind of embarrassed, too. Sunny introduces herself, but Connie keeps her mouth shut and a scowl on her face. The truth is, I owe Diane. I wish I didn't, but I do. And I can feel Connie Treadway breathing down my neck, judging all of this.

The morning bell rings, ushering us all to class. Diane follows as we troop up the front walk and head in through the main doors. I sense her trying to catch up with me, and it makes me irritable.

'Will I see you in English class?' she asks me, her voice low like she's trying to keep a secret, only she isn't very good at it.

'Sure,' I say. 'Yes.' I think back to yesterday at the park, when I fought so hard for Diane. Maybe there was a part of me that hoped this first meeting wouldn't feel so awkward. And maybe now there's a part of me that wishes it hadn't happened at all.

Connie and Sunny break off from us without saying goodbye, and Juanita, Diane, and I head as an awkward trio down the main hall, dodging jocks careening around us and bumping into lockers and teachers clapping their hands and urging us to get to homeroom.

'I'm this way,' Diane says, nodding her head up the nearest stairwell.

'Well,' I manage, uncertainly placing my hand up in a strange sort of salute, 'see you in English.'

Diane nods, her smile overeager, and she disappears up the stairs, her shiny hair bouncing up and down on her back like a Slinky.

'So she's definitely sitting with us at lunch?' Juanita asks, popping a perfectly shaped coal-black eyebrow at me.

'Yeah, I guess,' I start, realizing that I had a lot more confidence about my plan yesterday. Something about Diane in the flesh makes me feel uncertain and strange. I feel an obligation to her, sure. But how far should it go? And the idea of Diane and Connie seated together at the same cafeteria table is practically impossible to imagine. Like a nun and a criminal sharing a sandwich.

'Well,' says Juanita. 'I'm just real curious how it's gonna be.'

To be honest, so am I.

The tardy bell rings, but Juanita and I just stand there, obstacles in the way of students more dedicated than we are who are racing to class. Once the halls are nice and clear, Juanita and I dawdle down the rest of the main drag, neither of us talking much and both of us definitely trying to picture just what lunchtime will bring.

8

Of all my classes, English is the one I cut the least. I guess it's because Miss Odeen is honestly swell for a teacher. She's young and real pretty, with honey-blond hair and a big smile. And you can tell she's smart from the way she knows so much about the writers and other important people we talk about. On the first day of school she told us this was her first year as a teacher, which means she still likes teenagers, I guess.

'Evie Barnes!' she says to me as I walk into third period. And before the tardy bell, no less. 'I'm glad you're here.'

'Hey, Miss Odeen,' I answer, kind of bashful. I catch Diane from the second row, waving me down and pointing excitedly to an empty seat next to her, even though it's impossible to miss. Her expression is as cheerful as Miss Odeen's.

'Hi!' Diane says. 'How are you?'

'Hi,' I say, sliding into the seat. I haven't sat in a row this close to the teacher since the seventh grade. I can feel the kids around me boring holes into my back with their eyes. Surely they must be wondering what I'm doing talking to someone like Diane. None of them are really my crowd, but they're kids who understand the social system at Eastside. And girls like me don't talk to girls who look like Diane.

'It was nice to meet your friends,' Diane says, beaming at me. It's the same beauty-pageant grin she gave me outside. Too excited. Almost frantic. Like if she let it drop, her face might fall off. It makes me nervous.

I told Connie I wanted to stand up for Diane. I wanted to be there for her. But that was easy to say in the park, away from the rules and stares of everyone at Eastside. Here, with Diane next to me, I'm not sure exactly how to do that.

'Sure,' I say, gazing toward the front of the classroom, ready for this conversation to be over. 'I'm glad you met them.'

'And I can eat lunch with y'all?' she asks. 'It's all right?'

My stomach sinks. It's what I promised, and at the time I thought it would be the best way for the girls and Diane to get to know each other and figure out what to do next. Even Connie gave it the green light. But here on a Monday morning in the rows of desks, in the sea of faces that judge and stare and categorize, that idea seems as silly as going to the moon.

But I just mutter, 'Yeah, of course you can.'

Miss Odeen asks us all to take out a piece of paper and a pencil for a writing exercise. I have neither, but Diane leans over and quickly puts a fresh piece of composition paper and a pencil sharpened to a point on my desk when she realizes I'm without. She smells like soap and something floral and sweet. Maybe it's that Evening in Paris perfume I saw on her vanity. A boy behind me chuckles and says something about my new friend as I wince in embarrassment. I nod in begrudging thanks, and she whispers, 'It's no trouble.'

'Class,' says Miss Odeen, 'I'd like to read a portion of a speech to you and have you respond to it. How many of you have heard of a woman named Fannie Lou Hamer?'

I smile, glad for the interruption. Miss Odeen is always doing stuff like this. By that I mean introducing us to names and ideas she knows we don't know much about, even if she always asks us first if we do, I guess just to be polite. Like the other week when she told us about Jerrie Mock, the first woman to fly around the world. Miss Odeen assigned us a composition from the point of view of Mrs Mock after she made it all the way back to Columbus, Ohio, last spring in her Cessna airplane. Some of the boys refused to write it because they said a boy couldn't write from a girl's point of view, but they changed their minds after Miss Odeen threatened to fail them.

None of us answer Miss Odeen, who perches on the edge of her desk and crosses her legs at the ankles. She's so stylish and put-together, I bet Grandma and Mama might wonder why she hasn't found herself a husband yet, but something about Miss Odeen makes me think that's not the first thing on her to-do list.

'Fannie Lou Hamer is a Negro woman from Mississippi, fighting for her rights,' Miss Odeen begins. I shift in my seat and peer around me. I can tell from the smirks of some of the students and the nasty comments they mutter under their breaths that they don't like that Miss Odeen has brought up civil rights. Like every other high school in Houston, Eastside is only for white and Mexican kids. The Negro students in this part of town go to Jack Yates High. Juanita explained to me once that at some point the grown-ups in charge decided Mexicans counted as white, which she didn't particularly like. She gets her fair share of sideways looks from the fuzz and cruel comments from the kids at school, but I know she's always been proud to be Mexican.

Up north I know they have integrated schools, and everybody goes to school together, and I think that's the way things should be everywhere. But it's hard to imagine that ever happening here in Houston, even if a few years ago the city did integrate the buses and lunch counters and movie theaters. It doesn't seem right that a bunch of white grown-ups get to decide the when and the how of who gets to go where. I lean forward in my seat to focus on what Miss Odeen is saying.

'This past August, Mrs Hamer spoke at the Democratic National Convention all the way up in New Jersey,' she continues. 'And I want y'all to listen to this speech that she gave and write a response.'

Miss Odeen begins to speak, repeating what Mrs Hamer said. I peer over at Diane, who sits up straighter, listening to everything coming out of Miss Odeen's mouth.

In the words of Fannie Lou Hamer, Miss Odeen talks about not being able to vote in Mississippi because of the color of her skin, and of even being arrested and beaten just for trying. Some of the testimony makes me wince. What she had to go through was horrible.

'"I question America,"' says Miss Odeen, and her voice grows louder as she reads Mrs Hamer's speech. '"Is this America, the land of the free and the home of the brave . . ."'

After she is done reading, Miss Odeen takes a deep breath. 'Those words surely did make an impression on me,' she says. 'And I'm sure they did for you, too. So I'd like you to write a response to this speech. Reflect on it and write a brief composition explaining it in your own words.'

I bend over my paper, thinking about how to get started.

Fannie Lou Hamer is very brave. I think she is definitely braver than me. I pause, chew on a thumbnail, searching for a word. *Fannie Lou Hamer seems fearless, but she must have been afraid. Maybe it's not that she is fearless. It's just that she is courageous in the face of fear.*

Diane scribbles away next to me, humming softly as she completes the assignment. As we write, Miss Odeen starts making her way around the desks, checking on our work. That's another way you know she's new. The older teachers just yell at us from the front of the room.

I spy a few kids off to the side, their papers blank, the expressions on their faces ones of disgust. Miss Odeen goes over to quietly encourage them to get started on the assignment, but she doesn't seem to have much luck. I wonder how long before some parent complains to the school administration about this lesson.

Toward the end of class, Miss Odeen collects our papers so she can review them, and we spend the last few minutes going over our weekly list of vocabulary words. As we repeat *caterwaul* and *perspicacity*, I hear Diane cough. A sort of notice-me cough, not a real one.

I glance toward her desk, where I see she has a new piece of paper out. In careful script at the top, she's written *I'm so scared*.

I look up and meet her eyes. They're glazed over, wet with tears. She's still trying to smile. Something in me softens for this girl, and I feel bad about how I acted at the start of class. All I can think to do is quietly mouth back, *I am, too*.

She nods, blinks hard, and two tears snake down her rosy cheeks. She presses them away with her fingers, then turns her attention back to Miss Odeen.

9

I watched as Diane composed herself and tucked away the piece of paper with her secret message just to me, hoping she'd be all right before the bell. When it rings, I expect her to want to walk out with me, hover nervously, and ask about lunch. Instead, she gathers her books and says, 'I have to go. But I'll see you in the cafeteria. I promise.' Like the tears and the note never happened. And with that she slips down the hall, lost in a crowd of ponytails and crew cuts.

I have one more class before it's time to eat, but I'm in no mood to go. I'm feeling unsettled and uncertain, and that moment with Diane just made something in me crack a little. I don't like it. How I wish I could blink my eyes and find myself back at Winkler's before I decided to head to the bathroom. How I wish I could reach out and stop myself from going.

Feeling out of sorts, I head out back behind the gym, where some of my crowd cuts and smokes cigarettes. I find Sunny there, dressed in the red gym uniform that we all hate. It always bunches too tight at the waist and makes us look as boxy and ugly as possible. Well, most of us. Sunny somehow still manages to look pretty. She leans against the back wall and puffs on a cigarette.

'Hey,' she says.

'Hey,' I answer.

The two of us have probably the least to say around each other. If Juanita is my closest friend in our pack, Sunny is definitely Connie's. Sunny almost matches Connie note for note in loudness and boldness, even if she cares about her looks a lot more than Connie does. And she's probably the least scared of Connie, even when Connie goes after her for being a ditz. But she never crosses Connie. Ever.

I don't tell Sunny about Diane and English class. It's like I'm not sure I should just yet. And I don't really want to. I don't want to try and figure out how I feel about Diane. I don't want to talk about Diane's tears and how anxious I got over how easily she shed them. Something tells me if I let myself feel too much, I might never stop feeling. And I don't think that would take me anywhere good.

If it was Juanita, I would probably say something. We might try to make sense of it together. Maybe. But Sunny isn't Juanita. Instead we just smoke and hide out until at last she says, 'You know, that was a pretty tough move in the park yesterday.' She doesn't look at me when she says it. She just stares out at the empty football field and the black asphalt track surrounding it.

I know she means standing up to Connie. I shrug.

'It just seemed like the right thing to do, I guess,' I say.

Sunny drags her blue eyes toward me, slow as molasses. Even through her mascara and eyeliner, they sparkle. 'You've got something special, Evie,' she says. 'I don't think you realize it.'

I frown, confused. What do I have that Sunny or Connie or Juanita don't have? If anything, they've always been the older ones. The more experienced ones. I've always been the tagalong.

'I don't know what you mean,' I say at last.

'There aren't many girls at Eastside High who would dare talk back to Connie Treadway,' she tells me. 'I love Connie. You know that. But you were right to stand up for Diane. Even if she does look like Miss America. Only . . . I don't know if I could have done it. And you did.'

I let Sunny's words sink in and feel my cheeks flush in what might be pride. But then the bell rings for lunch, saving me from having to respond. Not that I would have known what to say. We stab our smokes out against the brick wall of the gym.

'Hey,' I ask Sunny, 'why did you change into your gym uniform if you were only going to cut?'

Sunny peers down at her red romper and her mouth opens in a perfect O of astonishment. Then she swears in frustration.

'I forgot I'd put this on!' She rolls her eyes at herself, and I can't help but laugh. Sunny *is* a ditz lots of times, but the truth is she's smart in her own way.

'You want me to come to the locker room and wait for you while you change?' I ask.

'No, that's all right,' says Sunny. 'Besides, I have to hurry and find Ray before lunch. He's probably cutting class with Dwight and Butch. So I might not see y'all in the cafeteria.' She grimaces as we walk in the direction of the locker room. 'You know how he is. Meet me here. Meet me there. Sometimes I get sick of his orders.'

'Have you ever told him that?' I ask. Juanita and I have whispered sometimes about how Ray treats Sunny, but we've never said anything to her face.

She shrugs. 'No, never. But maybe I should. Sometimes I wonder if having a boyfriend is worth it.'

I think about Mom and Grandma wishing I'd end up with the right kind of boy. Not a boy like Ray Swanson, mind you. But a boy nevertheless. A boy like Cheryl's husband, Dennis, who enlisted in the army and can provide a stable sort of future. *Pick a man who'll stick around*, my mother likes to say, *even if he isn't handsome or clever. Just pick a man who'll stay*. Not a man like my father is what she really means. Wherever he is.

I say goodbye to Sunny and head to the cafeteria, thinking of meeting up with Diane. There are lots of times my crowd doesn't even eat in the cafeteria. The boys rarely do. Sometimes

73

we spend the lunch period in the parking lot or getting yelled at by Mr Samperi of Samperi's Groceries, a little store by the school where we sometimes buy Dr Peppers and candy necklaces and then hang out for too long in the parking lot. But today Connie and Juanita and I gather at one of our tables, in the corner the farthest away from the lunch monitors. I take my cardigan and fold it up, putting it on the seat next to me to save it for Diane.

'So,' Connie says, letting her tray hit the table with a smack. She wrinkles her nose at what looks like tuna casserole, then eyes my folded sweater. 'Diane's got dibs on that seat?'

'Just keeping it for her,' I say, unwrapping my lunch and starting with dessert. I've tried to get her to stop, but Grandma insists on packing my lunch for me, and today, like always, she's included one of her homemade chocolate chip cookies. Sometimes the cookie makes me feel like a little girl again, and this makes me both pleased and sad. I scan the entrance at the back of the cafeteria, trying to spot Diane in the crowd.

Connie doesn't react, just sighs, leans back, bounces a bit, and says, 'I'm saying it again, just so you all hear me. I don't *like* her.'

Uncomfortable, I pretend I didn't hear Connie's proclamation and instead peer out at the sea of people. At last I spot her. Diane. She's standing at the entrance of the cafeteria, looking out on the mess of kids yelping and shoving one another. I watch her, wondering if I should try to get her

74

attention, but she spies us at last and waves with enthusiasm.

'Jesus, she looks like a cheerleader,' Connie says, rolling her eyes. Connie's right, and the truth makes me cringe, but I don't say anything in response.

'Hey, you can sit here,' I say to Diane when she arrives at our table. I scoot my cardigan off the seat next to me.

'Hi,' Diane says, carefully folding her skirt underneath her as she sits. She swallows, forces a smile, looks around at all of us.

'Hi,' Juanita says at last. She takes a loud crunch of her apple. I shoot her a quick smile of thanks for cutting through the awkward tension. She returns the smile, but then her eyes jump back to Diane and Connie, curious about whatever will happen next.

Diane has a small sack lunch in front of her. She carefully takes out a sandwich in waxed paper, an orange, and a thermos. She folds her paper sack down into a neat rectangle like a place mat, smooths it out, and lines the three items up carefully. When she's finished, she peers up at us.

Connie stabs at her mystery school lunch and stares at Diane. There's a thick silence. At last she says, 'I didn't tell you my name this morning, but I'm Connie. Connie Treadway.'

At this a strange look crosses Diane's face, a ripple of awareness. I wonder if Juanita notices it, too. I have no idea what to make of it, but I put a pin in Diane's expression. Something tells me it's a clue of some sort, but to what?

'It's nice to meet you, Connie,' Diane says, dipping her head down to stare at her lunch. Her cheeks redden briefly.

'So Evie told us what you did for her,' Connie says. Her voice isn't unkind. At least not for Connie.

But Diane just stiffens for a moment at Connie's words. She carefully peels back the waxed paper and smooths it out, too, over the paper bag. Diane's bedroom flashes through my mind. All perfect right angles and organized spaces. A quiet cocoon with not a single thing marking it as hers.

Finally she speaks.

'What I did for Evie,' she begins, her hands fluttering over the sandwich, picking it up and putting it down. At last she rests them in her lap and looks up at us. At Connie specifically. 'I . . . how could I not do it? I knew what Preston was going to do to her. So I did it. I *had* to.'

Diane's gaze doesn't waver. Neither does Connie's. I realize I'm holding my breath.

At last Connie gives in. Nods and briefly looks away. You'd have to know Connie to get it, but the way Diane just handled her has given Connie what she would begrudgingly describe as respect for Diane. I wonder if Diane realizes.

Connie takes a bite of her lunch, then pushes the tray away. 'So you don't think the fuzz have a clue it was you? Evie says you left the switchblade. That wasn't so swift.'

'I know that,' Diane says, her voice softening as she blushes again. 'It was stupid. I panicked.'

76

'I would have panicked, too,' says Juanita, and my heart swells in gratitude.

'So the blade,' Connie says, pulling us back, 'where'd you get it anyway?'

A stricken expression comes over Diane. The same expression that crossed her face when the topic of the switchblade came up on Saturday night.

'I can't say.' Her voice shakes, but she means it. You can tell.

'All right,' says Connie. 'I guess I get that. But you better promise us if the fuzz come around, you keep your trap shut. The last thing we need – or Evie needs – is for the police to think she had anything to do with it. They won't believe her and you know it.'

'I . . . I know,' Diane says, stumbling. 'I just have to say . . . I'm really scared. And . . . I need . . . friends. I barely know anybody here. And it's really, really lonely.'

The way she dumps it out there, spills her guts like she doesn't care who sees them. I can't imagine doing something like that. It's not that I don't trust the other girls. But I do worry sometimes about sharing too much. Being that open. What if Connie and the others thought I was a baby? Or weak? Not tough enough to run with them?

But Diane doesn't seem to care what anyone thinks.

Juanita's eyes are open and wide, staring at Diane curiously. I can see from the way her eyes soften that she does feel sorry for Diane. That she does want to help her. And I do, too. But part of me feels lost as to how to handle a girl who rips her heart out in the middle of the cafeteria.

It's briefly quiet until Connie shocks me by speaking up first. 'Listen,' she says, 'I'm not wild about this. I'm making that clear now. But if anyone messes with you, you tell us. We'll take care of it. But you have to promise if the police catch wind, you play dumb. Got it? Just keep your mouth sealed tight. The rest of us will, too.'

Diane nods, grateful, and she shoots me a small smile. She takes a bite of her sandwich and chews quietly.

'Thank you, Connie,' Diane manages. Connie nods briefly but doesn't respond. Instead she chews at a thumbnail, gazing out at the cafeteria, her body bouncing ever so slightly in her seat.

'That's it, I'm taking off,' she says all of a sudden, standing up. 'Gonna go find Sunny.'

'She had to meet Ray somewhere,' I say. 'That's why she's not here.'

Connie rolls her eyes. 'Someone needs to remind that dipstick that Sunny's not his maid.'

'Good luck with that,' mutters Juanita.

The three of us finish our lunch mostly in silence. It's awkward more than anything, but maybe a little less awkward after Connie is gone. After a few moments of silence, Juanita smiles at Diane and says, 'I like your dress.'

'Oh, it was a present from my grandparents,' Diane answers, smoothing out her skirt. Then she evens out the exchange. 'I like your eye makeup, Juanita.'

'Really?' asks Juanita, surprised but pleased. 'I can do my eyes up in five minutes flat, you know.'

'Wow,' says Diane, impressed. 'I couldn't pull off that eyeliner if I tried for days.'

'I bet you could,' Juanita counters, and Diane grins in response. I feel a flood of relief that lunch hasn't been a total disaster, and relax as Diane keeps the conversation moving by asking Juanita who her favorite Beatle is. When Juanita admits it's George because of his soulful eyes, Diane nods in eager agreement.

After we throw away our trash, I suggest hanging out on the front lawn. We head out and spy Connie and Sunny by our oak tree, smoking cigarettes with Ray and Johnny.

'I'm not sure,' Diane says, shifting uncomfortably next to me. 'I think I've worn out my welcome with Connie today.'

'Forget it,' says Juanita, 'it's cool. I mean it.' Maybe it's the exchange about Diane's dress and Juanita's makeup and the Beatles, but Diane pauses and stares at the foursome by the tree. Then she finally exhales and says, 'Well . . . all right.'

As we approach, Johnny spies us first, looking dangerous and mysterious and handsome all at once. Dark, angry eyes and greased-back black hair. Connie's hair would be that color, too, if she didn't insist on dyeing it an almost white blond. I imagine Grandma's voice in my head. *Connie's cheap dye job is trash.* If Connie knew my grandmother thought that, she'd just yelp with delight. I don't mind the color of my hair, but I think it's sort of tuff that Connie doesn't care if her hair is the type grandmothers might lift their noses at.

'Hey,' Johnny says to the three of us, but his eyes pause on Diane. I can sense him taking her in, probably noticing how pretty she is, all curvy and bright-eyed in her lime-green dress. Diane must be used to that sort of look from boys. I wonder if I'll ever know what those looks feel like.

'This is Diane,' I manage, nervous to say anything to Johnny even if he isn't looking at me. 'She's new.'

'Hi, Diane,' Johnny says, his voice soft. Gentle, almost. 'I'm Johnny. Connie's brother.' Never breaking his gaze from where it's directed – at Diane – he tips his head toward Connie, who observes the interaction carefully before taking a drag off her Salem. She doesn't move from her spot against the oak tree, set in a pose that's all cool and relaxed-seeming. But I know Connie. She's like a cat, ready to strike at any moment. Ray and Sunny are huddled off to the side, and they take a moment from their own private banter to observe this arrival.

Diane nods, tucks a lock of her auburn hair behind her ear. 'Hello, Johnny. It's nice to meet you.' She hugs her thermos close to her chest, blinks her green eyes once. Twice. Who knew some girls could even blink in a way that makes them seem prettier? As for Johnny's eyes, he doesn't take them off Diane. Not for a moment.

'So any word on what went down at Winkler's on Saturday night?' Ray says, oblivious to whatever it is that's happening between Diane and Johnny. 'The fuzz still haven't picked anyone up.'

'No clue,' Connie answers, tossing her cigarette butt onto the ground and letting it burn. 'But I'm sure they'll be creeping around this neighborhood, looking for someone to blame. That's what they always do.'

'Yeah, but this is different,' Ray says. 'Beefs between us and the tea sippers are nothing new, but murder sure as hell is.'

On hearing this, Diane grips her thermos more tightly to her chest and bites her bottom lip.

'I don't think it was anyone we know,' Sunny says, maybe too loudly.

'Shit, what do you know, Miss Detective?' Ray barks, laughing at Sunny's words.

Sunny scowls. 'I know a lot,' she protests, elbowing him.

'Don't get fresh,' Ray answers. 'You're too cute for that.'

At this Juanita and I glance at each other, but we don't say anything. Just then, the bell rings for fifth period, and Diane is the only one who jumps at the sound.

'I guess it's time for class,' she says, shooting a furtive

glance at Johnny, who has barely been able to keep his eyes off her.

'What's class?' Ray cracks. I wish someone would tell him he's not half as funny as he thinks he is.

'I guess I'll see y'all later,' Diane says, turning to go. 'It was . . . nice to meet you.' She glances at Johnny once more, then darts off across the lawn.

'Jeez, Johnny, drool much?' Ray says, noticing Johnny watching her go.

Connie pushes herself off the oak tree at last and draws up close to Ray.

'It would be so nice,' she says, her words coming slow and even, 'if someone told you once in a while to shut the hell up.' And then, without waiting for Ray's response or for any of us to follow, she marches off toward the school. I catch a glimpse of Sunny, who allows herself a tiny grin as Ray curses out Connie under his breath.

'Evie, do you feel like fifth period?' Juanita asks me.

I don't, but I do feel like getting away from Ray's stupid remarks.

'I guess I could make an appearance,' I answer.

'Same here,' says Juanita. She glances over at Sunny. 'You coming?'

'All right,' Sunny answers, defiantly tossing her blond hair over her shoulder as she walks away from Ray, for once not waiting for his permission. Ray's face is still frozen into a scowl over Connie's words, but he doesn't protest.

As the three of us head across the grass, Sunny says to us, her voice nothing less than gleeful, 'I know Connie can be a real piece of work sometimes, but I'm glad she's on my side.'

'Me too,' I answer, and I make a silent wish that she's on Diane's side, too.

10

When I get home, Grandma is snapping peas on the kitchen counter.

'Hello, Evelyn,' she says, looking over her shoulder at me, then back at the peas. *Snap, snap, snap.* Just then, along with the rest of the day's mail, I spy a slim white envelope on the kitchen table with my name written in Cheryl's unmistakably lousy cursive. I lunge for it and race to my room.

'A polite young lady would say hello back to her grandmother!' Grandma hollers down the hallway.

'Hello!' I yell as I shut the door behind me.

I can practically hear my grandmother sighing at me through the walls.

I used to share this space with Cheryl. Two twin beds, Cheryl's closest to the closet and mine pushed up next to the drafty window because Cheryl got colder more easily during Houston's brief winters. One old, cracked dresser from the resale shop with the top drawer that sticks. Two seen-better-days nightstands, mine littered with magazines and a pile of gum and candy wrappers the size of Mount Everest, plus my marble collection from elementary school in a jar, my Raggedy Ann doll, my eye makeup, and an empty water glass I've forgotten to return to the kitchen and that Grandma will soon be scolding me about. A brightly colored oval rag rug on the wooden floor sits between our beds. And on the wall space next to the window, above my pillow, a collection of ripped-out pictures and covers from *16* and *Teen Screen* stuck up haphazardly with pushpins. The best one is of Ringo Starr, my favorite Beatle. Everyone else loves Paul, but Ringo is the one for me. I don't know why. He just is. And I like that not everyone else likes him best.

I glance at Cheryl's side, stripped clean and bare, even her childhood quilt long gone, leaving behind a sagging mattress. I try to picture her there, on the other side of the room, spread out on her bed doing homework and sketching pictures or, years earlier, cutting out paper dolls. It's like I can almost see her sitting cross-legged, brow furrowing in focus, humming quietly to herself like she always did when she was concentrating on something.

My heart sinks with longing. It still feels strange to me that my sister isn't here, ready to talk over her day with me, share our private jokes. Cheryl is four years older than me – she's nineteen now – but she was the first person to treat me like I wasn't a kid anymore. Now she's gone and it hurts so much, I don't know what to do with the hurt.

I tug the letter out of the envelope and flop onto my bed on my belly, anxious to take in Cheryl's words. For the past year, we've mostly kept in touch through letters. Once in a while, she'll call late on a Sunday evening when the long-distance rates aren't too expensive, but we can only speak for a few minutes on the phone, with Grandma and Mama hovering around picking up every snippet of my end of the conversation.

Hey, favorite sister, her letter starts. I smile at the old joke. I'm her only sister, of course. I keep reading. *How are you? I'm doing all right, I guess. I know you'll get irritated, but just a reminder to HIDE THIS LETTER after you read it because you know Mama and Grandma will take a peek if they spy it lying open on your disgusting and messy side of the room. Anyway, things are all right, like I said. I started talking to the girl who lives next door to me on base. Her name is Mary and she's pretty nice. She's 20 and just had her first baby so that's sort of hard for me. I know you understand what I'm trying to say. Dennis is hoping we can try to have another one soon. I know it's what he expects and wants. I guess we'll see. I suppose it would give me something to do. I go over to Mary's to fold laundry with her or watch television, and that helps fill my time. Maybe I should take up a hobby or something. Maybe I should start drawing again? But that seems so pointless. Mary's baby is named Charles, but they call him Charlie Junior. He spits up on absolutely everything, you wouldn't believe it.*

I read on. Cheryl spends a paragraph or two talking about a

place called Vietnam and Dennis maybe having to go there. That part of the letter is sort of confusing, because I don't really understand everything Cheryl says about all of it, and honestly, I don't think she does either from the way she's writing it. I've heard about Vietnam on television a few times, and I know it's another country and maybe the United States will soon send more troops to this faraway place, but I haven't paid much attention. It all sounds scary to me. At the end of the letter, Cheryl adds, *Write me back soon don't forget LOVE CHERYL YOUR FAVORITE SISTER.* I go back to the beginning and read it through again. Most of Cheryl's letters sound like this. Confused. Lonely. She doesn't come right out and say it. I can just tell.

I flip over onto my back and turn my head to peer at Cheryl's empty bed again, and at the squares of clean white paint next to the closet that mark where her pinned-up posters of Dion and Frankie Avalon once were, along with the colorful sketches of flowers and birds that Cheryl sometimes liked to draw. I wonder what happened to the posters. Surely a married woman can't put up a poster of Frankie Avalon in the bedroom she shares with her husband, but I sure do hope Cheryl has saved her drawings. I wish she'd start drawing again, like she said she might in her letter. And that even if I'm not there to hear the soothing sound of her pencils scratching on her sketch pad, she soon finds the time to do it, even if she's a married woman now and supposed to be keeping house.

Like I often do, I think back on that moment, the summer before last, when Cheryl crawled into bed with me in the middle of the night, crying so hard she gave herself the hiccups. She was *in trouble*, she whispered. *Gotten herself pregnant*, was what the neighbors would say. It had happened the night of the senior prom, she confessed, and now it was just a few weeks after her high school graduation and she couldn't ignore the truth anymore. She was going to have a baby.

'You're sure?' I whispered, rubbing Cheryl's back, running my hand up and down her spine and trying to get her to calm down enough that I could understand her. Cheryl was only able to nod, and I felt a strange mixture of panic but also pride that she thought I was old enough to share this terrible secret.

'Do you think Dennis will do the right thing?' I asked, thinking of her prom date, a quiet boy with constant ruby-red blemishes on his chin who lived down the street and read *Archie* comics and mowed our lawn for pocket change. He seemed nice enough, I supposed. But now Cheryl was going to have to *marry* him. *If* she was lucky.

'I told him today,' she managed between hiccups, sobbing into my white cotton nightgown so hard it would still be damp when the sun came up. 'He said he would marry me. He enlisted the day after we graduated, you know. After boot camp, I can join him and we can live on base.'

I hugged her back hard. 'That's a relief, I guess,' I answered, but was it? It meant Cheryl would be leaving. Leaving *me*. It was impossible to accept. Too painful to be true. But it was true. And it was incredible to me how suddenly Cheryl's whole life had been decided for her. All because of a few minutes in the back seat of Dennis's father's Mercury Monterey station wagon on the night of her senior prom.

Not long after that evening, she and Dennis exchanged vows in our backyard, surrounded only by our families and with Cheryl wearing a simple white dress Grandma had sewed together in a matter of days. Then she and Dennis moved away.

'Don't be silly, Evie,' my mother said when I'd asked her if Cheryl might ever come back to Houston for good. I'd broached the question one evening after dinner while the two of us watched *Bonanza* and she patched a small hole in the maid's uniform she wore to the Shamrock Hotel. 'She might, but now she has Dennis, and a husband decides where a family is headed. Dennis is a good boy, you can tell. He did the right thing by marrying her, after all, and you can't go wrong with marrying a man in the military. They're very stable. You should be so lucky.' Then she took her small rose-gold sewing scissors and snipped a loose thread, and that was that. Conversation over.

But the snap of my mother's scissors signaled much more than the end of the discussion. It was clear what Mama wanted for me and what I had to look forward to – but even clearer was how strongly I knew this wasn't the life for me.

I didn't want what Mama wanted and what Cheryl had, and this scared me. I could feel my throat closing, strangled by that loose thread that had drifted to the ground.

I wasn't sure what to do to make it less scary. But I had an idea. Something I'd wanted to do for some time. Something that could get me closer to the girls I'd spotted in the hallways at school and at the park. The girls I'd never had the guts to talk to before, but who I knew didn't seem to care so much about the rules.

Sometimes it was like they were even looking to break them.

The next day I wandered across our driveway to Juanita Barajas's back steps, where she sat smoking a cigarette and watching her baby niece toddle around the backyard. Juanita and her friends had always seemed fierce to me. Powerful. But I'd never admitted that to anyone. Certainly not to my old friends — sensible girls with sensible lives — who sneered at Connie and Juanita and Sunny and called them trash.

But there was something about Juanita Barajas and the rest of them.

And I wanted that something.

That afternoon I made my way to the Barajases' backyard, and I asked Juanita just how she made her eye makeup look so tuff. What I meant was how did she make those dramatic, delicious curves? How did she draw those smoldering black lines? How did she transform her eyes into a set of rebellious identical twins?

Juanita took a slow drag off her cigarette and examined me carefully. 'It's easy,' she said, after exhaling a tight stream of smoke, 'but I don't think your mother and grandmother are going to like it much.'

I shrugged, hoping I looked nonchalant and cool even though inside my heart was hammering, hoping I could pull this off.

'I don't care what they think,' I said, which was partly a lie but mostly the truth. I quickly crossed my fingers behind my back to make up for the lie part, a girlhood habit I didn't realize then that I'd soon be giving up. And as it turns out, the untruth didn't matter because Juanita believed me, and she went inside to get her makeup.

After a silent dinner of peas, rice, and meat loaf with Grandma, my mother comes home late from her shift at the Shamrock. As I'm helping clear the table, I hear her opening the front door, followed by the predictable *thunk-thunk* of her shoes hitting the floor. Next will come the squeak of our old couch as she collapses into it to rub her feet.

'Marjorie, do you want your dinner now or should I put it up?' my grandmother asks as she plates the leftovers.

'I'll eat later tonight, Mama, thank you,' my mother answers.

'Hey,' I say, venturing into the den. 'How are you?'

My mother looks up at me and smiles, then pats the spot next to her on the couch for me to join her. I know Mama worries about me. Loves me. And there's still a part of me that wants to please her. Make her proud. So from time to time, I find myself skating around her like this, searching for the closeness we once had when Cheryl and I were tiny.

It sure is hard to find, though.

As I curl up by her side and fold my feet underneath me, I see she has today's *Houston Chronicle*, the evening paper, folded up in front of her on the coffee table.

'How I am is tired, Ladybug,' she says, using my childhood nickname. She doesn't do that much anymore, or at least she stopped doing it so often after I started running around with Juanita and Connie and Sunny and teasing my hair and wearing eye makeup. The nickname tugs at my heart and irritates me at the same time, and I wonder if there's something really wrong with me to feel both emotions at once.

I remember when I was little and Cheryl and I would cuddle into her soft spots after one of her long shifts at work, not caring that she smelled of bleach and the city bus. She has more soft spots than she did then, I imagine, but it's been a long time since I curled up next to my mother.

'Long day?' I ask.

'Yes, always,' she says, rolling her neck to one side and then the other, setting off a series of pops. 'But I survived.'

Grandma joins us, pausing to turn on the television set before she settles into her corner armchair.

'*I've Got a Secret* is on soon,' she says. Grandma loves her television programs.

'All right,' my mother agrees, tipping her head back and closing her eyes.

I sigh and draw my knees up to my chin. All of a sudden, my brain flashes on something strange – me, fifteen years into the future and still in this house, my mother in my grandmother's place and me in my mother's, me calling out for the leftovers to be saved for later. Something about the image makes me shudder, and then I feel guilty.

'Cheryl wrote Evelyn a letter,' my grandmother announces, her eyes trained on the end of the episode of *To Tell the Truth*. 'It arrived today.'

I roll my eyes and hope neither one of them sees, or I'll get scolded for being fresh. But now my mother's going to want to know what Cheryl wrote. Sure enough, Mama immediately opens up her pale blue eyes – naturally, I inherited my boring brown ones from my good-for-nothing father – and peers at me, curious.

'Is she all right?' Mama asks, her voice eager for news.

'She met a neighbor,' I say. 'A girl around her age named Mary? She seemed happy about that.' Remembering Cheryl's demand that I keep her letter private, I don't mention Cheryl's obvious loneliness or Mary's baby or the unsettling unknown

93

of Vietnam. My mother takes a deep breath and draws a thumbnail up to her mouth, then quickly drops it back to her lap. Grandma is always after her not to chew her nails. 'I'm glad to hear it. It's so good she ended up with Dennis.' She pauses. 'I know it's expensive, but maybe we can call her on Sunday night, just to hear her voice for a few minutes,' my mother says. The last time my mother and Cheryl spoke on the phone, Mom teared up a bit after she'd hung up, even though she said they were tears of joy from knowing that Cheryl was settled and safe somewhere. That's what she said, anyway, but I couldn't help but sense that Mama might feel a lot better about the situation if she could see Cheryl with her own eyes and hug her with her own two arms and know for sure that her oldest was all right.

'It would be nice to hear her voice,' I say, letting the truth about Cheryl tickle the tip of my tongue. What if I told Mama right now how worried Cheryl's letter made me? What if I spoke up about how scared I was that Cheryl's life is the only future Mama sees for me?

But I just keep my mouth closed tight. Something about doing that feels easier, even if it's not exactly easy.

Suddenly my mother sits up, remembering something.

'Evelyn, did you know about this?' she asks, reaching for her copy of the Chronicle. 'This murder that happened at Winkler's on Saturday? Weren't you there that night?' She unfolds the paper, revealing a headline over a picture of

Preston Fowler. My stomach lurches at the sight of him and his rich-boy smirk, and a bitter taste of bile tickles the back of my throat. I look away, down at the nubby green couch, squeeze my eyes shut for a moment.

'Evelyn, are you all right?' my mother asks, and I feel her hand on my shoulder.

My eyes flutter open, and I focus them on the television set, the headlines of the newspaper blurring the edges of my vision. 'I'm fine,' I say. 'And yeah, I heard about that, but I'd left Winkler's before the fuzz . . . I mean, before the police showed up.'

I sense my mother nodding, and then she folds up the paper and tosses it back onto the coffee table. 'That's good,' she says, 'although I don't like the idea of you just hanging out at Winkler's with those friends of yours, frankly. I wonder if you were even really watching the picture.'

I nod, my heart racing, my eyes unable to block the image of Preston Fowler from my mind. Anxiety grips me, makes me want to move. I feel the urge to run right out of the house and into the black night, outpacing the memory of that boy's face until it can't catch up with me ever again.

'I need to finish some homework,' I manage at last, unfolding myself from the couch and heading toward my bedroom. Both Mama and Grandma eye me curiously. Homework hasn't been a priority for me in ages.

'Well, good,' my mother answers uncertainly as I head

off down the hallway, squeezing my hands into fists until I feel my fingernails slicing into my palms. My tongue feels thick in my mouth.

Moments later I'm inside my bedroom, and I quietly shut the door behind me. I switch off the light and bury my face in my hands, trying to disappear somehow into the inky darkness.

Breathe, Evie. Breathe. You're all right. He didn't get you. That monster didn't get you. You're here now, in your bedroom. You're safe.

And I imagine Cheryl and her once constant presence in this space that we shared for so long. And I think about Sunny and Connie and Juanita and their flashing eyes and bold hearts and loud laughs, and Diane with her guts and her bravery that night outside the bathroom. Hell, I even picture Miss Odeen, my English teacher, who always seems so confident and sure of herself. And I wish that any one of them could be with me now, right now in this bedroom of mine where I feel so trapped and alone. So ashamed and sick. I imagine they would tuck an arm around the small of my back, lean close, and whisper into my ear, 'Evie, it's all right. You're all right. Listen, Evie, it wasn't your fault. You didn't do anything wrong.'

And in my imagination, I believe them.

11

Miss Odeen slips my paper about Fannie Lou Hamer into my hands as I walk out of English class the next day, and I peer down to spy a *Lovely thoughts! I agree!* written in perfect red script at the top.

'Nice job, Evie,' she says, smiling, her honey-blond hair perfectly set, her pink lipstick neat and crisply lined. 'It's so good to see you making an effort. I hope you keep it up!'

'Thanks, Miss Odeen.' I nod, my cheeks warming. The way some teachers would say that stuff about my effort might make me feel sort of lousy, like it's a rare thing for me to try in school. I mean, I guess it sort of is. But the way Miss Odeen notices my work, it almost makes me want to try more for her.

'She's really lovely, isn't she?' Diane asks as we filter into the crowded hallway, our shoulders practically bumping up against one another's. I catch a whiff of her Evening in Paris perfume and wonder how much it costs.

'Yeah, she's my nicest teacher, and she's new, so she doesn't hate us yet,' I say.

Diane nods. 'My fifth-period algebra teacher, Mr Morris, seems to hate us, but I hate him, too.'

'Oh, he's the absolute worst,' I say, grimacing. 'He picks on Juanita all the time for the dumbest things. She can't stand him, and I don't blame her. He's just horrible.'

'He's mean to all the Mexican kids in class,' Diane says. 'He accused Julia Delgado of cheating just because she got the highest score on the last test.'

I frown, disgusted. That sort of thing isn't even the worst sort of stuff Juanita has to endure at Eastside. An impulse grips me and refuses to let go. It comes on all of a sudden — the same urge to run that I felt last night when that monster's smirk invaded my mind.

'Hey,' I say, 'let's cut.'

Diane's eyes widen. 'What?'

I shrug, Miss Odeen's comments about my effort slipping away. 'Wouldn't you like to avoid Mr Morris this afternoon?' I ask Diane. I don't tell her that I also want to get away from school, away from too much time in classroom after classroom with blocks of boredom stretching out in front of me, making it too easy for Preston's drunken, slurred voice to snake into my brain.

Maybe I only need a minute.

Diane is still insisting she isn't sure as we head down the

stairs and out of the building, students spilling out onto Eastside's lawn for lunch. I grab her by the hand and tug her toward Telephone Road.

'Come on,' I say, consumed by the need to run. To *go*. 'I bet you've never cut. Not even once, right?'

She shakes her head no, and it strikes me how strange it is that this girl took a boy down with a switchblade to protect me, but she's never skipped a single minute of school.

'It's just this once,' I tell her, 'just for today.' I don't know why it's so important to me to leave school now with Diane. There's something freeing, maybe, about taking off with the one other person who was with me that night at Winkler's. Who knows exactly what happened to me and how terrible it was. Even if there is a part of me that wishes I could have been the one to defend myself.

'Well,' says Diane, following me and not protesting all that much, 'all right, I guess.'

Still hand in hand, we prepare to cross Eastside's perimeter near an edge of the campus I know few adults will be monitoring, when suddenly I catch a glimpse of Johnny Treadway heading out of a side door of the school building all by himself.

'Hey,' he shouts, nodding his chin in our general direction.

I turn and meet his eyes with mine, and I feel Diane grip my hand, and hard, too.

'Hello,' she says, her eyes homing in on him, her face

99

breaking out into a soft, uncertain smile.

'Hey, Johnny,' I say, still leading Diane off campus. 'If you see Connie and the others, tell her we're taking a vacation, will you?' I applaud myself for such a witty comment in front of a boy as cute and tuff as Johnny Treadway, but I realize he's not all that interested in what I'm telling him. Instead, his eyes are set on Diane, following her, just like they were yesterday during lunch.

'Okay,' he finally manages, never losing focus. 'I'll tell them.'

Diane is still peering at him over her shoulder as I lead her toward the closest bus stop, and when the city bus lumbers closer and we climb on, I can tell she's still lost in thought, or at least in Johnny Treadway's deep brown eyes. Not that I blame her for that, of course. Then again, part of me thinks a girl like Diane wouldn't ever give a boy like Johnny the time of day.

As the bus moves, the thick, sweet scent of gasoline and exhaust cuts through the air, but I just sit back and feel the rumble of the bus's wheels under us, drawing us farther and farther away from school and crowded halls and complicated cafeteria conversations and teachers who aren't Miss Odeen frowning at me, their eyes full of fake concern.

For the first moments of our ride, Diane hums to herself, deep in thought. First a Beatles song I recognize, then something I don't. Her face is relaxed and open, maybe

100

the most at peace I've ever seen it.

At last she turns to me and says, 'I can't believe we cut class.' She offers an exaggerated frown. 'You're a bad influence, Evie.' But then a smile cracks her face in two, revealing her perfect white teeth. She winks.

'I guess I am,' I say, and I smile, too. I turn and peer out the window, smudged with fingerprints. 'This bus goes downtown,' I say. 'Where do you want to go?'

Diane sits up straighter, grinning even more widely. 'Oh, let's go to the Jive Hive. Please? Do you know it? On McKinney and Main?'

'The record store?' I ask. 'Yeah, I know it.' I've been there a few times with Connie and the others, and one time we got kicked out for loitering too long and not buying anything, but it seems as good an idea as any.

'I love that place,' Diane says. 'I'm absolutely mad about music.'

I smile at her, because of course she is. That must be why she's always humming to herself. But then why didn't her sad little bedroom have a single record in it? I want to ask, but something stops me, and instead I turn my attention out the window.

As the bus lurches through downtown, we pass Sakowitz and Foley's, and the Loew's State Theater on Main. I can remember the ruckus last year and the anger among some white people when it integrated and everyone was allowed in through the big brass doors up front. I heard about the students from Texas Southern University, the Negro college in town, holding sit-ins to finally integrate the lunch counters at Mading's Drugs and Union Station. But I also remember Fannie Lou Hamer's words and the terrible things that happened to her when she tried to vote. It seems some things are changing for the better, and other things aren't changing at all.

As this jumble of thoughts floats through my mind, I ask Diane what she thought about Miss Odeen's assignment on Fannie Lou Hamer.

'I really liked that Miss Odeen taught us about her and everything she had to go through,' she answers. 'I feel stupid that I didn't know about her before. But I could tell some of the kids didn't like the lesson.'

'I could tell, too,' I answer, shifting in my seat. 'Diane, don't you think it's strange that we don't go to school with everyone like they do up north? Don't you think it's not right?'

Diane ponders for a moment before she answers. 'Yes. But I do know parents like mine would get so angry if that happened. They say the most awful things when they see the news.'

It's odd to have Diane mention her parents, and I can tell when she does that she's caught herself off guard. Like she didn't mean to bring them up at all.

'I don't think my mother would be angry,' I say. 'At least I hope she wouldn't be.'

When it was in the papers this past July that President Johnson had signed the Civil Rights Act, my mother said she was proud that it was a Texan who had done it. But my grandmother didn't say anything at all.

'My parents are hateful people,' Diane murmurs, her mouth in a firm line, her eyes suddenly clouded with concern. I feel guilty that the topic has come up, and I mutter a quiet apology.

'It's all right, Evie,' Diane says as she reaches up to ring the cord and let the bus driver know we want to get off. 'I'm used to thinking of them that way.' The way she says it, I can tell it's not really true, but I don't press. Instead, I follow her as we hustle through downtown, passing businessmen racing through crosswalks and shopgirls gossiping and smoking as they head off for their lunch breaks. By the time we reach the Jive Hive, with the painting of a cheerful bumblebee playing a saxophone on the front window, Diane's good mood seems to be returning. Just as we reach the door, she pauses and touches me lightly on the arm.

'I'm sorry, I didn't mean to get so prickly on the bus,' she says. 'I just do sometimes when I think about them.' Then she nods toward the record store. 'Anyway, we're here now, and that's certainly helping.' She offers me a smile and I return it, but as we head inside, I can't help but wonder one more time what this girl is hiding.

12

As Diane and I flip through records, the only patrons in the store, I can tell she's a bigger music fan than I am. Sure, back in February I watched the Beatles on *Ed Sullivan* – that's when I decided Ringo was my favorite. Everyone else already had crushes on John and Paul and George, and I thought liking Ringo the best made me different. And of course I know all the words to 'I Want to Hold Your Hand' like everyone else on the planet, but Diane's knowledge of music runs deeper than all of that. She asks the quiet, bespectacled man at the counter what's come in that's new, and she shuffles through 45s, gazing at pictures of Mary Wells and Roy Orbison and Martha and the Vandellas, her mouth twisted in serious thought.

'Oh!' she says suddenly as she flips through a bin. 'Irma Thomas!'

'Who is she?' I ask as Diane holds up a record.

'She's a soul singer from New Orleans,' she says, her voice

growing wistful. 'I used to adore playing this.' She flips the 45 over and over, transfixed. I can't help it anymore.

'Diane,' I say, suddenly feeling bold. 'If you love music this much, how come you don't have any records in your bedroom?'

She swallows hard and doesn't say anything right away, and I wonder if I've made a huge mistake. But she just looks at me and whispers, 'Evie, can I trust you with something?' She peers over her shoulder, even though there's no one around but the man behind the counter, and then turns back toward me, steps closer. I can still smell her perfume. 'I mean,' she says, her soft voice insistent, 'can I *really* trust you?'

My heart picks up speed, knowing I've come close to finally discovering at least something about this strange girl from the right side of the tracks who had the guts to save my life. I owe her something. At the very least I owe her my word. That and my friendship are all I have to offer her, and it hits me hard that maybe it's what she needs more than anything else right now.

'Yes, Diane, of course,' I say.

She takes my hand in hers and leads me to one of the listening booths in the back of the shop, holding up the copy of Irma Thomas's record in her hand. The bespectacled man nods, and as we enter the tiny, musty, closet-sized space with the turntable and bench seat covered in cracked red vinyl, Diane slips the record on and gently dips the needle down to play it.

'This song is called "Ruler of My Heart",' Diane intones, her face serious. 'Just listen to how beautiful her voice is. I mean, it's heavenly.'

We sit side by side, our shoulders pressed tight against one another's. I can still spy the rows of records through the glass window in the listening booth door.

Irma Thomas's throaty, rich voice swells around us as she talks about waiting for the man she loves to return. A piano builds, and so does Irma Thomas's yearning. It gives me shivers.

'I really like it,' I say.

And Diane looks at me and says, her voice a whisper, 'Johnny Treadway and I used to dance to this in my bedroom back when I lived in River Oaks with my family.'

I blink once. Twice. I realize I'm holding my breath.

Johnny Treadway. Connie's twin brother. Johnny with the wounded eyes and the dark hair and the bad home life. Johnny who wouldn't look twice at me, a kid. Johnny, the tuffest boy in the entire neighborhood.

Johnny and Diane?

It's like trying to picture the beaches of Galveston covered in mountains of snow or my mother the maid wearing the crown jewels.

'What?' I manage, and it comes out like a croak over the music.

'Evie, he would hold me so close to him,' she says. 'And it

was the best feeling in the whole wide world.' Diane's eyes fill with tears and then spill over, but she's smiling at the same time. In fact, she's almost laughing. It reminds me of the sort of laughter that comes with staying up too late and not getting enough sleep. Mama always calls it *punch-drunk*.

'God, it feels good to tell someone,' she says. 'It feels good to tell *you*, Evie.'

My mind flies through yesterday and today, remembering the way Johnny and Diane stared at each other, how Johnny couldn't take his eyes off Diane. How her cheeks pinked up and her voice softened around him. But they acted like they didn't even know each other.

The record ends, and Diane starts playing it again.

'I bet you're wondering how, huh?' she asks. She sniffles and takes a tissue from her skirt pocket and blots her reddening eyes.

'I'm wondering a lot,' I say, trying to make sense of everything I'm feeling. Astonishment? Worry? Maybe even a thin slice of envy?

'I'll tell you – I want to – but do you promise to keep this between us? At least for now? Please? The others are sweet, but I just met them.' The way she says that last bit, like she expects and hopes to one day be close with them, sort of crushes my heart. She's so lonely. It's enough for me to promise Diane she has my word. I even cross my heart for emphasis.

'We met the summer before last,' she begins, clutching her tissue. 'We met here, of all places. We're both crazy about music.' I know that much is true about Johnny. For all his delinquent habits, he's held a regular job at the Texaco in our neighborhood for a few years now, and Connie always says he spends his money on three things – hair grease, cigarettes, and new records. They're the three things he comes by honestly.

'I was here this one Saturday in June,' Diane says as I lean in, anxious to catch every detail. 'I went with some girlfriends. And at the time I was going steady with someone. Actually, a friend of Preston Fowler's.' She bites her lip and looks away at her own mention of the dead boy. At the sound of his name, my stomach drops.

Maybe I only need a minute.

I shake my head at the sound of his voice in my mind, and Diane lightly touches my knee.

'I'm sorry, Evie, I shouldn't have mentioned him.'

'It's okay,' I say. 'Go on.'

Diane sniffs a bit, starts the record over. 'I knew Johnny wasn't from my neighborhood,' she says, and she grins at a private memory, her eyes wrinkling up around the edges.

'And he must have known you weren't from ours,' I say.

Diane nods, and she unfolds her story. She shells out tiny details – the way Johnny admired her choice of a King Curtis record. How she caught him staring at her through the glass

108

window of the listening booth when she tried it out to make sure she liked it.

'It was this very booth,' she says, peering out the window. 'I caught him peeking in here. And I knew we were from different worlds. But . . .' She blushes. 'There was something about him.'

I smile, wanting to say something about how Johnny is dreamy. But I don't know if I should.

Diane keeps talking in a whisper over the music, describing how Johnny managed to catch her in a corner of the Jive Hive and invited her to play a game with him.

'A game?' I ask, confused.

'Yes,' Diane says, her face wearing a full-fledged smile now. 'He said if I gave him my telephone number and he could remember it, I would have to go out on a date with him.'

At this I grin back briefly, wondering what it must be like to have a good-looking boy like Johnny Treadway do something so bold to catch your attention. Of course, if you're a girl as pretty and stylish as Diane, maybe you're used to that sort of behavior from boys.

'Anyway, I gave him the number,' she says, still smiling at the memory. 'And you can guess the rest.'

I can, but fortunately for my curious mind, Diane keeps talking, and one chapter leads to the next. Diane sneaking out to meet Johnny. Lying to her parents. Meeting up at Winkler's with her friends and then pretending to feel sick and head home, only to meet up with Johnny in the shadows of our neighborhood. Heading over to Playland Park and kissing at the top of the Ferris wheel. Venturing out to see construction on the fancy new Domed Stadium being built on the west side. Heading to Galveston for the night, sinking their feet in the cool sand and imagining what lay out beyond the waves.

I realize I'm still as a stone while Diane spins her story, and totally transfixed. It all sounds like something out of a Hollywood picture, and it reminds me of the movie *A Summer Place* that I saw at Winkler's when I was a kid. It was a steamy romance about two teenagers named Molly and Johnny who fall in love even though they aren't supposed to, and they end up sneaking off to get married. Mama and Grandma took Cheryl and me as a treat, and when Grandma made us cover our eyes during all the kissing scenes, Cheryl and I peeked through our fingers, both of us practically holding our breath so we could hear every single whispered promise. Every sad cry of lovers kept apart.

'It's like a movie,' I say.

'It sure felt like one,' agrees Diane. 'Like the biggest romance ever. And I got to star in it. With him.'

Tears keep falling, and she clutches her tissue to her face again. The image of Diane gently shaking me awake that night at Winkler's, Preston Fowler's blood fresh on her pink dress, plays in my mind. So does the image of her handing me some of her clothes to change into later on at her aunt's house.

You can keep these. I've got heaps of clothes.

Her cries ring much louder than the record playing. I do all I can think to do, which is to reach out and hug her, letting her weep into my shoulder. I remember the way I held Cheryl the night she told me she was going to have to marry Dennis. Diane's sobs are like Cheryl's. Heavy and hard. Devastated.

'Diane, it's all right,' I whisper, rubbing my hand up and down her back, wishing I knew what to say. Imagining what it must feel like to be able to spill out all your emotions, to lay them out in front of another person without knowing how the other person will respond.

Finally, after a few shaky breaths, Diane gets her composure back, and she withdraws a bit.

'Thanks, Evie,' she says, squeezing her eyes shut briefly and taking a deep breath. 'I bet you're wondering how the hell I ended up at *school* with Johnny, huh?'

'I guess I was, yeah,' I say. 'And why you acted like you didn't know each other yesterday.' Seeing my chance to ask another question that's been on my mind, I screw up my courage and say, 'And what about Connie? Does she know?' Suddenly Connie's insistence at the park that she just didn't *like* Diane, and her cold, careful stares, make more sense.

Diane nods, wordless for a moment, still trying to calm down from her crying jag. 'I think she does, yes. I mean, I don't know how much, but I know Johnny told her about me, and he swore her to secrecy. We knew my parents would

111

never understand us being together. My mother and father are all about appearances. They've been planning my match since I was in primary school.'

'Your match?' I ask, confused.

'You know, the right sort of boy. The kind of boy whose parents go to the club with my parents and whose father does business with my father and whose mother plays bridge with my mother and . . .' She pauses and scowls. 'It's all so awful. My parents don't believe in true love, like what Johnny and I had. They believe in mergers.'

I think about Mama wanting to pair off Cheryl and me with boys who'll stick around. And I wonder if it's any different than what Diane is describing.

'So you had to keep Johnny a secret?' I say.

Diane nods vigorously. 'Yes. We would sneak away to be together. Only . . .' She pauses, takes a deep breath. 'Ruler of My Heart' stops spinning, and Diane doesn't pick up the needle again. We just sit, huddled in the booth, our whispers and breathing and Diane's sniffles the only song we have.

'One Saturday evening a few months after we met, my parents were gone at some charity event and my younger sister, Patty, was at a girlfriend's house,' she says. 'And I had Johnny come over. He'd been over before a few times when I was home alone. He'd . . . been to my bedroom.' At this her cheeks blush a deep scarlet, and she glances down at the tissue clutched in her lap. I can't possibly imagine working up the courage to ask Diane what I really want to know. Me and the girls don't have the words for such conversations. Not even Connie talks about it all that much, and she can talk pretty dirty when she wants to. But Diane's burning cheeks answer my buried question, and the idea of being in love and holding a boy like Johnny Treadway behind a shut bedroom door makes my body thrum with a strange, almost delicious sense of possibility.

'Anyway, that night my parents came home earlier than I'd expected,' Diane says, not making eye contact. 'They tossed him out. My father threatened to shoot him, he really did. And then they called me a whore.'

I gasp. Maybe my mother does want to set me up with a boy like Dennis, but not even when Cheryl admitted to Mama through tears in our tiny kitchen that she was in trouble did Mama say anything so cruel.

'A whore?' I manage, lowering my voice. For some reason that word sounds dirtier than any of the dirty words Connie says and any of the ones I've tried saying before. 'Really?'

Diane nods, her face threatening to collapse into tears again. 'They said I was trash to be with such trash. That I wanted to ruin my family's good name and embarrass them in front of all their important friends. I'm telling you, all they care about is what other people think.' She twists the tissue, her fingers gripping it hard. Then she rips it in frustration.

'After Christmas they sent me away.' She breaks her gaze

and stares off, her face falling, something unsettling clearly crossing through her mind.

'Where?' I ask, worried that perhaps I'm pestering her for too much information. Then I realize Diane's face has gone blank all of a sudden. A shiver runs up my spine. Something about her bleak expression is frightening.

She shakes her head. 'I can't . . . I don't want to talk about it.' The way she says it is firm, settled.

'All right, you don't have to,' I say, not sure what to do next. I'm dying to hear more of Diane's story, of course, but it's also obvious how difficult it is for her to unfold this part of it.

'I got home in July,' she says, and I can tell she's picking her words with caution. 'But my parents decided I wasn't done being punished. They told me it would be better if I had a fresh start. If I came to this side of town to live with my aunt Shirley. She's always been . . . I guess you would say the family outcast. She's my father's half sister, and she's a mean drunk. She lives on whatever is left of her part of the family trust, and I'd honestly only met her once or twice before I came over to live with her for good. I think she only took me in because my parents give her a little money for it every month.'

I remember the cluttered, filthy home. The empty bottles of wine on the kitchen counter. The tiny, clean oasis that was Diane's room. Another piece of the Diane puzzle has slid into

114

place, even if the picture being revealed is hardly pretty.

Diane wipes at her eyes. 'And do you know what?' she says, her voice ratcheting up in volume and anger. 'When I got back, my parents had emptied my room of my record player and my magazines and my records. My records! All the records I'd played all my life and when Johnny came over were gone. *All* of them! They said they were a bad influence.' She starts to number them on her fingers, and her tears return. 'The Cascades and the Chiffons and Little Stevie Wonder and Mary Wells and Dusty Springfield and Lesley Gore and everyone,' she says, like they're all old friends. 'I know maybe it's stupid. But the records really mattered. I sobbed and sobbed, and I begged Patty to tell me what had happened to them, but she avoided me like I was contagious.' She takes a shaky breath. 'She's always been the good one, if you know what I mean.'

I nod, and I can't help but think about Cheryl for a minute. Which one of us is the good one? Which one of us is bad? What did Diane do that was wrong but decide for herself who she was going to love?

'Anyway,' continues Diane, sniffling, 'my parents sent me to my aunt's house, only they didn't realize it was Johnny's neighborhood they were sending me to! They never even bothered to learn his name. They just threw him out of the house that day, and I never saw him again or talked to him again until I moved in with my aunt and started at Eastside. Before I left, I tried to talk to some of my old friends who I

115

thought would care, but they didn't want anything to do with me.'

A realization strikes me. 'Wait, Diane, were some of those girls the ones who were giving you a hard time at Winkler's on Saturday? I mean, before . . .' I don't finish my sentence. We both know what I mean.

Diane nods, frowning. 'Yes, those were my friends. Or rather, my former friends. I'd told my best friend, Betty, about Johnny. She was one of those girls that night. I guess she couldn't keep her mouth shut. I'm sure her vicious, awful mother helped spread the rumors, too.' I remember what those tea sippers at Winkler's said. How they couldn't believe Diane had the guts to show her face in public again. All for loving a boy from my side of town. It makes me want to spit nails.

'So why do you and Johnny act so strange around each other?' I ask, confused. 'I mean, shouldn't you be happy to be together again? And at the same school?'

Diane looks away from me and presses her hand up against the listening booth wall, then leans her head against it, too, like this conversation has completely exhausted her. Maybe it has.

'I know, you would think so, wouldn't you? Only . . . I never got a chance to tell Johnny goodbye. And I think he believes I abandoned him. I just disappeared, and months ago, too. I think it's why Connie doesn't like me. And when Johnny and I have tried to talk since . . . well, everything feels off. Like that night at Winkler's? Before you stood up for me at the concession stand? We got into a big fight about everything.'

Johnny skulking around the fence line at Winkler's. A drunk Connie threatening to spill the beans about something until Johnny hauled her away. Now it all makes sense.

'Couldn't you explain it was your parents' fault?' I ask.

Diane nods. 'I did. And he wants to be together again. Only . . . oh, Evie, I don't have the words. It's so complicated.'

I couldn't venture a guess as to how complicated, or even begin to try. Suddenly Diane seems so old to me, older even than Cheryl, who's married and everything.

Diane takes a deep breath. 'Evie, I need to stop for a bit,' she says. 'I haven't really talked about any of this with anyone. Not like this, anyway.'

I squeeze Diane's hand. 'I understand,' I say. 'Let's just sit here for a little bit, all right?'

Diane offers me a soft smile of agreement, then reaches out and restarts the Irma Thomas record. The two of us barely make a sound as we wait for the song to begin, aching to hear the longing in her voice again.

CHAPTER

13

After the record finishes, Diane takes it and slides it carefully back into its sleeve. In the past twenty minutes, it feels like we've lived through two lifetimes together. So much has changed – at least in the way I see Diane.

'Could you buy it?' I ask, suddenly aware of the silence. 'I mean, I know you don't have a record player anymore, but just to have it?'

'It would hurt too much to have it and not be able to listen to it,' she says. She sighs as she stands up. 'Let's just leave, all right?'

I stand up, too, and tentatively reach my hand out and place it on her back for a moment as we open the door. It's strange how a conversation in a listening booth has changed how I see Diane. She's not just some tea sipper I'm obligated to anymore. Is she my friend? Three days ago we didn't know each other, and based on her appearance, I wouldn't have given her the time of day. But now? My heart is breaking for her like it would for Juanita or Connie or Sunny.

After we exit the listening booth and then the Jive Hive altogether, we head toward the bus stop. I notice just how red and blotchy her face is from crying. I imagine her in that dark, messy kitchen with an aunt she barely knows and who doesn't seem to care about her. A strange idea grips me. Before I have a moment to doubt it, I hear myself asking, 'Diane, by the time we get back, school will be almost over. Do you want to come home with me? You could maybe have dinner with us?'

Diane turns to me, her eyes wide. 'Oh,' she says. 'Are you . . . that would be swell, Evie. But I wouldn't want to put you out . . . even if I have to say that I'm not really ready to go to my aunt's house yet.' I notice she doesn't call it home.

'No, it's all right,' I say. 'It would be nice. But you're going to have to meet my mother and my grandmother.'

'What about your dad?' Diane asks.

'I don't know him,' I admit. 'He took off when I was small.'

'Oh. I'm sorry.'

'It's nothing,' I say, even though some days it feels like everything. At least when it comes to how my mother views my future.

After a quiet bus ride home, we walk down Munger Street to my small green house, with the white shutters that have needed a paint job since I was in elementary school. When I lead Diane inside, where Grandma is in the kitchen preparing

119

dinner as usual, I realize I'm so nervous my palms are suddenly slick with sweat.

'Hello,' my grandmother says, not looking up right away. When she does, she startles. I never bring people home.

'Hello, I'm Diane,' says Diane, stretching out her hand as smooth as you please, catching my grandmother by surprise. But Grandma is pleased, too, you can tell, and her eyes crinkle up at the sides as she carefully wipes her hands on her red gingham apron and extends the right one to Diane.

'Hello, I'm Evelyn's grandmother,' she says, 'Helen Davis.'

Diane's face grows confused at the sound of my full first name, but she just nods and says, 'It's nice to meet you, Mrs Davis.'

'I wondered if Diane could stay for dinner?' I ask, already knowing that the answer is yes, already sure that my grandmother is quietly praying to God that this clear-eyed, well-scrubbed girl rubs off on me. If only she knew about Johnny Treadway, I think to myself. How funny that Grandma is so concerned with how proper ladies should behave. If she knew about Diane's past, she'd probably be begging that I bring Juanita over instead.

'Yes, of course,' my grandmother answers, smiling.

'We're going to my room,' I tell Grandma, and I guide Diane down the hall. Juanita's only been over once or twice, and Connie and Sunny never have. Mama and Grandma wouldn't like it, of course.

I can sense Diane taking in the space as soon as I shut the door behind us. 'Wow, you're messy, Evie.' But it's not a judgment, just an observation. She grins a little.

'I know I am,' I say, shoving a pile of dirty clothes off the bed and onto the floor so Diane has a place to sit. 'My mother and my grandmother hate it.' For some reason, I don't care that Diane is seeing it like this.

'Does she always call you Evelyn?' Diane says, slipping off her shoes and delicately folding herself onto my bed.

'She thinks it's nicer than Evie,' I answer, making a move to sit down on Cheryl's stripped bed.

'Oh, come over here next to me,' Diane says, pushing herself over, moving my pillow and leaning up against the wall. I smile at the gesture.

'You don't have a desk or anything?' she asks.

'I don't do homework,' I say, trying to make a joke. The truth is we probably wouldn't spend the money on a desk when there are bills to pay. I slide off my shoes and sit at the foot of the bed, leaning over to open the window before crossing my legs. A cool breeze floats near us.

Diane reaches out and touches a picture I've pinned up of Ringo Starr.

'Ringo's cute and all, but George is still my favorite,' Diane says, tracing her finger around Ringo's chin. 'I know everyone loves Paul, but George really is a hunk.' She sighs and adds, 'His dreamy eyes remind me of Johnny's.'

'It's not that I think Ringo is the cutest,' I say, frowning. 'But I like that he's the drummer. It seems like such a tuff instrument to play, you know?'

'Do you play anything?' Diane asks. 'I mean an instrument?'

'Just the recorder when they made us in elementary school,' I say. 'Do you?'

'When I was small, I had to take piano lessons from this woman named Mrs Taylor, who smelled like brussels sprouts,' Diane answers, wrinkling up her nose. 'My parents thought an elegant young lady should be able to play the piano. But I was never very good at it, even though I'd have given anything to sing like Irma Thomas or Dusty Springfield.'

'My grandmother thinks an elegant young lady shouldn't do any of the things I do,' I say, shrugging.

Diane eyes Cheryl's empty bed. 'Whose is that?' she asks.

'My sister's,' I say. 'Cheryl. She graduated from Eastside a year ago and lives on base at Fort Hood with her husband.' And then, because I feel like our conversation in the listening booth has given me permission, I glance at my lap when I say, 'She had to get married.'

Diane doesn't say anything for a moment. Just stares at Cheryl's sagging mattress and empty nightstand covered with nothing on it but fading water rings.

'Did she have a boy or a girl?' Diane asks, her voice low. She peers down at her hands, not at me, when she asks the question.

'She lost the baby, but they stayed married,' I answer, and as the words tumble out, I realize how good it feels to trust Diane with them.

'Oh, I'm so sorry,' she answers. 'That's terrible.'

'It was really sad,' I say. 'And she didn't know Dennis – that's her husband – all that well when they got married. It's not like they'd been going steady for years or anything. He's nice and all, but . . .' I trail off, uncertain how to describe Cheryl's letters and phone calls, the loneliness laced through every single one. Part of me wants to tell Diane how angry it made me when Cheryl lost her baby. After it happened, she had a reason to leave Dennis, a reason to come back home. But she wouldn't do it, no matter how much I begged her. It was like Cheryl had been tricked into playing a game she'd never have the chance to win. And it terrified me that I'd someday get tricked into it, too.

'So your mother wasn't angry at her?' Diane asks, peering at me carefully, her green eyes curious. 'I mean, if you don't mind me asking. Maybe I'm prying.'

I shake my head. 'No, it's all right.' I honestly never talk about Cheryl much. I love Connie and Juanita and Sunny – they'd do anything for me and stick by me no matter what – but sometimes it seems we're too busy running wild to sit around having heart-to-hearts. Maybe because running wild is a way to forget what put our hearts through so much pain in the first place. Or maybe because even though I can let my guard down with Juanita at least once in a while, there's a big part of me that worries if I let it down too much – especially in front of Connie – I won't fit in.

'My mom wasn't thrilled about what happened with Cheryl,' I admit at last, thinking back to those days of disappointed sighs and tear-soaked breakfasts. 'But she wasn't blowing her top over it, either, I guess. I mean, ever since our dad walked out on us when me and Cheryl were small, my mom's pinned all her hopes on the two of us finding good, stable husbands. She thinks a girl's ticket out of this neighborhood is a decent man with a decent job, and in her opinion, Cheryl got that.' I pause for a minute and then, not caring that Diane is a tea sipper with a father as rich as King Midas, I add, 'My mom supports us by cleaning rooms at the Shamrock. And we get a little from my grandpa's pension. He died when I was a baby.'

Diane nods. The comment about my mother working as a maid doesn't seem to surprise or bother her. She mulls over what I've shared, drawing her finger around the faded blue delphiniums that dot my bedsheets.

'I understand,' she says. 'I think my parents want me to graduate from Eastside out of sight from all their friends at the club, and then they'll send me to college far away somewhere. And after that's all done, they're hoping everything that happened will be forgotten enough that they'll be able to pawn me off on some respectable young man who either likes me or likes my father's money.' She pauses, her index finger pressing into one of the delphiniums extra hard.

'I don't have any idea what happens to me if I graduate from Eastside,' I offer with a shrug.

'Why *if*?' Diane asks.

'I'm not exactly top of the class,' I say, rolling my eyes, frustrated at myself. Maybe even a little embarrassed. I know what's waiting for me. Maybe graduation. Maybe getting a factory job or joining my mother cleaning rooms at the Shamrock. And if Mama has her way, marrying some guy I'm not wild about and having babies who will grow up to one day maybe graduate from Eastside, and on the weekends I'll sit on the porch with Juanita and Connie and Sunny and retell the same stories over and over and over until we can't remember what happened to who and when, just that it happened, and maybe it was fun.

'Well, you could still finish,' says Diane. 'I bet you could. And then, who knows?'

'Yeah, I'll move to California like the Beverly Hillbillies,' I crack. 'I'll get a cement pond.' That last sentence I say in my silliest hillbilly accent.

'I despise that television program,' Diane says, frowning. 'It's so corny.'

'I hate it, too!' I say. 'But my mother and grandmother love it.' I pause to consider something. 'So that show isn't how rich people live?' I'm joking, of course, but it's worth it when Diane laughs. The sound fills the room, which suddenly doesn't feel so empty anymore.

Soon we're talking at almost the same time, Diane's sentences sliding over mine and mine over hers, like they're getting to know each other, too. I can see Diane relaxing a little in front of me, dropping her shoulders, dropping the ends of words. As for me? The last time I felt this comfortable spilling secrets and talking things over in this room, it was with Cheryl. It's nice.

'Isn't it funny, you hanging out with a tea sipper like me?' she asks.

'How'd you know we call you that?' I ask, surprised. 'Tea sippers.'

'I live on planet Earth, you know,' Diane says, smiling. 'Even if most of that time was spent in River Oaks.'

I hear the front door open, Mama's work shoes hitting the floor, and some low talking between my mother and my grandmother. I'm sure Grandma is alerting Mama to Diane's presence. Then my bedroom door opens. Diane pops up on both feet, tucks her hair behind her ear.

'Hello, Mrs Barnes,' she says. 'I'm Diane Farris.' I can't believe how quickly she can put on her company manners.

'Hello,' my mother says, more softly than normal. 'Evie,' she says, peering at the floor, 'you could at least straighten up a bit if you're going to have a friend over.' She looks at Diane again, tips her head a little. I know she's trying to understand

126

how Diane is here in her house with her bad daughter who wears too much eyeliner and has too little common sense.

'Diane doesn't mind,' I say. 'Really.'

'I can help her tidy up if you'd like,' she says.

My mother pauses, stares at Diane, and blinks. 'My goodness, any influence you could have on my daughter would be much appreciated,' she says. 'Now I need to get cleaned up before we eat.' After she walks out, Diane and I share a glance and a grin.

'You've impressed my mother quite a bit, in case you couldn't tell,' I say.

'I live to please,' Diane says, before putting her hands on her waist and peering around. 'And I really can help you fix this room up if you'd like, you know.'

I shoot Diane a *no way* look and slide off my bed.

'Maybe next time,' I say, smiling wider, and we head into the hallway toward the kitchen.

Dinner is pork chops and butter beans. Grandma and Mama aren't sure what to make of Diane, who pulls her pageant-queen self out again and chatters on, making up a story about coming to our part of town to 'help a sick aunt' and going on and on about how much she's enjoying Eastside High. But they seem impressed, smiling and nodding as she fills the empty pauses with observations and questions about just how my grandmother gets her pork chops so tasty. This gives Grandma an opportunity to elaborate on her cooking skills. Skills, she notes, that she wishes I would be more interested in learning.

'I should learn more about the kitchen, too, Mrs Davis,' Diane says, in between careful bites, and Grandma smiles. When dinner is over, Diane insists on clearing the table and doing the dishes. I help, and I quickly make Diane take over drying because she clearly hasn't washed many dishes in her life.

As we finish up, we hear Mama and Grandma turn on the small television in the living room. Diane takes this as her cue to leave.

'It was so nice to meet you both,' she says, smiling broadly.

'You're welcome in our home anytime, Diane,' Mama says.

'Thank you so much,' she says, nodding. I'm almost surprised she doesn't curtsy.

I walk Diane out to our porch and shut the front door behind me.

'Good grief, Diane,' I say good-naturedly. 'My mother and grandmother are going to be all over me about how come my manners aren't as nice as yours.'

Diane sighs in embarrassed acknowledgment. 'I can't help it. I'm like a well-trained show horse around adults, especially when I meet them for the first time.' She snaps her fingers for emphasis and then mimics a voice I can only guess is her mother's, high-pitched and snooty. 'Diane, dear, please come in and say hello to Mr and Mrs Cullen. Now parade around and open up your mouth so they can see how well you trot and how nice your teeth look.'

I snort, and loudly, too. Diane can certainly be funnier than I expected. I suspect this is one of the things that made Johnny Treadway fall in love with her. And I think about how it's something that might make Connie and the other girls like her a lot more, too, if only they would give Diane a real chance.

'Anyway, Evie,' she says, 'I should be leaving.' The weight of our conversation in the listening booth at the Jive Hive feels heavy between us, but neither one of us mentions it. Diane just reaches out and hugs me. 'Thanks for being my friend,' she whispers into my ear.

'Thanks for being mine,' I say, and I stand on the sidewalk watching her walk all the way down the street until she rounds the corner.

When I head back inside, I find Mama and Grandma watching *The Andy Griffith Show*. 'What a lovely young lady she was,' Grandma says, managing to pull her eyes away from the set to look at me. 'You should bring her by more often.'

'You can bring her by whenever you'd like,' Mama echoes, then pauses and frowns a bit. 'Although I have to tell you, she reminds me of some of those society ladies I see at the Shamrock. She talks like she's . . .' Mama struggles for the right phrase, then simply says, 'Like she's got plenty of money.'

I shrug, hoping if I ignore the comment Mama will let it

drop, but as I head toward my bedroom, she presses me. 'How did you meet her, exactly?'

I hover in the space between the living room and the hallway, tucking myself around the corner so I don't have to make eye contact.

'Just at school,' I say. 'We have the same English class.'

Mama doesn't say anything at first. I don't think she believes me – after all, what's a girl like me doing bringing home a girl like Diane Farris? But she doesn't push the issue.

'I'm going to my room,' I say.

'Come back if you want to watch *The Joey Bishop Show*!' Grandma shouts as I make my way down the hall.

In my room alone, I crawl into my bed and under my bedspread. I'm by myself now, with only my thoughts as company.

If Cheryl were here, maybe I could tell her how Diane and I *really* met. And if Cheryl were here, I could tell her about Preston Fowler and his rough hands and his slurred threats. I could tell her about the smirk on his face that's been burned into my brain every waking moment since Saturday night.

I shiver. I wish I could tell Mama, but how would my mother ever understand? She thinks a good girl should get married, find a nice boy. What would she think about a girl who let herself get caught by a boy outside the bathroom at Winkler's? What kind of girl would make a boy think he could get away with what Preston Fowler wanted to get away with?

My chest tightens, and the lump that's suddenly blossomed in my throat strains until it aches. Diane was the one who spent most of the day crying, but now it's my turn. Only I don't have anyone to cry with. I sink my face into my pillow, desperate to scream, to sob – really sob – but I can't because I don't want Mama and Grandma to hear. I let myself cry as much as I can, as loud as I can manage through my pillow, until hot tears and snot cover my face and my sheets. I don't care. I cry until I'm too tired to keep crying, and I end up falling asleep in my school clothes.

CHAPTER

14

Juanita and I walk to school together Wednesday morning, and the entire time my mind can't let go of what I've learned about Diane. But I can't say anything, of course. Even if Juanita knew I was carrying a secret, she'd never pressure me to spill the beans. Loyalty is part of our code.

'What happened at Winkler's was still all over the front page of the *Post* this morning,' Juanita says, clutching her notebooks close to her chest. 'I didn't read it, but I saw the photographs.'

My stomach twists. 'I wish all of it would disappear,' I say.

'I shouldn't have said anything,' says Juanita.

'No, it's all right,' I say. 'The cops aren't going to ignore this. That boy's father is too big of a deal in this town.' I pause, thinking back to yesterday with Diane and trying to square the funny, damaged, kindhearted girl I spent the afternoon with and the understanding that this same girl is the reason a boy is dead. 'She didn't mean to kill him, you know,' I say. 'She was only trying to scare him and protect me. It was totally self-defense.'

Juanita tucks a loose black curl behind her right ear, revealing her expertly lined eyes. The same eye makeup that drew me toward her the summer before last with the promise of a life that could feel different, somehow. I can still remember the moment Juanita finished making me over on her back steps, and she pulled out her compact and opened it. I peered into that tiny, dirty mirror and smiled. A girl with eyes like that can be a girl who takes chances. Who breaks rules.

'Of course she didn't mean it,' says Juanita. 'But it's strange how she and that boy both came from River Oaks. How'd she end up on this side of town anyway?'

I mumble something about needing to help a sick aunt, borrowing from Diane's easy lie at dinner with Mama and Grandma the night before. I don't get the sense Juanita believes me, but of course she doesn't pry.

'At the very least, if the police find out it was her, which I hope they don't,' says Juanita, 'she'll have better luck at convincing them that she never meant to kill him. I mean, that bastard wanted to hurt you!'

I nod in agreement, trying to push out the image of Diane getting caught and blamed because I was dumb enough to go to the bathroom at Winkler's alone. It must show on my face because Juanita peers at me, concerned.

'Are you okay, Evie?' She pauses, uncertain. 'Everything's been so wild I feel like we haven't really had a chance to talk.' She makes a space for me, but something stops me from taking it.

'I'm fine,' I say. Maybe if I say it out loud, it will be true.

I can sense Juanita deciding whether she should press the topic, but by this point we've approached the school. I'm relieved when we spy Sunny and Connie hanging out under our oak tree. Connie is smoking a Salem, and Sunny is peering at her reflection in her compact, no doubt making sure her makeup is on just right.

'Hey,' Connie says. 'How's tricks?'

Juanita and I shrug, and I nod at Connie, trying not to eye her too much as I think about what she knows about Diane and her brother, and whether I know even more.

'Nothing new,' says Juanita, her eyes scanning the lawn. 'Look, there's Diane heading over here.'

Connie sighs, annoyed, but at least she doesn't say anything mean. There's a tension inside me, I realize, born out of standing here in my usual spot with my usual friends and having Diane – my new friend – join us. I want to fit in with everyone. I want Connie and the other girls to respect me, hang out with me, consider me one of them. And I want Diane to like me and feel like she belongs with me, too. It's a strange and uncomfortable feeling.

'Hi,' Diane says brightly – maybe too brightly – as she approaches us. I sense Connie tense up, but again, she doesn't say anything mean. Juanita and Sunny and I say hello.

'I had so much fun having dinner at your house last night, Evie,' Diane says, shining a broad smile in my direction.

Connie snorts under her breath, and immediately I wonder if the other girls are angry with me. After all, Juanita is the only one who's ever even been inside my house, and certainly not for dinner. Diane senses maybe she's done something wrong, and her face falls a little, her eyes gazing down toward the ground.

I swallow hard, remembering Diane crying in the listening booth at the Jive Hive, trusting me with her secrets. Curling up on the foot of my bed and talking about Cheryl and music and dumb television programs.

'I had a lot of fun having you over, Diane,' I say, and I mean it. Maybe it takes guts to say it out loud in front of Connie. Actually, I know it does. But I say it, even if my heart is racing a little when I do.

No one responds, but Connie lights another cigarette. Diane lifts her eyes and smiles back at me, and I wonder who is going to speak next.

Just then, our awkward calm is destroyed. I hear a boy's voice shout Connie's name from several yards away, and when we all turn to hear where it's coming from, we spy Ray Swanson careening toward us, followed by his buddies Dwight and Butch.

'They've got Johnny,' Ray manages as he and the two other boys brake suddenly to a halt right next to us, barely able to breathe. 'The cops, I mean. At least five cars. I think it has something to do with what's been in the papers. That rich boy at Winkler's. Come on!'

What happens next happens so fast I can hardly keep up. Without stopping to think or even say anything in response, all of us, including Diane, are racing through the yard past teachers and fellow students shouting at us to slow down and watch where we're going.

Our shoes clatter as we run down the sidewalk, and nobody says much as we move in a pack. Our breathing is shallow and loud, and I can hear soft, whispered curses coming from Ray Swanson.

Diane runs alongside me, her face white as paste. Her eyes are wild.

We reach the corner of Diez and Dumble, not far from Connie and Johnny's house, and skid into place next to some more of the boys in our crowd, all of them dressed in their faded jeans and dark jackets. There are several cop cars on the street, keeping us from moving any farther in.

Johnny is in handcuffs, leaning up against one of the cars but facing us. His long dark hair, normally greased and combed back, is falling into his face, but I can still see the defiance in it. His eyes are cold and staring at nothing. His mouth is a sharp line. One of the police officers is writing something in a little notebook. Two others are off to the side, muttering to each other. One of them laughs and says, 'He must be all kinds of stupid to think he can kill a Fowler in this town and get away with it.'

It takes only a few seconds to absorb all this before Connie explodes.

'Damn you!' she screams, running toward the police, her face red. Ray grabs her at the last moment and holds her back, tight around the waist, and she kicks and screams in his grip so hard one of her loafers goes flying.

I'm so focused on Connie I barely hear Diane next to me when she gasps, sharp and loud.

'Johnny!' she shouts, even louder than Connie. Diane's hand is on my forearm, her grip is cool and tight. I feel her start to sink next to me, almost pulling me down with her.

Her cry is loud enough that even Connie stops to stare, but the one who really notices is Johnny. Something in him cracks. Breaks. His suddenly sad eyes fixate on Diane, noticing her there for the first time, and he opens his mouth for a moment, like maybe he's going to shout back her name.

But he doesn't say anything. Doesn't yell back. Not at Connie or Diane. He doesn't have the time, really, before the fuzz are shoving him into the back seat of one of the patrol cars, his broken eyes still focused on Diane.

I grab her and haul her up to her feet. She's sobbing now, sobbing even harder than she did yesterday in the listening booth. She's crying so hard she's barely making any noise. Just gasping for air. Juanita and Sunny stare at her, confused. The boys are still too busy shouting at the fuzz to notice much.

Just then the biggest, burliest officer wanders over and tells us to scram. Ray and Butch and a few of the other boys act tough and curse and in general act like roosters on a farm, but they know they've lost. The officer is met by his buddies, who smirk in our general direction, pushing us off as the car carrying Johnny speeds away. Kids around me mumble in protest, but the crowd finally starts to break up and leave, and in the mess of it all I see Connie bullet toward Diane and grab her tight by the arm, so tight it must hurt, and her voice turns low and seething like a fire that refuses to be put out. I'm the only one close enough to hear what Connie has to say.

'Listen to me, little rich bitch, there is no way my brother is going to pay for what you've done, do you understand me?'

In her misery I'm surprised Diane is even able to respond, but she does, her voice soft yet earnest. Sad but certain.

'Oh, Connie,' she says, finally spilling her secret out loud in front of all the girls, 'you have no idea how much I love him.'

After Diane declared her love for Johnny in front of the girls, Connie nodded coldly, a look of what seemed like relief spreading across her face. All the cards were finally on the table. Juanita and Sunny simply stood frozen in shock. Then Connie looked at me and ordered, 'Take her you-know-where. Don't be obvious about it. I'll be there with the others real soon.'

So down Wesley Street I hustle with a still-weeping Diane, checking over my shoulder every so often to see if anyone is behind us. A housewife hanging laundry in her backyard and a few stray cats are the only living creatures we spot, but they ignore us.

Surely most of our crowd didn't go back to school, but it's doubtful any administrator will be after us. Not after they find out it was Johnny Treadway who's been arrested. They'll roll their eyes and look at each other knowingly. We're just typical Eastside trash and not worth doing much of anything about.

I guide Diane like a lost toddler, holding her hand. As we walk at a quick clip, I keep picturing Johnny's tortured eyes as he stared at Diane moments ago. I keep hearing Connie's screams and Diane's sobs.

'In here,' I say, speaking at last.

It was Connie who discovered this vacant house at the end of Monroe near Telephone Road, a few blocks from her house. A treasure uncovered on some nightly escape out of her sorry excuse of a home. Maybe she'd been running away from her parents' knockdown fights or her mother's hard slaps or her father's nasty jokes about her figure. Whatever it was, she found what she started referring to as our hideout, and the fact that I was too rattled to recall it the night Diane stabbed Preston Fowler is one more reason Connie Treadway usually calls the shots, not me.

It's a junky place, once painted white and now a dingy, depressing gray, complete with busted-out windows and a sagging front porch made up of splintering floorboards through which we've spotted possums and raccoons scuttling. The electricity has been cut off, but the water is still on, somehow, and the first night Connie took us there, she used the tap water to stretch out the half bottle of bourbon she'd brought to share.

'The boys were too stupid to find it,' she told us as we sat in a circle on the well-worn, filthy carpet, 'and I want to keep it that way.'

And we did, of course, using the house to drink and gossip. Not even Sunny spilled the beans, even though it would have made a perfect place for her and Ray to sneak away to when Ray couldn't get the car.

I take Diane around back and kick open the stuck door with the doorknob that often doesn't turn. We enter the kitchen, all grease stains and faded yellow wallpaper. Inside it smells musty and foul, like old cigarettes and fresh mold. Diane wrinkles her nose and tries to get her tears under control.

'Does someone live here?' she manages.

'No,' I tell her. 'I think the family that did was evicted.'

We head through the kitchen into the living room, where an abandoned jelly jar Sunny rescued from one of the kitchen cabinets sits in the middle of the carpet, full of butts and ash. Diane collapses onto the floor. She doesn't cry, though. She just presses her face into her hands. I sit next to her and slowly draw my hand up and place it on the small of her back. I don't say anything. It's silent except for the yapping of dogs and the low thrum of cars passing by on the main drag of Telephone Road.

At last Diane raises her face, peers through her fingers. Her pretty green eyes are glassy with tears. Her features sharp and fine. Pretty. Even in this mess, she's one of the prettiest girls I've ever seen. I imagine Johnny spotting her for the first time. Handsome Johnny. So handsome as to be almost pretty, too.

'Connie's going to make me tell her everything, isn't she?' Diane says, her voice a whisper. She wipes her tears with the cuffs of her sweater. 'She's going to want to know every detail.'

'I'll be here,' I say, 'so don't worry too much. I won't let her hassle you. She already knows about the two of you, but I'm sure she's wanted to ask questions. And now with . . .' I pause, unable to say the words *Johnny being arrested* out loud. I just stop, uncertain.

We sit in silence for a few more moments, until at last we hear noise coming from the back of the house.

'It's cool,' says Connie, walking through the kitchen, 'it's just us.' And there she appears with Juanita and Sunny at her side, the three of them red-cheeked and wide-eyed, Juanita smoking a cigarette and Sunny staring at Diane with an expression that's almost wonder.

Connie peers down at Diane, examining her with fresh

eyes that don't register any emotion. Not yet. I've known Connie long enough to realize she's calculating something and keeping the solution all to herself.

'Okay, so now we all know about it,' she says at last, joining us on the filthy carpet and sliding out a fresh cigarette. 'And not just me.' Juanita and Sunny sit down, too, crossing their legs and huddling close.

'Evie knows, too,' Diane murmurs. 'I told her yesterday.'

Sunny sighs, frustrated. 'Can someone *please* catch me and Juanita up?'

Connie lights her cigarette and takes a puff. 'Don't worry,' she says. 'Diane is going to lay it all out for us. Before my brother got carted off downtown for a stunt *you* pulled' – at this Connie nods pointedly at Diane – '*you* claimed you loved him, but you abandoned him months ago, and you never said a word. You never even sent him a postcard, and you broke his damn heart. And then you show up at our school this fall, and you can barely give him the time of day? I mean, you act like you don't even know him?' Connie flashes her angry brown eyes at Diane. 'So don't worry, Sunny. She's going to explain *everything*. Right here and right now.'

After this speech, Diane peers at me, then Connie. She takes a breath and lifts her head up, looking around at our small circle.

'I'm glad it's out,' she says at last, and there's a boldness beginning to build in her voice. 'The truth is, Connie, it's been killing me not to be able to talk about it. But listen. I'm only opening up my mouth if you promise to believe me first.'

Connie scoffs at anyone trying to set the limits of a conversation with her, but Diane doesn't waver. Just stares back at Connie evenly.

'Believe me or nothing,' she says.

Connie takes a slow drag, leaving us in suspense. She nods first at Juanita and then at Sunny, who flank her like an Eastside version of ladies-in-waiting.

'I believe you, Diane,' I say, breaking the silence. My heart is pounding, but I say it anyway.

Connie glares at me, then nods almost imperceptibly in Diane's direction.

'Fine,' she says. 'Just talk.'

For Sunny's and Juanita's sake, Diane explains how she and Johnny met at the Jive Hive the summer before last. She fills in some of the blanks for Connie, too, who admits she hadn't known every single detail. When Diane recounts how Johnny picked her up at the record store by proposing the game where he'd be forced to remember her phone number, Connie smirks.

'That's my brother, all right,' she says, and she softens, if only for a moment.

Diane keeps talking, and as she describes the places she and Johnny used to go to and the time they spent together, her voice chokes up, and she gets tears in her eyes. Juanita reaches out, tentatively at first, and rests her hand on Diane's back. I'm grateful.

'Connie,' Diane says, taking a deep breath and trying to regain control, 'you have to believe me. We really did care for each other. We loved each other. I . . . I still love him.'

'So what the hell happened?' Connie says, leaning forward.

Diane gets up to the part of her story where her parents walked in on her and Johnny in her bedroom. Her cheeks flare up red just like they did with me in the listening booth, only this time they burn an even brighter red. In a rare moment of good manners – or maybe because the boy involved is her own brother – Connie doesn't say anything nasty. She just listens as Diane describes her father threatening to shoot Johnny.

'We'd kept it private until then, of course,' Diane says. 'My parents would have killed him. Killed *me*. My mother's been planning my coming-out at the club since I was in first grade. Do you think they would have approved of someone like Johnny?'

Upon hearing these words, Connie mutters, 'My brother's not trash, you know.'

Diane's eyes flash at Connie, unafraid, and her voice is angry. 'I know that, Connie! Your brother wasn't trash to me. He . . . he was everything to me. We could spend forever talking. About music. About our families. About what was going to happen to us when we were old enough not to care what my folks had to say about how I lived my life.'

At this Diane stands up suddenly and moves to one of the living room windows. A crack snakes through the glass pane. Diane brings her finger up to it. Traces it slowly. Her back is to us.

'But a few weeks after they caught us together, my parents sent me away to this place up in Dallas,' she says, her face still turned toward the window, her voice so soft we can barely hear her. 'It was really terrible.'

After a beat or two of silence, she finally turns toward us. Her flushed cheeks have faded quickly, and her expression is blank. Vacant, really. An eerie feeling settles over me, and I doubt I'm the only one sensing it.

Sunny frowns, confused. 'A terrible place? Like . . . ?'

'Like the state school in Gainesville where they sent me?' Connie asks, her voice quieter than it's been since Johnny was hauled in. Her brow furrows. 'Like a place for . . .' It's rare to find Connie at a loss for words, but her voice trails off and she's silent.

My mind wrestles with what Diane is telling us. This place. I can tell from Diane's face that it hurts her just to think about it, much less talk about it. I try to make eye contact with her, to let her know that I'm here for her, listening to her. But she just keeps staring out at nothing. Eventually I glance toward Juanita, and she looks at me, her beautiful, lined eyes wide with confusion. I respond with a look that is equal in its bewilderment.

'It was like a place for bad girls,' Diane offers at last. 'Girls who . . . broke the rules.'

Connie snorts ruefully, then nods in understanding. 'Yeah, the rules,' she says. 'It seems they're different for girls, though.'

Diane finally looks at Connie, and maybe I'm dreaming it, but it feels like a sense of quiet understanding is passing between them. Diane hesitates, then walks toward us, takes a seat on the floor, and stares at her hands folded up in her lap.

'It was an awful place,' she continues. 'I was watched every minute, and the women who ran it read all the mail. Every letter anybody wrote or received.' She scowls at the memory.

'Up in Gainesville they forced me to write two letters home to my parents every week,' Connie scoffs. 'Like those assholes even wanted to hear from me.'

'I think my parents were perfectly happy not to get a single letter from me the whole time I was up there,' Diane says, that empty look returning to her eyes. 'So I never sent them one. But I also couldn't send any to Johnny. That's why he didn't know where I was.'

I wonder, not for the first time, what sort of place Diane was sent to. Maybe there are special, private versions of Gainesville for girls from rich families.

'You have to believe me, Connie,' Diane continues. 'And when I got back, my parents wouldn't let me out of their sight. I couldn't call Johnny. I tried to mail him a letter, but they caught me and ripped up what I'd written. I even tried to bribe my little sister, Patty, to help me get a message to him, but she called me awful names and said she was ashamed to be my sister.' At this Diane's voice cracks.

'I'm just confused about Dallas. Was it like . . . like a jail?' Sunny asks.

'Do you think she really wants to talk about that?' Connie snaps. 'God, Sunny, please.'

'Sorry,' Sunny says, shrinking back, wounded. Then, defensively, she shoots back, 'You talk about Gainesville all the time, Connie. Like how you were the toughest girl up there.'

'Gainesville was hell,' Connie says, her voice cool and even. 'Don't bring it up again.'

Sunny frowns, opens her mouth to protest, then thinks better of it and shuts it. Juanita and I glance at each other, surprised.

'I don't really want to talk about Dallas,' says Diane to Sunny gently. 'But I'll just say it was hell, too.' The word *hell* coming out of Diane's mouth strikes me as strange, but when she says it, Connie nods in understanding.

'How long were you there?' Juanita asks.

'I came back to Houston in July,' Diane says. 'Then they sent me to this side of town to live with my aunt, who's sort of the family outcast. She's a drunk, too. My mother and father don't care,' Diane says, her voice breaking. 'They explained me away to their friends, and their friends believe whatever lie they tell them. They have Patty to focus on now

147

anyway. She can be their perfect princess and marry the right man. And anyway, I almost think . . .' She pauses, then doesn't keep speaking.

'What?' Juanita presses.

Diane's cheeks redden. 'I think . . . I think they thought having to live here would be some sort of . . . punishment.'

'You mean having to live on the east side,' Connie says knowingly. 'With kids like us.'

'No,' Diane protests. 'That's not what I think. But . . . yes, I suppose . . . I suppose that's what they think.' Her voice drops slightly. 'But I don't agree with them. And anyway, if they think this is punishment, they don't know what it was like for me up in Dallas.' She shudders, and several beats of silence follow. I wonder if the other girls are filling up that silence with their imaginations like me.

'But why didn't you talk to Johnny when you got here?' Sunny asks, and I notice she's sliding closer to Diane now, her mouth turned downward with sadness. Sweet Sunny.

'We did talk, but . . . it's been . . . it's difficult. Connie, you have to believe me. I still love him so much. And we tried to be with each other when I came back, but . . . that night at Winkler's when everything happened' – at this she looks over at me – 'he and I had just had an argument. It's so complicated. It had been so long since we'd really been together, and . . . it's . . . I don't know.' She gives up trying to explain. This is just what happened in the listening booth at the Jive Hive, I realize. Just when Diane got to the part of her tale that put her at Eastside High with Johnny, she was hesitant to offer any more details. Just that things were *complicated* between them.

'What happened to your old friends in River Oaks?' Juanita asks.

'They dumped me,' says Diane, her voice a whisper. 'They thought I was beneath them, I guess.'

'Then they're lousy people,' says Sunny, looking at us. '*We* would never do that to each other, no matter what. *We* stick by each other. Right?'

'Right,' says Connie as quick as the question is asked.

'There's something else, though,' says Diane.

'What?' I ask, my stomach knotting up.

'It's . . . oh, Connie, I'm so sorry,' she continues, stricken. 'I made an enormous mistake. I know why they took Johnny.'

Connie frowns, confused. 'The cops hauled him in because they haul him in for just about anything that happens in this neighborhood.'

'There's more to it,' Diane says, her voice catching. 'The switchblade I used to . . . well. The one I stupidly left behind? Johnny gave it to me that night at Winkler's when we had that fight. It was *his*. He said he was giving it to me for protection, that he'd feel better knowing I had it. I thought it was ridiculous at the time. That was part of our fight.'

There's a stunned silence as we absorb this news. Not even Connie says anything or reacts at all.

'But dozens of kids around here carry blades like that one,' I offer, my heart racing a bit, worried that any uneasy truce between Connie and Diane is about to shatter. 'There's no way they can link that blade to Johnny, right?' After all, it's commonplace for the Eastside kids to carry switchblades, even some of the girls, like Connie. I never do. Grandma and Mama would flip if they found one on me or in the house, and anyway, I never felt the need so long as I was with Connie and the others. And something about carrying one scares me a little, I guess.

'I don't think so,' Connie answers, but she's antsy and bouncing all of a sudden. She gets up and wanders to the window, peering out it like she's expecting someone, even though I know she isn't. At least she doesn't explode at Diane.

'They can't press any charges based on flimsy evidence like that,' Juanita argues. 'They're just hauling Johnny in to scare him into spilling something.'

'Does he know it was you?' I ask. 'I mean . . . what happened.'

Diane shakes her head. 'No. We never talked again after that night. I mean, except for before when we pretended not to know one another.'

'So he couldn't say anything even if he wanted to,' Sunny suggests brightly.

'Even if he could say something, he *never* would,' Connie snaps, turning to look at us from the window.

'You're right,' Sunny answers, chastened.

'So let me think,' I say. 'If there's no real way they can connect the blade, and they always haul Johnny in for everything just to try and scare out some information they're never gonna get, there's a real good chance that if we keep quiet – if we don't let on to any of the boys or anyone else about any of this – Johnny will be out soon?'

No one answers right away, but Connie walks back to our group. 'Get close,' she commands, and we all scoot in on our knees. Connie leans into us so tight I can see her black roots peeking out from under her blond hair. I can spy a mean red blemish beginning to erupt on her chin, and when she speaks, I can catch a glimpse of the cracked incisor she got from jumping a girl at a party who Connie thought bumped into her on purpose.

'Listen,' she begins, 'the only people on the face of the earth who know what happened at Winkler's are in this room. The five of us.' She pauses for emphasis, dragging her gaze across each one of our faces. Her voice is cutting and insistent. Her dark eyes as mean as an alley cat's. 'And not a single one of us is talking, right?'

'Right,' says Sunny immediately, anxious to prove her loyalty.

'Right,' says Juanita.

'Right,' I say.

We look at Diane. The one who has the most to lose. The

one who has already lost so much.

'Right,' she says, her voice quavering only just.

'Good,' Connie says, passing judgment on us.

At this we sit back in silence, each of us lost in our own thoughts. It's so quiet I can hear the traffic on Telephone Road, a few car horns peppering over the rush of the wheels. Finally, out of her pocket Connie pulls an open pack of Salems. Before she takes one for herself, she wordlessly tips it forward to Diane, who somehow understands the gesture and accepts. Connie lights Diane's cigarette for her, and we sit there quietly for a while.

'If my parents only knew what would happen when they sent me away,' Diane says, shaking her head. 'They thought they were going to make me better, but they just made me worse. At least in their eyes.'

'That's something we have in common,' Connie answers, her voice rueful. 'We both got sent away. You to that place in Dallas and then here, and me to the state school.'

'Bad girls get sent away, I guess,' says Diane with a shrug of cold acceptance.

'To hell with that,' says Connie, throwing her head back and laughing a loud Connie laugh before looking Diane in the eye, giving her respect. 'Maybe we do get sent away. But you know what else is true about us? Bad girls never give in. And bad girls never say die.'

CHAPTER

15

The five of us smoke and talk for a little while longer – going over the possibility that Johnny will be released soon, saying it enough that it's like we're willing it to come true with our words – before we figure we might as well head home even though school isn't out yet. We leave through the back door of the abandoned house, promising to meet up at our tree in front of the school tomorrow. And to keep our eyes peeled and our ears open for any news about Johnny's arrest.

'Are you all right getting back to your aunt's place?' I ask Diane as Connie and Sunny split off toward their houses.

'I'll be all right,' says Diane. 'I'd like some time to think anyway. Just by myself.'

'I get it,' I answer. Diane gives us a wave, her auburn hair bouncing as she turns to leave. I overhear her start whisper-singing some song to herself while she walks away. I imagine briefly what I'd think of her if I'd never met her before. A priss. A nasty tea sipper. A rich, spoiled brat. But Diane isn't any of those things. I know that now.

Juanita and I walk together. We head through the neighborhood in silence until at last Juanita breaks it.

'I'm still sort of in shock,' she says.

'I know. So am I,' I respond. 'It didn't feel any less strange hearing Diane's story the second time, I'll tell you that much.'

'I'll bet,' says Juanita. 'You know what? I like her, though. I like Diane. I know she's sort of supposed to be my sworn enemy from the other side of town, but she seems pretty tuff.'

I laugh. 'I know. I feel the same way. I think maybe even Connie likes her after today.' Something about this realization makes me happy. And maybe a little proud that I was the one brave enough to stand up for Diane and bring her into our circle.

'I remember being new and meeting Connie for the first time,' says Juanita, smiling at some private memory. 'Back in junior high. I'd moved here from Clayton Homes. I'd never gone to school with so many white girls, and I sure had never met one like Connie before.'

Clayton Homes was public housing a few miles away on Navigation Boulevard and close to Our Lady of Guadalupe Church, where the Barajas family go to church sometimes. (But not often enough, according to Grandma, even if it is a Catholic church.) I remember being in grade school when Juanita and her family moved in next door and peering through a window, anxious to get a good look at the new neighbors

154

and thinking Juanita struck me as pretty and tuff. Before I approached her that day, she'd offered me a friendly smile from her yard sometimes, but I'd always been too intimidated to talk to her.

'What happened when you met Connie?' I ask, curious.

Juanita laughs. 'Well, all my teachers at Anson Jones Elementary had been white ladies, so I was used to that. I had one nasty teacher who made kids sit in their own mess if they didn't ask to go to the bathroom in English.'

I wince at this story. 'That's awful, Juanita.'

'I know,' she says. 'But it happened. And when I moved here, you know, the teachers were white ladies, too, and some white men. But it was weird to have white kids in class with me also. Anyway, this one teacher over at the junior high, on the first day of seventh grade she kept on insisting that she wanted to call me Janie instead of Juana, which is my real first name, you know, because Janie was easier for her to say. And I kept fighting her on it. I told her to call me Juanita because it was what I liked to be called.'

I nod, thinking of some of the Mexican kids I've had in class with me over the years. How lots of times on the first day of school Jorge becomes George and Lupe becomes Lucy. And no one ever says anything. It's like it's just normal. But I know it's not *right*. After all, no teacher has ever given *me* a hard time when I ask to be called Evie instead of Evelyn. They just call me whatever I ask for.

'Anyway,' Juanita continues, 'I keep protesting that my name is Juanita, like really fighting back, and this witch comes over to me with her wooden ruler, and she grabs my hand and starts swatting it.' Juanita scowls at the memory. 'You know, palm up so it will *really* hurt.'

I ball my fists up protectively, thinking about how much it must have stung. 'That's terrible,' I say.

'It *was*,' Juanita agrees, 'but then you know what happened?'

'No, what?' I ask, eager to find out.

'I grabbed that ruler and snapped it in half and went over and threw it out the window!' Juanita says, her face lit up by the memory.

I howl in appreciation, imagining a smaller, younger version of Juanita rebelling like that. 'I wish I could have seen it,' I say.

'Well, that wasn't all,' Juanita says. 'Right after I toss the ruler out, I hear this noise from the back of the room. I turn back to look, and it was Connie. This was before she started dyeing her hair blond, by the way. I just see this tiny blur of brown hair and skinny arms and legs jump up from her desk as fast as gossip.'

'What did she do?' I ask. With Connie, I know anything is a possibility.

'She stood up and started cheering and applauding!' A big grin spreads over Juanita's face as she gets to this part of the story.

The two of us giggle at this, and Juanita's face holds her

smile for a few more beats as she stays lost in the memory.

'I've had Connie on my side ever since,' she says. 'I know she can be scary sometimes, but I'm glad she's with me.'

I nod, agreeing, but I ask a question I've been considering since we left the abandoned house. 'Do you think she's with Diane?'

Juanita pauses before she answers. 'I think so,' she says slowly. 'I think the fact that Diane got sent up to Dallas like that? Connie gets that. But . . .' She stops, frowning a bit. 'I have to say, I feel like there's something else going on. Something Diane isn't telling us. I can't put my finger on it.'

'I know what you mean,' I say. We're almost home. Grandma is sure to wonder what I'm doing back in the middle of the school day, and I'll have to make up some story about being sick. She'll take my temperature and know I'm lying, and then she'll have one more piece of evidence to add to the list proving my lack of good-girl behavior.

'Maybe I'm wrong,' continues Juanita. 'But my gut's telling me she's keeping something a secret.'

I reach our front stoop, and Juanita lingers on the sidewalk in front of our house. I think about Diane's green eyes filling with tears, her tortured glances at Johnny as he was hauled in. The way she spoke about Dallas with such doom in her voice it makes me wonder how she ever made it back alive at all.

'I think you're right,' I say to Juanita. 'But I also don't think we can push her to tell us what it is. That girl . . . it's like she's about to break all the time, you know?'

'Yeah,' says Juanita. 'But at the same time, it's like she's tougher than nails, too. And that's what makes her one of us.'

I nod, grinning at Juanita and grateful for her, too. For the briefest moment, I want to stay outside with her. Maybe try and talk things through with her. Sort through the shadows in my mind that have only been building since that night at Winkler's. I know Juanita would listen and she'd be kind about it, more sensitive than Connie or Sunny might be. But if Juanita thinks being 'one of us' means being tough as nails, what would she really think of me if I cried?

'I gotta get inside, I guess, and face my grandmother,' I say at last.

Juanita tips her head toward her own house next door. 'I have my own firing squad waiting for me,' she says.

'Bye, Juanita-not-Janie,' I say, heading toward my front door.

'That's Miss Juanita Barajas to you!' Juanita exclaims, flashing me a big smile and striking a brief, exaggerated pageant-queen pose for good measure, causing both of us to laugh before we head inside our homes.

Either Grandma believes that I had a stomachache and came home from school early because of it or she doesn't want to deal with the possibility of a lie, because she doesn't fight me when I show up unexpectedly during lunch. She's sitting on the couch watching *Search for Tomorrow* and eating a sandwich when I head inside, but once she buys my story, she lets me crawl into bed. Of course, my 'stomachache' means I can't have anything to eat, and I have to find a way to calm my growling tummy as I curl up under the covers and stare at my ceiling, wondering how this can honestly be my life. How just four days ago everything turned upside down when that monster caught me.

I clench my fists and roll over, punching my pillow hard once, then twice. It feels good, so I keep doing it until I run out of energy and slump down face-first, my heart thumping, my eyes shut tight, my nose filling with the peculiar scent of the bargain detergent Grandma uses to wash our sheets. I try not to think.

Eventually I fall asleep, waking up only when I hear an urgent knock on my bedroom door, followed by my grandmother.

'Evelyn,' she says, crossing my messy floor, her face creased with concern. 'Cheryl is on the phone and wants to speak with you.'

Groggy and fuzzy-brained from my nap, I blink hard a few times and try to grasp what my grandmother is saying.

'What time is it?' I ask, stumbling out of bed. I realize I'm still wearing my scuffed loafers.

'After four o'clock,' she says, leading me toward the kitchen.

Long distance is so expensive there has to be some reason

159

why Cheryl would call in the middle of a weekday. Our Sunday evening calls last for a few minutes at most, just enough for all of us to stand around in a circle in the kitchen and pass the phone to say hello. It always feels forced and uncomfortable, not like a real conversation at all, and I've been dreaming of Christmas when she can visit in person and the two of us can have real talks, like we used to. That is, if she can stay with us. What if she has to stay at Dennis's house?

I shake all these thoughts from my mind as I grab the telephone.

'Cheryl?' I say, any remaining sleepiness instantly gone. Grandma hovers in the doorway of the kitchen, observing. I turn toward the wall, trying to create some sort of privacy.

'Oh, Evie, I'm glad you're home,' she says, her words cracking a bit. 'I just needed to hear your voice.'

'Cheryl, is everything all right?' I ask, conscious of Grandma's presence behind me.

There's a pause, and I imagine Cheryl in the small kitchen of her on-base housing, trying to keep herself together. Of course, I have no idea what Cheryl's kitchen looks like, but I try to make a picture in my mind of my older sister standing in the middle of it, clutching her phone to her ear, her dark hair pulled up off her face, her brown eyes filling with tears. Whatever she has to say, I will her to be okay.

Cheryl sniffs, then whispers, 'I don't know. Maybe it's nothing.'

My heart aches for my big sister, who suddenly sounds awfully young to me, her voice so staticky and far away. I consider Grandma's eavesdropping and try to think about how to encourage Cheryl to talk without giving too much away.

'Maybe it is or it isn't, but . . .' My voice trails off, but I hope Cheryl hears the encouragement in it. The permission to tell me what's wrong.

'It's just . . .' She takes a deep breath, her voice increasing in volume. 'Dennis and I got into an argument this morning. He wants to have a baby. And . . . I'm not ready. I'm just not. And I feel like . . .' She pauses again.

'Yes?' I ask, and at this I peer over my shoulder, where Grandma still stands in the doorway of our kitchen, her expression worried, her hands twisting the gingham apron tied around her waist.

'I feel like a bad wife, I guess,' Cheryl says. Her voice draws my focus back to the phone, and I turn and curl toward the receiver.

'No, of course not,' I tell her, hoping my end of the conversation sounds as vague as possible.

'Grandma's listening, isn't she?' Cheryl asks.

'Yeah.'

Cheryl manages a soft laugh and then a deep sigh. 'Of course she is.'

'But I mean it,' I say. 'It's all right that . . . you feel . . . the way you feel about that.'

161

'Mary next door said I should do it,' Cheryl says. 'She said it would be fun for the two of us to have kids together so they could play in the front yard.'

'That's not enough of a reason,' I say, turning back toward the wall, my voice hushed.

Cheryl sniffs. 'Thank you, Evie. I know that. I think I just needed to hear you say it.'

'I'm sorry I haven't answered your last letter,' I tell her, feeling like a terrible sister and wishing I could explain everything that's been happening in my life that's prevented me from doing so. What I wouldn't give for Cheryl to be here, at home with me, just a whisper away across our shared bedroom. What I wouldn't give to be able to have her to spill all my secrets to.

'It's okay,' she says, her voice steady again. 'Write when you can, but I have to get off the phone. This call is costing a fortune. But make something up for Grandma and Mama. I don't want them to worry. You can think of some explanation.'

I can? I'm not sure about that, but I promise Cheryl, and after an exchange of I-love-yous, I hang up. Just then I hear my mother walking in the front door.

'Is Cheryl all right?' Grandma asks me as I turn away from the phone, my mind racing for some false reason she phoned us.

'Why wouldn't Cheryl be all right?' Mama asks, heading into the kitchen. She pulls a Salem from a pack in her purse

162

and grabs an ashtray from the kitchen counter. She only smokes after work if she's had a really hard day.

'She just called,' Grandma says. 'Maybe I was imagining it, but she sounded upset. And she called on a weekday afternoon. She asked for Evie.'

My mother puts down the cigarette she was about to put to her mouth to light, and she looks up at me, clearly nervous. 'What did she say, Evie? Tell us.'

'We only spoke for a minute,' I say, trying to avoid my mother's eyes as I grasp for a plausible lie. 'She . . . she and Dennis had an argument about . . . about how he isn't as romantic as he was when they first got married.' It sounds absurd as I say it. I stare at my mother's hands paused above the pink plastic ashtray, her unlit Salem in one hand and a book of matches in the other. I can feel her uncertain gaze, and Grandma's, too, but I'm too nervous to look up.

'That sounds . . . strange,' my mother says. 'Are you sure that's what it was about?'

'Yeah,' I say. I finally look up.

My grandmother is looking at me, her head tilted, her eyes trying to read mine. 'Well,' she says, 'young marriages can be tricky sometimes.' She says this like she doesn't believe it but has to say something to break the awkward silence.

'Yes,' Mama says. 'They can.'

A beat later I beg off to the bathroom, where I stand and stare at my reflection in the mirror before flushing the toilet

163

and running the water to avoid suspicion. When we sit down for dinner later, I keep hearing Cheryl's sobs in my right ear. I keep playing her words over and over.

Why is Dennis pushing her to have a baby, and so soon, too? To make her stay with him? I think he's lucky to have Cheryl – she's pretty and smart and kind – and she only went to the prom with him because he asked first and early, and she didn't want to hurt his feelings by saying no. Maybe he thinks without a baby to tie her to him, she'll leave. Cheryl promised me he was nice to her, but now I don't know.

'Evie, you've barely touched your chicken,' Mama says.

'She came home early with a stomachache,' Grandma offers, and I realize my hunger has disappeared since Cheryl's telephone call.

'I'll have a few more bites,' I say, trying to ward off their concern.

After dinner and washing up, we head into the den to watch television, namely the evening news. My mother and grandmother like Channel 11 best, and I figure I'll watch, too. Maybe there'll be something about Johnny.

He turns out to be the lead story. The anchor, in a suit and spectacles, says an arrest has been made in the killing of the son of Lamar Fowler, and suddenly a picture of Preston Fowler pops up on the screen, staring at me like he knows me. He's dressed in a madras shirt and a smirk, and my mind is flooded – the image of Preston's blood flecked on Diane's dress that night. The feeling of total helplessness as he dragged me into darkness. The skittering sound of my feet kicking up gravel.

Maybe I only need a minute.

'Oh,' I say, surprising even myself. Before I know it I'm down the hall, crouching over our toilet, all of my grandmother's chicken making its way back up.

There's a knocking on the door. My mother is calling my name. 'Evie! Are you all right, sweetie?'

I wipe my mouth with the back of my hand and flush the toilet. Shaking, I stand up and manage to cry out that I need a moment. After I splash my face with cold water, I open the door and Mama immediately has her hand on my forehead, her face lined with concern.

'You must really be sick,' she says. 'Do I need to call Dr Curtis?'

'It's nothing, just a bug,' I say, wanting to sink into my mom's arms and cry even though I can't remember the last time I did such a thing. I swallow, the taste of bile strong in my mouth. I feel warm tears start to prick behind my eyes.

'Maybe you need to lie down. You look so pale.' She doesn't seem to be connecting what just happened with what was on the news broadcast.

'I will,' I say. 'I'll go lie down. But . . . Mama, that boy on the news? The one they arrested? What happened to him?'

My mother's face grows grim. 'I recognized the last name,' she says. 'That's that girl Connie's brother, isn't it? The one who works down at the Texaco when he's not off doing God knows what.'

I nod, not wanting to get into all that. Just wanting to know what's happened. Just hoping for confirmation that all they've done is called him in to scare him or get him to talk.

'Mama!' my mother shouts from the hallway toward the den. 'What'd they do with that Treadway boy? The one who they arrested today for that stabbing at Winkler's? Evie's asking.'

'Is Evie all right?' Grandma shouts back, ignoring the question.

'Grandma, what about Johnny Treadway?' I shout. 'He goes to my school.'

'Oh, that,' she answers, her voice as calm as can be, like I've asked her about the weather report. 'It said he's being charged with murder.'

16

Miss Odeen is sitting quietly at her desk, reviewing our compositions, while we're supposed to be working on some grammar exercises. Normally, I don't mind Miss Odeen's grammar work, because she makes an effort to write funny phrases for us to correct, sentences that include mentions of the Beatles and the Supremes and her pet cat, Mr Whiskers.

But today, I can barely focus. Ever since we heard about Johnny's murder charge the other night, it's been impossible for any of us to think straight. This morning Mama tried to get me to tell her why I was acting so out of sorts. She'd be even more worried if she knew I cut school yesterday and spent the day with Juanita and Sunny at the park, smoking and talking in circles about Johnny's murder charge. Juanita and Sunny want to believe that the charges can't stick. That there isn't really enough evidence to hold Johnny. After all, the switchblade couldn't be connected to Johnny for sure, and lots of kids carry blades like that. But we'd read in the paper that some of

Preston Fowler's friends had claimed they'd spotted Johnny and Preston in an argument earlier near the bathroom. It had all been made up, of course. But who was going to believe a bunch of kids from the wrong side of the tracks over tea sippers with daddies in important places?

Diane cut school yesterday, too, but she'd been too upset to join us at the park. The same for Connie, who cut again today.

Diane did drag herself to Eastside High this morning, though, her face pale and her eyes red-rimmed from crying. As I glance at her from my desk in Miss Odeen's class, my heart sinks. She's seated next to me and keeps staring straight ahead, her expression bleak. She won't pick up her pencil to try and complete Miss Odeen's assignment.

But when I peer back at her again toward the end of class, I find her looking over at me. She looks magazine-pretty as always, her auburn hair pinned back in a ponytail, dressed in one of her many sharp dresses, this one dark blue with tiny mother-of-pearl buttons running down the front. When our eyes meet, she glances down to the floor. Beside her bright white Keds, I spy a folded-up piece of composition paper. She slides it toward me with her right foot, and in one quick and hopefully graceful swoop, my eyes on Miss Odeen, I reach down and grab it.

I unfold it carefully in my lap and peer down. Diane's script is schoolteacher perfect.

I wish I knew how we could help Johnny. Could you please meet me after school at the tree and we'll walk home together? I want to come up with something. Please don't tell the other girls. xoxoxo Diane

I fold the note back up as tight as I can and slip it into my pocket as I nod yes at Diane. She offers me a smile of gratefulness, and her eyes glass over again, but she simply turns her focus forward before she lets tears fall. I look down again, Miss Odeen's exercises on semicolons and adverbial clauses floating like jellyfish before me. I can't concentrate. At last the bell rings, and Diane and I file out.

'Girls, can I see you a moment?' Miss Odeen asks as we pass her desk. She stands and tucks a loose curl behind her right ear, and I notice red smears of ink on her fingers from marking our papers.

'Yes, Miss Odeen?' Diane says, somehow managing to turn on her Miss America pageant grin she uses with adults. But I know her well enough by now that I can tell it's not her best performance.

'Well, you were both absent yesterday,' she says, tilting her head and frowning just a bit. But it's an *I'm worried* frown, not an *I'm angry* one. She waits a beat but neither of us responds, and I sense Diane tense up with nerves. She isn't used to this sort of interrogation from a teacher, I know, but I am. Sometimes you can play dumb and they just give up. Even though I feel sort of lousy doing that to Miss Odeen.

'Were you two cutting class together?' she asks, softening

169

her voice just so, almost conspiratorially. I like Miss Odeen, but I know this trick. Get the kids to believe you're just wanting gossip, that you're all on the same side, and maybe they'll spill the beans.

'No, ma'am, we weren't together,' I offer, which isn't really a lie. Diane was at home, and I was at the park with Sunny and Juanita. I flash a weak smile.

'I'm sorry, Miss Odeen,' says Diane, her voice suddenly crisp and together. 'It won't happen again. Not with either of us.' She looks over at me and nods. 'Right, Evie?'

'It won't,' I say. Now this *is* a lie. The odds of me never cutting class again, even English, are not low at all. But at least Diane can get us out of here.

'Girls, listen,' says Miss Odeen, leaning against her desk, crossing her feet at the ankles. 'I know I'm just an old lady English teacher, but if something is wrong . . . if you need help . . .' At this she pauses, and I wonder if she's thinking back to teacher school and what she learned there to deal with unruly girls like me. Like us. 'Listen,' she says, starting again, 'I'm *not* an old lady English teacher, so let's not pretend. I'm a grown-up, yes, but it wasn't that long ago that I was around your age, and . . . anyway, I just want you to know if you ever need to talk . . . I'm here.' She smiles, her pink lipstick perfect as ever. I wonder for a moment what Miss Odeen was like in high school and how long ago it was.

'Yes, ma'am, thank you,' says Diane, and I offer my

thanks, too.

'All right, you're excused,' she says, and as soon as Diane and I are out in the hallway, Diane takes a deep breath.

'I don't like lying to Miss Odeen,' she says, 'but I couldn't have come to class yesterday. Or to school at all. Not with everything going on.'

'I know it,' I say as we make it down the hallway. 'I'm surprised you're here today.'

'If I didn't come,' says Diane, 'I'd be trapped at home all day with my thoughts. It's too much. Plus, I wanted to talk to you.'

I touch my pocket where Diane's note is hidden. 'I want to help you, but what can we do?'

Diane's shoulders slump. 'I don't know. But we have to do something.' We're making our way through the crowd, getting closer to where we'll have to head our separate ways to fourth period. 'Please promise me you'll help me.'

'Of course I promise,' I say. 'You know that.'

Diane smiles, then tips her head onto my left shoulder for just a moment. 'I know,' she says. 'Of course I know.'

After school, I show up at our regular meeting place, the big oak tree on the front lawn, but I don't spy Diane. I do spot Sunny and Ray Swanson, smoking and waiting for me.

'Hey,' says Sunny, 'how are you?' Ray ignores me.

'I'm all right,' I say. 'Any word from Connie?'

'That's why we're here,' says Sunny. 'Let's not let her be alone, okay? My stepdad isn't around and my mom is working, and Ray thought we could all head over to my place and hang out or something. And get Connie to join us. You know, to distract us.'

'I lifted some whiskey, and Sunny can get something from her stepfather's stash,' Ray says, barely looking at me. 'Butch and Dwight can score something, too.' I wonder if he's even upset his friend is locked up or if he just sees it as an excuse to get blitzed.

'Well,' I start, thinking of Diane, who just then approaches us on the lawn.

'What's going on with this girl anyway?' Ray says, scowling. 'Suddenly she's your little mascot. She's not even from around here.'

Sunny protests, 'She's really sweet, Ray. I swear.' But Ray just frowns as Diane draws nearer.

'Hey, Evie,' she says. 'Hey, Sunny . . . and Ray.'

Ray grunts.

'Diane, come with us, please,' Sunny says, grabbing Diane's hand and tugging it toward her. 'Just for a little bit. Juanita's joining us later, and Connie, and some of the boys. I know we're all miserable about Johnny, but it's Friday. Let's hang out for a while and forget about everything for a little bit.' She waggles an eyebrow and whispers conspiratorially, 'We have booze.'

'I was . . .' Diane starts, making eye contact with me. I don't know what to do. I know Diane wanted to spend time with me alone. Should I make an excuse so Diane can come with me? Say I can't go to Sunny's because my grandmother is expecting me? Not that I've ever acted like I'm worried about a curfew or anything in front of the girls – even if secretly sometimes I am.

'Diane and I were . . .' I start, waiting for my mouth to make up the best excuse. But then Diane surprises me.

'We'll go,' she says with a nod.

I eye her, surprised.

'Maybe I want to forget,' she says as we follow Sunny and Ray off campus toward Sunny's house on Leeland.

'All right,' I say, leaning closer and lowering my voice. 'But what about coming up with some plan?'

'We'll talk about it later,' she says, then reaches out to give me a squeeze. 'Right now let's just escape.'

It's good to feel the warmth of the liquor spread out in my cheeks and my chest. To feel the edges soften.

'Hold it, little sister,' Connie says, sliding the bottle of Four Roses out of my hand. But she's been drinking, too, and her fingers slip reaching for the bottle. She laughs a classic Connie laugh – loud and honking – but it's forced, too, somehow. Her eyes are bleary. Her face is tired. A week or two ago, Connie Treadway referring to me as her little sister would have sent a thrill of belonging down my spine. Now, I'm so foggy with sadness it barely registers.

I blink, trying to get my head on straight. I manage to hand the bottle back to Connie and stumble out of the kitchen into Sunny's living room. Someone has the radio on too loud, or maybe I've just had too much to drink. It's that song about the house of the rising sun, and the lead singer's growling voice is full of desperation and sadness. As if he knows exactly how I feel.

My friends are all here, and so is the rest of our crowd — lots of Johnny's friends and some of their girlfriends, too. Tough girls like Connie and the rest but not part of our tight inner circle. There's already been two fistfights in the backyard, one lovers' quarrel in the bathroom, and several beer bottles smashed against the chain-link fence. In a different neighborhood, someone might call the cops. But not in this one.

Even though Sunny and Ray thought this would be a good way to blow off steam and forget about how miserable we all are about Johnny, it's all everyone at school can talk about, even kids who aren't part of our crowd. I've even heard some of the teachers gossiping about it in the hallways, and when Mama tried to find out what was going on this morning, she couldn't stop with the questions.

'Evie, honey, I'm worried about you,' she said, perching uncertainly on the foot of my bed as I stared up at my bedroom ceiling. 'You're not yourself. Is this because of the arrest? Connie Treadway's brother and that boy from River Oaks?'

That boy from River Oaks. All that made me want to do was start crying as I remembered Preston Fowler's rough hands and terrifying taunts. I turned toward my bedroom wall and curled up, hot tears threatening to sneak out of my eyes. My throat ached. I wanted to say something but couldn't figure out the words. And besides, I didn't want to start crying in front of my mother. She worried about me enough as it was, and I was pretty sure Cheryl's phone call had her worried already.

'Evie?' my mother tried, a hand hovering over my knees, then anxiously resting on my leg. 'Evie, won't you talk to me?'

I'd already let Mama down so much. I already wasn't the daughter she'd imagined having, and something in me doubted that I was ever going to find a clean-cut, sensible guy and settle down like she seemed to want so much. How could she ever understand a girl who'd gotten caught in such a terrible position with Preston Fowler? Instead of saying anything, I just buried my face into my pillow and shook my head until my mother gave up and walked out, shutting my bedroom door softly behind her. Her steps sounded heavier than ever.

Mama didn't know what to do with me, and Connie's brother was going to pay for a crime he didn't commit. A crime that started because I'd gone to the bathroom alone and hadn't been tough enough to make it out of there on my own. Connie would have fought off Preston. Sunny and Juanita, too. Even Diane had managed it.

I knew thinking like this was absurd. Stupid, even. But I couldn't help it.

So it's no surprise I'm half-drunk at this Friday afternoon party, numb and weirdly giddy as I stumble through the living room, trying not to trip over people. Pushing open the front door, I find Sunny and Juanita on the stoop, smoking and talking.

'Evie, sit,' says Juanita, patting the empty space next to her.

I obey, but as I collapse onto the steps, I almost fall over.

'Watch out, Evie!' Juanita says, holding out a hand to steady me.

'I'm all right,' I offer. But here, on the cool cement steps, I realize how swimmy the yard in front of me seems. I put both hands down and brace myself.

'No more for you,' Juanita says. She reaches over and puts an arm around me.

'You're not my mother,' I say, surprised at how forceful I sound.

Juanita just laughs. 'No, I'm not,' she says. 'But I do know when you should probably slow down.'

Sunny glances at me and smiles. 'Hey, you can't blame

Juanita for looking out for you. After all, she's the reason you even hang out with us.'

I roll my eyes. I always feel like a kid when the girls bring this up. The way they like to remind me of how Juanita adopted me like one of the stray dogs that roam our neighborhood.

'Don't roll your eyes!' Juanita says in protest, laughing. She lights a fresh Salem. 'And anyway, it started with your eyes. You came across the yard that one Saturday and asked me how I did my makeup. You wanted eyes just like mine. I still remember the way your voice shook a little. I knew right then I was going to make you my little pet.'

I bat my eyes at Juanita, and she and Sunny start laughing. As they laugh, I lean into Juanita, rest my cheek on her soft shoulder. She smells like cooking vanilla, which she sometimes dots behind her ears as perfume. Juanita is right. My voice did shake that Saturday afternoon when I saw her outside smoking and babysitting her niece. My heart, still breaking and confused over Cheryl, did thump as I took a handful of steps across our property line, like I was crossing into some unknown world. And my smile did explode as Juanita turned to look at me, her head bent in curiosity, her eyes wide as I asked her just how she made her eyes look so tuff.

And so Juanita helped me after she'd warned me Mama and Grandma wouldn't like it. She sat there on her backyard stoop, her pink tongue pinned between her teeth as she painted my eyes with her kohl eyeliner. I felt like I was being inducted into some secret society. Some new way of being. Something that didn't involve having to get married and moving to some army base in Killeen with a boy you barely knew.

'You loved the way it looked,' Juanita says. 'But I was right. Your grandmother sure didn't.'

'She was sure my new eyes meant I was headed straight for hell,' I say. At this the three of us laugh. When we run out of laughter, Sunny exhales and rests her chin on her hand.

'I feel bad for laughing,' she says. 'I mean, with everything that's happening.'

Juanita and I nod in agreement. It does feel bad to laugh. Things have been so rotten.

'If they would only let someone visit him,' Sunny says. 'Isn't it against the law that they haven't been able to visit? Connie says she couldn't get in yesterday.'

'The fuzz are going to do whatever they want,' Juanita replies. 'That boy's daddy can pull all kinds of strings.'

'Did you know that Johnny's parents didn't even try to go downtown to see him?' Sunny mentions, lowering her voice even though we're the only ones out here. 'Their own son.'

'Doesn't surprise me,' I say, remembering the fresh bruises I've sometimes seen on Johnny and Connie. Not bruises they earned on the streets, either.

'Yeah,' Sunny says. 'It's still sad, though.'

The sun has started to set just a little – Grandma has to be so upset that I'm not home yet – and the dip in October temperatures has started to sharpen my fuzzy thinking. 'What I don't understand,' I say, 'is how they can possibly have enough evidence to charge Johnny.'

'You read the same papers we did,' Sunny says. 'They knew the blade was the same type Johnny carried from the other times they'd hauled him in, and they got enough of those tea-sipper kids to lie and say they'd seen Johnny threatening that rich boy at Winkler's earlier on that night.'

'But they couldn't pin that exact blade on him,' I protest. 'Lots of kids carry a blade like that.'

Juanita shrugs. 'Like I said, that boy's daddy can pull a lot of strings.'

'I guess,' I manage. 'I feel so lousy about it. So guilty.'

'Hey, you've got to cut that out,' says Juanita, putting her arm around me. 'Honest, Evie.' Our eyes meet, and I offer her a grateful smile.

Just then we hear the front door open behind us. It's Diane, her cheeks red, like maybe she's been drinking, too.

'Evie, can I talk to you privately for a minute?' says Diane. Her voice is soft and just this side of slurred, and suddenly I'm *sure* she's been drinking.

'Of course we can talk,' I say, standing up, thinking of her note in my pocket.

I wish I knew how we could help Johnny . . . I want to come up with something. A wild image of Diane trying to spring Johnny

179

from prison while I drive the getaway car pops into my mind. The idea is ridiculous, I know.

Juanita and Sunny glance at us as I follow Diane to the side of Sunny's house, our shoes sinking a bit into the cool, wet ground. I can hear yelps and bottles breaking and laughter coming around the corner from the backyard.

'How are you?' I ask. Diane's face is cast in the strange shadows of a setting sun, making her look sadder and more lost than she does even in the daylight. She's still pretty, though. The sort of pretty that would make a boy like Johnny Treadway take notice.

'Evie, I can't take this anymore,' she says. She closes her eyes and manages a shaky breath. 'I can't take knowing I'm here, free, and Johnny is in prison for something I did. I can't stand it!' She clenches her fists, brings them up to her chin, and squeezes her shut eyes even tighter.

'I know, Diane,' I say, reaching out for her, touching her shoulder lightly. 'But we have to hope that the case against Johnny will fall apart somehow. They don't have any real solid evidence.' Even as I say these words out loud, I know how foolish and hopeless I sound.

'I can't wait for something that will never happen,' she says, reading my mind. 'Forget talking here. Can you walk home with me?'

'Sure,' I answer, drawing my arms up around myself to guard against the cool evening and my building anxiety about just what Diane is thinking. 'I should be getting home anyway, before my mother and grandmother have a fit apiece.'

'Let's just head off,' she says, growing more upset by the moment. Her breath stinks like cheap alcohol, and she presses her fingertips to her cheeks, wiping away a few tears that have escaped. 'I don't want to have to talk to anyone else. Just walk with me. Please?'

'All right, okay,' I say, trying to reassure her. We decide to cut through the backyard, and I worry whether Sunny and Juanita will be concerned about us, but Diane is so clearly in distress I don't have time to think about that much. As we move, she drunkenly trips and stumbles a few times, and I have to help her catch her balance.

Diane's aunt's house isn't far from Sunny's, and by the time we get there, Diane is crying, hard. Wordlessly, she leads me to the back door and holds up her hand for me to wait. She heads inside and then comes out a moment later.

'She's not here,' she says, sniffling. 'As usual. I think she has a new boyfriend or something, and she's been staying with him. Will you come and sit with me in my room for a little bit?' I nod, and Diane drunkenly leads me through the dark and gloomy kitchen, which she's managed to clean up a bit in her aunt's absence, I guess. We retreat to her oasis of a bedroom, still neat and tidy. But this time sadder to me. The practically blank walls and no records, the cosmetics and perfumes set in their rows, like they're desperately holding on to a sense of order in the middle of all the gloom. All of it is depressing. We sit on her bed, me toward the foot, Diane toward her pillow.

'Evie,' she says suddenly, and her tears start again. 'Oh, Evie.' At this she falls over, sobs into her pink chenille bedspread, and reaches out for her tiny teddy bear and clutches it close to her chest. I want to reach out and touch her, pat her comfortingly on the back. But I also wonder if she wants to be touched. Something tells me maybe she doesn't.

'Diane, what is it?' I ask. There's something fresh and urgent in her tears, and I find my heart starting to race.

'Evie, do you know what?' she manages through her tears, sitting up so I can see her face. 'I think you know this, but I want to say it anyway. I don't regret Johnny. No matter what happened. I loved him. I *love* him. I mean, it was hard to be with someone from another world, but it wasn't hard, either, do you know what I mean?' She doesn't give me time to answer, just plows ahead. 'When we were together, we could talk about anything. We would trip over each other to finish each other's sentences, be the next one to speak. We talked about music, and he took me seriously, you know? Maybe that's dumb, but it mattered.'

She dabs at her eyes with her teddy bear. 'And we could make each other laugh, always. Johnny thought I was funny, too. Not just a laugh machine for *his* jokes. Even though he was funny, too.' She smiles briefly at some private memory.

I nod, wondering where this speech is headed and why she's delivering it now. Just then, Diane sits up, wipes at her nose with her bare hand. She takes a deep breath.

'And Johnny . . . he made me feel good,' she says, looking me right in the eyes when she says it. 'He told me he would, and he did.'

She says this without any shame.

'I understand,' I say. And then I surprise myself when I add, 'I'm glad it was like that for you.'

She nods, grateful.

'But . . . Evie, I never thought about . . .'

She stops talking and my mind races, trying to fill in the blanks.

'What?' I whisper, barely able to hear my own voice.

'Evie, I never thought about . . . a baby.'

A baby. Oh my God.

The hair on my arms jumps to attention. My eyes widen. I'm sure I gasp, loudly, too.

'Diane, did you . . . Were you . . . ?' I manage at last. But I can't say it. I'm not sure how to say it out loud myself. I remember Cheryl's sobs when she told me about Dennis and the prom, and I think about something that happens every so often at Eastside High and probably at every high school in the country. A girl comes around to each class with a withdrawal slip clutched in her hand, asks her teachers to sign it, then turns in her textbooks. As she stands in the doorway of the

183

classroom, face toward her feet, cheeks pinking up fever-like, everyone pretends they don't know why she's leaving. Why she's being forced to walk like a criminal through the halls of her own high school. We don't talk about it, of course. But we know.

Sent to help a sick aunt.

Left to go live with family friends who need a mother's helper.

Disappeared as if by magic trick, possibly never to be seen again.

Or in Diane's case, being sent to someplace in Dallas.

I remember those mean girls by the concession stand at Winkler's, making fun of Diane and questioning how she could ever show her face in public again after what she did, and my heart breaks for her again.

It wasn't just that she was in love with a boy from a bad neighborhood. That wasn't all that happened.

'When did you find out?' I ask.

'Just after Christmas,' Diane says, pausing, maybe taking in how I'll react. 'I started getting sick all the time. My mother took me to the doctor, and that's when I found out for sure.'

She eyes me carefully. Will I be like those heartless girls at Winkler's? Will I tell her she's nasty? Dirty?

A bad girl?

'You must have been so scared,' I say at last, still grappling with my surprise.

'Oh, Evie, I was terrified,' she says with a sigh, and I'm not sure if she's sighing from the memory or relief that I haven't acted like her old friends at the drive-in.

'And you didn't tell Johnny?' I ask.

Diane sniffs, shakes her head no. 'My parents watched me like hawks afterward. There was no way to get to him. My sister wouldn't help, like I said. And then maybe there was a part of me that didn't want to tell him. I thought maybe he'd want to get married. In fact, I'm sure that's what he would have wanted. And I wasn't ready for that, even though I loved him. I *love* him. I felt so . . . trapped.'

Suddenly I can hear Cheryl's worried voice on the other end of the phone. Her lonely letters from Fort Hood.

'What was it like in Dallas?' I ask, immediately embarrassed by my question. 'Maybe you don't want to talk about it,' I add. But Diane waves away my concern and spills out her story in the soft, slow voice of a girl who's had too much to drink at a party and too much heartbreak in her life.

She fills in all the blanks I've been wondering about. The days in Dallas were long and terrible, she tells me, spent learning shorthand and playing cards. Torn from everything familiar, even the familiarity of her stuffy, stilted homelife. Night after night she was surrounded by other sad girls and their swollen bellies, trading their sorrowful stories like prisoners trade cigarettes and stamps. There were pinch-faced matrons who told Diane and the other girls they were bad, that this was their punishment, that a mother wasn't supposed to be a girl like them.

'We spent hours just bored out of our skulls, taking classes in secretarial skills because girls like us sometimes don't find husbands, and we'd have to find a way to survive in the world,' Diane says, her teddy bear still tight in her hands. She grimaces at the memories.

Diane's story ends with a baby, of course. That's the natural finish to it. But this baby isn't with Diane. I don't know if she'll want to tell me that part. We just sit in the quiet. At last Diane peers out the window next to her bed. It's dark now. I try to imagine Grandma and Mama angry at home, but I can't leave Diane right now. There's no possible way I would.

'When the pains started,' Diane begins, still gazing out the window, 'the maternity home put me in a taxicab and sent me to the hospital alone. I was in a dark room by myself, with a nurse coming in every so often. The nurse was chewing gum. That's what I remember. I was having a baby and she was chewing gum as calm as you could.'

'Oh, Diane, all by yourself?' I ask. She nods, and I feel tears well up in my own eyes. Just imagining it seems awful. I can't imagine living it. And Diane did.

'At the end a doctor came in, and I finally had my baby,' she says. 'What a sweet little gumdrop with fingers and toes. A little piece of Johnny and me, and I got to hold that angel for

186

just a moment. Those two little eyes stared up at me, and I remember thinking that they hadn't seen the stars or the ocean yet, but at least they'd seen my face.'

Tears are rolling down my face now, and I wait for Diane to cry, but she doesn't. Her drunken voice has somehow grown still and measured as she tells me this part. Like she's bearing witness. Testifying. Like she has to make sure someone knows exactly what happened to her. I listen, barely able to breathe.

'Then not long after that, this woman from the adoption agency in a gray suit and hat came and took my baby right through the door and out of my room. And that was it.' This comes out as the slightest of whispers. Her gaze out the window is vacant.

I don't know what to say. We're both just quiet for what feels like forever. Diane breaks the silence at last when she says, 'Thank you, Evie. It feels good to tell someone.'

I reach out and squeeze her snotty, wet hands. 'I'm glad you could tell me.' I pause, struggling to find the words for something I've just realized. 'You're so brave to tell me that.' If I'd never gotten to know Diane, would I have thought she was brave based on how she looks? No. But bravery takes a lot of different forms. I know that now, and I'm glad I do.

She squeezes my hands back, too. 'I don't feel brave, really, but all right, I guess,' she says, the tiniest, briefest of smiles on her face.

Her hands still in mine, I ask her if Johnny still doesn't know what happened.

Diane shakes her head. 'He doesn't have any idea. I told you it was complicated when we ended up at Eastside together. Johnny was hurt. He thought I'd just disappeared. And for me . . . I didn't know if I could tell him about the baby when it was so painful for me to even think about it myself, much less talk about it. And . . . as much as I love Johnny, I guess there was a part of me that was . . .' Her voice trails off.

'A part of you that was angry?' I guess, thinking back on how resigned and resentful Cheryl seemed when she understood she would have to marry Dennis.

'Yes,' Diane says, letting go of my hands and clenching her fists for emphasis, relieved by my answer. 'Yes. I was angry at him. I know he was miserable when I disappeared, and that's why Connie hated me at first. But *he* didn't get stuck in that awful place in Dallas. *He* didn't have to carry our baby for all those months and then sit there, helpless, while our child was ripped away. And *he* didn't have to take being called a slut by his own parents because he wasn't the one who'd *gotten herself pregnant*.' At those last words she scowls, her face twisted up with anger.

'It's different for boys,' I say, thinking about what would have happened to Cheryl if Dennis hadn't offered to marry her and she hadn't lost the baby. He could have said no and joined the army anyway, disappearing into a brand-new life. Cheryl would have been the one trapped. Stuck. Just like Diane.

'It sure is,' Diane says. 'A girl doesn't get herself pregnant, you know. I mean, it wasn't Johnny's fault. And it wasn't my fault, either. But I paid for it.'

'You sure did,' I say. 'I'm so sorry, Diane.'

'So you don't think I'm' – she lowers her voice – 'a slut?'

'Diane, no, of course not,' I say. 'Never. You were in love.'

Diane surprises me with a big hug, pulling me in tight. One of Miss Odeen's vocabulary words slides into my mind. *Surreal*. It's surreal that tomorrow will mark one week since the night Diane and I first met at Winkler's. It feels like one year ago with all that's happened.

But Diane Farris is my friend. And I'm so glad she is.

Pulling back, she eyes me carefully. 'Please don't tell the others yet. Or anyone, promise? If I tell anyone else, I want them to hear it from me. Especially Johnny.'

'I won't tell,' I say. 'But as for Johnny, you still want to help him, though, right?'

'Yes, Evie, I do,' she admits. 'I'm still in love with him. I still want . . . I think maybe we can be together again one day. Somehow. And Evie, he's been charged with murder! He might be stuck in prison for the rest of his life. For something I did! Even if it was an accident and I was only trying to help you.'

'So what can we do?' I ask, wishing I could go back in time

and decide never to go to the bathroom at Winkler's at all. 'It feels impossible.'

Diane nods. 'I know. But sitting here, talking to you, I think I've come up with an idea. But I have to think it through first. And write something down.' She yawns, and I check the small alarm clock on her nightstand. It's almost nine o'clock. Mama and Grandma are sure to be furious. 'Can you meet me tomorrow morning at the park? Around ten? I think my head will have cleared by then.' She winces. 'I drank too much from Connie's bottle tonight.'

She flops down onto the bed, closes her eyes. I ease off the foot of the bed.

'Can I get you a glass of water?' I ask.

Diane shakes her head. 'No, that's all right. I'm just . . . I'm exhausted. I need to close my eyes. But tomorrow. At ten o'clock? The park. Please?'

'Of course,' I say, heading toward her bedroom door.

'And Evie,' she says.

'Yeah?'

'Thank you. For being a real friend.'

'Thanks for being mine,' I answer. And I mean it from the bottom of my heart.

17

When I get home, my heart is hammering as I open the front door. I find Mama pacing in the living room, smoking a Salem. She doesn't smoke a lot. When she's tired or worried, mostly. I don't have to guess which one it is this time.

'Evelyn,' she shouts, spotting me. 'Where have you been? We haven't seen you since you left for school this morning!' She stabs out her cigarette.

'Is she back?' My grandmother's voice travels down the hallway, soon followed by my grandmother herself, wrapped tight in her baby-blue bathrobe, a scarf tied around a head full of curlers.

'I'm sorry,' I say. 'After school a bunch of us went over to Sunny's and—'

'Your friend Juanita was home an hour ago!' Mama shouts, motioning in the direction of the Barajases' house next door. 'I went over there and pestered her to tell me where you were. She said she didn't know.'

'She didn't!' I argue. 'She really didn't. She didn't see me leave.' I immediately realize my mistake.

'Leave and go where?' my grandmother presses, frowning.

'Mama, let me ask the questions, please!' my mother shouts.

'She's headed straight for perdition,' Grandma says, her hands on her hips. 'She's going to end up Lord knows where if you don't get a handle on her, Marjorie!'

'Mama, I told you to stop!'

I take advantage of this argument to race past them and toward my room, shutting the door behind me. Moments later, I hear my mother on the other side, and I brace myself for her to come barging in to keep yelling at me.

'Evelyn, it's late. I don't have the energy for this. But we are going to talk in the morning. Do you hear me?' Her words are frustrated, but her voice is tired.

'Yes, ma'am,' I say, just to make her go away.

There's a long pause, and I wait until I hear my mother and grandmother go back to their bedrooms, shutting their doors behind them. This gives me a chance to wash up for bed, but it takes me a while to fall asleep. When I do, I dream I'm running through an empty Winkler's, with no cars in sight. In my arms is a crying infant, and a shadowy figure is chasing me, threatening me with his presence. In the nightmare I know I have to get away from him and somehow manage to get the baby back to Diane and Johnny, but when I trip and fall, the baby evaporates out of my arms as the figure approaches. I wake up sweating, my heart thudding hard.

I blink, still trying to catch my breath and erase the disturbing images from my mind, and as my gaze comes into focus, I see my mother sitting on the edge of my bed, a plate of bacon in her lap. She doesn't seem angry, but I wish she weren't here. I need a moment to collect myself. But I can't exactly send her away after last night.

'Grandma made breakfast,' she says, her face neutral. Her voice almost flat.

Wordlessly, I sit up and take a slice of bacon, then stick it into my mouth. It tastes warm and crisp. 'Thank you,' I manage to mumble through bites. My head is throbbing just a little from the evening before. Mama takes a bite of bacon, then carefully rests the plate on my nightstand after clearing a space for it in all the mess.

'Evelyn, can't we talk? Like we used to?' Her face is pained, and she almost seems nervous to ask. My own mother is scared of me, and maybe I can't blame her.

When she says she wants to talk like we used to, she means like back in fifth or sixth grade, when Cheryl and I still told her everything. Or most everything. Back when my big sister and I would crawl into bed with her early on Saturday mornings and she'd whisper stories about the Shamrock, like how fun it was to catch a glimpse of the Corkettes practicing one of their water shows in the enormous pool, or how one rich guest got so drunk he accidentally fell asleep in the hallway and Mama and another maid had to help several bellhops drag him to the right room. I'd tell her stories, too, like how Bobby Finnegan put a thumbtack on Miss Carter's chair or how Marilyn Caldwell did a backflip on the playground and everyone saw her underpants. And Cheryl would compete with me for Mama's attention with stories of her own, and then the three of us would laugh until Grandma poked her head in and asked us when we were going to get up and face the day.

'We can talk, Mama,' I say, studying her face. She's still so pretty to me, even though she's tired all the time. When she grins, she reminds me a little of Diane, the way it's equal parts hopeful and sweet. Her dark brown hair has a few wisps of gray in it, but just a few. And her eyes can really bore into you if you let them.

As she gazes in my direction, the old worry starts gnawing at me, impossible to ignore.

Am I a terrible daughter?

'I'm just sad, Evelyn,' she says, 'like you don't trust me anymore. You're running around all the time, not coming home until late.' She snatches another piece of bacon and pulls herself all the way onto my bed, then takes a deep breath. 'I'm trying not to lose my temper. I just want you to tell me what's wrong.'

'Mama, I trust you,' I say. Suddenly I *am* filled with the urge to tell my mother what's wrong. Everything from Johnny getting arrested to Diane's secrets to what happened with Preston behind the bathroom building at Winkler's. I even open my mouth, push my tongue against the back of my bottom teeth. Then I shut it almost immediately. Everything I would say to her would crush her. Break her heart. Plus, it might put Diane at risk.

'If you trust me, why don't you tell me what's going on with you?' she asks. 'I can tell something is. Or lots of things, maybe.'

I break eye contact with her because it's too painful. I peek out the window, past the threadbare yellow curtains that have been washed and ironed so many times that they're paper-thin. I hear my voice say, at last, 'Mama, what do you want for me?' It's a surprise, even to me.

'What do you mean, what do I want for you?' she asks, and I manage at last to draw my eyes back toward her, toward the deep wrinkle that cuts between her eyes as she frowns in my direction.

'You know what I mean,' I try again.

'Well,' she says, her voice resigned, 'I'd like it if you didn't end up like me, smelling like bleach and rich people's garbage.'

'Don't say that,' I push back. 'It's not true.'

'It is,' she says. 'I'm used to it. But I want your life to be easier than mine. Settled. A life where you don't have to work so hard and you can have someone to take care of you.'

I know she means a nice boy. A good man, not like my

father. Again, I'm struck with the urge to open my mouth, spill everything that's been going on. But what could my mother do for me except worry? She can't get Johnny out of prison. She can't make Diane innocent of killing Preston Fowler, even if she did do it to protect me. And she can't go back in time and stop Preston from trying to hurt me. I want to believe Mama would understand what happened that night, but wouldn't she think a girl who couldn't keep herself out of a situation like that would also be a girl who'd never find the right sort of boy? Wouldn't I end up being an even bigger disappointment if I told her the truth?

And at the thought of the truth about Preston Fowler, I close my eyes and feel a rage coursing through me without any place to put it. The shadowy figure from my dream feels very real all of a sudden, even though now I'm awake. I'm gripped by the urge to run again. Somewhere. Anywhere.

'Evelyn, are you all right?'

My mother's voice pulls me back, forces me to open my eyes. She tilts her head, confused.

'I'm all right, Mama,' I say. I push out a smile and free my hand from hers. Suddenly I feel irritable. Unsettled. I need to get up. Move. 'I need to wash up. I'm going to the park later.'

'Oh, Evie, I wish you'd stay put today,' she says, defeated.

'Mama, please,' I fight back, annoyed and hating myself for being annoyed all at the same time. 'It's Saturday.'

I head out into the hall, leaving my mother on my bed, the plate of bacon on the nightstand.

'Evelyn?' my mother tries again.

If I move fast enough toward the bathroom, maybe I can shut the door behind me before the urge strikes to turn and race back into her arms.

I spy Diane on the park bench, waiting for me. She's early, of course. And she's wearing one of her pastel sweater sets.

'Hi,' I say, walking up to her. I notice she has a piece of paper folded in her hands.

'Hi, Evie,' she says. Her face is pale, and there are slight, purplish half-moons under her eyes. As I sit down, I notice her fingers pressing tight against the paper, the tips almost white from the pressure. I think about last night and all she shared with me, how much courage it must have taken to share it.

'How are you feeling?' I ask.

'I'm all right,' she says, offering a shy smile. 'I'm so glad you were able to walk home with me last night.'

'Me too,' I answer, and we both know exactly what we mean, even if we don't say the words out loud. 'What's that?' I ask, motioning to the paper in her hands. 'A letter?'

Diane turns the paper over a few times, like she's attempting a magic trick she's not sure she can pull off. 'Evie, you know the part of town I come from, right?'

'I know it exists, sure,' I say, trying to crack a joke. 'But I don't know it much more than that.'

Diane doesn't laugh at my poor attempt at being funny. 'No, what I mean is, you know the kind of people who live there? Folks who have money? Power?'

Of course I know that much. The name River Oaks even *sounds* impressive. Rivers can be strong, dangerous, cutting courses however they wish. Oaks are broad and tough, towering above other trees. River. Oaks. Just a mention of that neighborhood and it's easy to picture homes like palaces with big fat columns out front and green grass as thick as carpeting and rows of maids and butlers in matching sharp black outfits marching up the drives to fetch tea and slippers and whatever else maids and butlers fetch for the mighty and the rich.

'Yes, I know, Diane,' I say, cutting the humor out of my voice and matching Diane's tone. 'Of course I do.'

Diane takes a deep breath. 'So you've heard the name Howell? Tom Howell?'

The name is familiar, but I can't place it. 'Yes, but why do I know it?' I ask Diane.

'He's the police chief,' Diane says. 'And he's married to Lynn Cullen Howell. All that oil money. Anyway, I'm friends with their daughter Betty. Or . . . I was.' She peers at the paper in her lap.

'Was she one of those mean girls at Winkler's that

night? The ones I tossed my cigarette at?'

Diane manages a brief grin at that memory, then says, 'Yes. She was the one who came up later. Who tried to get Vickie and the other girl to leave me alone. But she didn't say anything to me.' She hangs her head for a moment, clutches the paper in her hand. 'Like I told you, Betty and I were best friends once. She was the only one who I trusted to know about me and Johnny and about what happened to me.' Her voice cracks, and I picture two fancy River Oaks girls having slumber parties in matching silk pajamas and staying up late and breaking into their parents' liquor cabinets.

'But after I got sent away, it was all over,' Diane continues. 'Those few weeks I was home after I'd—' She stops, and I wait for the words *I'd had the baby* to spill out of her mouth, but she pauses, takes a breath, and corrects herself. 'Those few weeks I was home after I got sent away, the few weeks before I moved to my aunt's house . . . no one came around, but Betty was the only one decent enough to sneak a phone call to me to tell me her mother wouldn't let her talk to me anymore and she was sorry. She hung up before I could say anything, but . . . I guess that's why I'm hoping this harebrained plan will work and she'll help me.'

'So what's the plan?' I press.

At this Diane hands me the paper. It's thick and cream-colored, and when I open it, I see the name *Diane Amelia Farris* embossed at the top in shiny black lettering.

'Amelia?' I say, surprised.

'Don't. It was my great-grandmother's, and I hate it,' says Diane, knocking into me only slightly. 'Just read it, Evie.'

The letter is written in Diane's careful, even script.

To All Concerned,

I swear to God that everything in this letter is true and correct. I want it to be known that on the evening of Saturday, October 10, 1964, I stabbed and killed Preston Fowler behind the bathroom at Winkler Drive-In because I was protecting a girl who Preston was trying to hurt. I did not intend to kill Preston, only to scare him off, but he was very intoxicated, wouldn't listen, and everything happened very quickly. If I hadn't acted, Preston could have hurt a girl very badly. I am sorry for the pain I've caused the Fowler family, but I had to do it. It must be known that Johnny Treadway is completely innocent of all charges and should be freed immediately. I take full responsibility for what I have done.

At the bottom of the paper, Diane has signed her name, all careful loops and perfect slants.

I read it twice, then a third time, and then I peer up at Diane as I hand it back to her.

'I'm going to go to Betty's house tonight to give her this letter and beg her to give it to her father and convince him of the truth,' says Diane. 'I'm going to ask to borrow her car. I don't have a license yet, but I know how to drive. Well, I'm going to ask to *take* her car, I guess. If she'll let me. And I'm going to drive somewhere and hide until all this blows over and we know that Johnny is free.'

I don't have any response. Diane's plan sounds wild. Impossible. And from the determined look in her eyes, I know she is deadly serious.

'Evie, will you come with me tonight to take this letter to Betty? If she hears from you, she'll know for sure that this' — she holds up the letter, waves it in the air — 'is all true.'

'Diane, there has to be another way,' I say even as I scramble to figure out what it is. 'Where on earth will you go?'

'I have Christmas and birthday money saved. Maybe I'll drive to Mexico.'

'Mexico!' I shout, and then clamp my hand over my mouth, even though there isn't anyone else at the park.

'Evie, I don't know everything yet, but I do know I . . .' Her voice gives out. 'I do know that I can't sit here, breathing in the fresh air, talking to you, and the entire time knowing Johnny is in prison for something I did. I can't stand it anymore!' She squeezes her eyes shut tight, manages one tortured sob. 'After everything — *everything* — I have been through . . . please, Evie. Please say you'll come with me tonight to Betty's. If she hears what happened from you, too, I think she'll help me.'

I reach out, put one hand on Diane's shoulder. I was never going to say no. Before I even got to the park, I knew that whatever Diane asked of me, I was going to say yes.

'I'll come with you,' I say, and she opens her eyes.

'Oh, Evie, thank you!' she says, cracking a smile at last and leaning over and pulling me into a tight hug, just like she did last night. Juanita and Connie and Sunny and I don't hug much. I'm not sure why. We just don't. But Diane throws her arms around me like we've known each other for ages, not just a little over a week.

'We'll have to take the bus,' Diane says, pulling back and carefully folding her letter to Betty in half again.

'How do you know Betty will be there tonight?' I ask. 'It's Saturday.'

'Chief Howell is police chief for a reason,' explains Diane. 'He's strict. She always had a ten o'clock curfew. If we get there after that, she's sure to be home. We can throw pebbles at her bedroom window. I know which one it is.'

I nod. It all sounds absolutely bonkers, but I can't see what other choice we have. Diane tells me that as soon as she's able to deliver her letter to Betty, I can come back home and play dumb and she'll get on the road, far away from River Oaks and the east side and Houston and maybe even Texas. She'll get away from every rotten thing that's happened to her in all those places these past few months, and in doing so, she's sure she'll help one of the few good things that's happened to her – Johnny – see the light of day again.

'Be at my aunt's house tonight at eight o'clock, all right?' Diane says, standing up and straightening and smoothing her skirt reflexively. I picture her staying prim and proper on a solo trip to Mexico, and while my first reaction is to smile at the thought, I'm immediately gripped with the realization that Diane is leaving. *Leaving*.

'Diane,' I say, 'are you sure about all this?'

Diane nods. 'It's the only way, Evie. Don't tell a soul, all right?' Before I can argue, she reaches out, squeezes my hand, and says, 'I'll see you at eight.' And then she heads off, still clutching the letter like a life preserver.

When I get home, Juanita is on her porch steps with her little niece Celia, sharing a box of Lemonheads.

'Only one more,' says Juanita, carefully handing Celia a tiny yellow ball. 'Or Abuelita is going to let me have it when your teeth rot out.'

Celia laughs and snatches the candy, then races around back to play.

'Hey,' Juanita says, standing up and walking toward me, holding the box in my direction. 'Want some?'

'No thanks,' I say. I remember Diane's words. *Don't tell a soul*. How desperately I want to tell Juanita. But I promised Diane.

Diane.

On the walk home from the park, all I've been able to think about is her wild plan. Her determination to take such a tremendous risk. And I'm struck again by how brave she is.

But I'm also imagining Diane driving Betty's borrowed car down to Mexico all alone in the middle of the night, her hands gripped tight on the steering wheel, no one in the passenger seat to help her find her way.

I bite my bottom lip.

'Why didn't you say goodbye last night?' Juanita asks, pulling me out of my thoughts. 'Your mother came over here, looking for you.'

'I know,' I say, embarrassed. 'I'm really sorry.'

'It's all right,' she says, popping a Lemonhead into her mouth. 'But she was upset and scared.'

'Trust me, I know,' I say, gripped with guilt. 'But Diane needed to talk to me about something after the party.'

'I figured,' says Juanita. 'Is she all right?'

I take a deep breath and stare at my feet, sure that Juanita can tell there's something I'm not spilling. I want so much to tell Juanita what Diane said to me. I really have been her pet, it's true, and it really did start that day I gathered up the courage to cross into her yard and ask for help with my makeup. Juanita would listen. She's even tried to get me to open up. And lately I've been feeling less like a mascot, I guess, given everything that's happening.

But I promised Diane I wouldn't talk about tonight, and I want to keep my promises.

And anyway, Juanita might also try to talk me out of an

idea that's swimming inside my mind.

'Do you hate me that I'm not telling you something I swore I wouldn't tell?' I ask, glancing at her as she tucks a lock of her black hair behind her ear and studies me.

'You know, Evie,' she says, 'you're as tough as Connie in a way.'

At this I laugh out loud. Me as tough as Connie? It's not true, even if I admit there's something about Juanita's declaration that I like hearing. 'Trust me, I'll never be as tough as Connie Treadway.'

'Maybe not in some ways,' Juanita answers. 'Not when it comes to throwing a punch or sassing back, but you hold your ground. You listen to your heart. You follow it.'

I remember what Sunny said about me that day behind the gym. That I had something special. I wish I could see what Sunny and Juanita see in me.

'But you listen to your heart,' I say, protesting. 'You do.'

Juanita shrugs. 'Yeah, maybe I do. I don't know. I don't know how to explain it, Evie. But Sunny probably would have told me what Diane said. Connie, too. Hell, even I might have. But you keep your word when it counts. And you speak up when it counts. You helped Diane when the rest of us probably wouldn't have. You'd never leave a friend in a fix. That's all I'm saying.'

My heart swells with gratitude, and her words bury themselves in my brain.

Suddenly I know what I have to do.

'Thanks, Juanita,' I say.

'Just promise me one thing,' she says. 'If you need us, you'll get us. Okay?'

'Okay.'

'No, you have to promise,' she says. 'Cross your heart and hope to die.'

I roll my eyes, but I find myself dragging a finger over my chest in an X.

'Say it,' orders Juanita, her mouth curling up into a grin.

'Fine,' I say. 'If I need you, I'll get you. Cross my heart and hope to die.'

'Good,' says Juanita, nodding with satisfaction. Just then Celia races around from the backyard.

'Tía, I wet myself,' she cries. And sure enough, the little white socks she's wearing under her jumper look soaked.

Juanita grimaces. 'Let's go inside and get you cleaned up,' she says, tugging Celia toward the front door. When she gets there, she tosses her hair back over her shoulder and eyes me one more time.

'Remember, Evie. Cross your heart and hope to die!'

'I know!' I shout back. And then, just after Juanita's gone inside, I notice the hair on my arms is standing at attention. I've got goose bumps even though it's not all that cold. Something about those words makes me feel funny inside. *Cross your heart and hope to die*. I remember that night at

Winkler's before I left for the bathroom. The sense that something wasn't right. Woman's intuition, like my mother says. I peer out onto my street, but there's no one. I think back to Diane at the park, her plan and all that's to come tonight, and I wrap my arms tight around my body, squeezing myself in a hug. Then I head for my front door.

CHAPTER

18

I set the last of the dinner dishes on the dish rack, dry my hands on the red-and-white-checked dish towel, and check the kitchen clock one more time. It ticks along much more slowly than my heartbeat, which is racing. 7:40 p.m.

If I don't do it at this moment, I may never do it. I might lose my chance, or lose the guts to pull it off.

So I have to do it now.

I can hear *The Jackie Gleason Show* playing in the den, and Grandma laughing so hard she starts coughing. That program has been on since I was a little girl, and even though I think it's silly, with its tired chorus girl acts and all of Jackie's ridiculous characters, Grandma never misses an episode. Normally I'd find the whole thing sort of charming, but tonight the shouts from the television and even Grandma's laughter make me cringe.

I leave the kitchen and find Mama in the den, too, curled up on the other end of the couch, dressed in her cream-colored nightgown, her feet tucked under her. She has a paperback novel in her lap, but her eyes are focused on the television.

My heart is pounding, and now my mouth is dry as dirt.

'Mama, how can you stand this?' my mother asks my grandmother, and then she gives me a knowing look. I remember this morning and the bacon and her push for closeness and how I didn't give her what she wanted. How I never do. All of a sudden I feel guilty and angry and sad all at once, afraid I'll never be the girl she wants. Or maybe afraid that one day I'll have to be.

My heart starts to beat even faster, and my breathing grows shallow. It's time.

'I'm going to Diane's,' I say, and I'm irritated at my own voice. At the way I practically shout it out, determined.

'Oh, Evelyn, now?' Mama says, shutting the book she's not reading and sighing.

'Evelyn, listen to your mother,' Grandma says, not peeling her eyes away from Jackie Gleason. 'It's too late.'

Tension between us arrives like a match has been struck. Its presence can't be ignored.

'I told you I'm going to Diane's,' I say, and I head for my bedroom, my cheeks heating up. My heart now not just thumping but cracking.

There's something I've got to do, and my mother doesn't know I'm going to do it.

Not even *Diane* knows I'm going to do it.

But I'm going to.

Juanita's voice from this morning runs through my mind.

You'd never leave a friend in a fix.

My shoes are heavy on the hardwood floor. I throw my door open so loud it bangs up against the wall of my bedroom, but I don't even jump. I just know I have to move. *Now.*

'Evelyn, no!' my mother shouts from the den, already knowing she's lost. 'I want you to stay in tonight. Please!'

In my bedroom, I shove my mother's voice out of my head and tug on a cardigan, slipping the little babysitting money I have left into one of its pockets. I glance around my bedroom, still a mess, just as it was on the day Diane came over. I take a shaky breath and remember being tiny in this bedroom, cutting out paper dolls with Cheryl and telling secrets to Raggedy Ann. Not knowing I was poor yet. Not knowing I was destined to be bad. Not knowing I was sure to break my mother's heart.

I try to sear this bedroom into my mind.

Suddenly a firm hand is on my elbow, the fingers cutting into the skin.

'Evelyn, listen to me, you're staying in tonight. That's an order.'

I pull away and turn around to face my mother. My mother, who deserves someone better than me. Who deserves to start over with a new daughter. A daughter who would never be so dumb as to head to the bathroom at Winkler's alone or get mixed up in anything like what I'm mixed up in now. A daughter who just wants to settle down and be good. Whatever that means.

But that isn't me.

'I'm not Cheryl,' I yell, upset. 'I won't just do what you say!' I break free from her grip and head for my bedroom door, but she blocks me.

'Evelyn, I am demanding that you tell me what is happening with you!' my mother shouts, anticipating my movements so I can't get past. 'What on God's earth is happening?' Her voice is thick with anger and sadness. It climbs up the walls and covers me. I want to wrestle free from it and pretend it never existed.

My throat constricts. My stomach churns.

'Let me go, damn it!' I stamp my foot like a child. I've never cursed in front of my mother before.

Her slap is hard and sharp, slicing into my face like a cold wind. It's so hard it knocks the breath out of me. As soon as she slaps me, my mother brings her hand up to her face as if she's just smacked herself.

'Evelyn,' my mother whispers. 'Oh my God, I'm so . . . Evelyn, I didn't mean . . .'

My grandmother switched me a few times when I was small, but my mother has never hit me once in her life. Not ever.

All I can think to do is scream, long and loud.

My grandmother appears around the corner, shouting for answers. Screaming for Jesus to help us.

My mother turns her head to look at her own mother, and I take my chance. I push past her and make a break for it, but I must push too hard, because suddenly my mother is on the floor. I've knocked her down. She stares at me from where she's fallen near my feet, her face crumpling. Her eyes wounded. She's never looked at me like this in all her life. Not ever.

No one says anything. No one does anything. I stand there, in between my mom and my grandmother. The only noise is studio audience laughter from the Jackie Gleason program hunting us down here in the hallway, mocking us.

My mind tells me one thing. *Go.*

And so I do. I race past my grandmother, who has pushed herself, terrified, against the wall like I might knock her down, too. And I burst through the front door and rocket down the street, my feet pounding as hard as my heart as I run all the way to Diane's house.

When I arrive at the back door, I'm still catching my breath. As I knock and wait for Diane to answer, I find myself pressing my fingers to my cheek where my mother slapped me. I press my fingers into where her fingers were. I press and press instead of letting myself cry.

'Evie, is that you?' Diane's voice slides through the door.

'Yeah, it's me.'

Diane opens the door and I walk in.

'I'm so glad you ca—' she says, but I interrupt her. Before I can lose my cool. Before I can break down.

'Give me the letter,' I say to Diane. 'The one you're giving to Betty.'

'What? Why?' Diane wrinkles her brow. Looks at me uncertainly. 'Evie, are you all right?'

'Just trust me.'

Diane has a knapsack by her feet, and from one of its pockets, she slides out the cream-colored paper she showed me earlier at the park. She hands it to me.

'Do you have something to write with?' I ask, my voice insistent. Bossy.

'Why?' Diane asks, frowning now.

'Please. Just hand me something.'

Diane doesn't push back at that. She finds a pencil on the cluttered kitchen counter and gives it to me. I open the letter, make room on the counter, and press the pencil tight between my fingers. In the space underneath Diane's signature, I add my own words, pushing the lead into the thick paper as if that somehow makes them extra true.

The words are easy to write because I've been rehearsing them all afternoon and all evening. Ever since I left the park. Ever since I saw Juanita's niece sucking on a Lemonhead and ever since I ate Grandma's tuna casserole and ever since my mother's hand hit my face and I ran and ran down Coyle Street like I was being chased by the devil himself.

I know just what to say.

Everything Diane Farris has written is completely true. She was protecting me from Preston Fowler, who was trying to hurt me. She didn't mean to kill Preston. Please release Johnny Treadway. He didn't do anything. I swear to God all this is true.

Then at the bottom I sign my full name, Evelyn Ann Barnes. For good measure I add Evie in quotes. I hand it to Diane and give her a moment to read it. She lifts her face from the paper and looks at me.

'Now there can't be any question,' I say.

Diane nods, her eyes wide.

'And Diane, there's one more thing I need you to know,' I tell her. 'I'm going with you.'

'Of course you're going with me,' Diane says, confused. 'You're going with me to Betty's.'

'No,' I say, and my voice is firm even if my heart is pounding, 'you don't understand. I'm going with you when you *leave* Betty's. You're my friend, Diane. And I'm going with you to Mexico. To the moon. To anywhere. I'm going with you like that.'

Diane opens her mouth to speak, then closes it and squeezes her eyes shut for a moment.

'Oh, Evie,' she whispers at last. 'Evie, thank you.'

19

My hand is tucked inside Diane's as she leads me, silently, around the back of Betty Howell's house. She glances over her shoulder, flashes me a serious look, and holds one finger up to her lips to remind me to be silent.

As if I'd even dream of making a noise.

Even though I'm anxious, I try to take in my surroundings. River Oaks. It's as grand as the black-and-white pictures in the society pages have promised, only now it's here, in color. Under the cast of moonlight it's not as vivid as it must be during the day, but even in the dark of night I can spy the manicured lawns and flower beds, the sprawling homes, the shimmer of backyard swimming pools rich people must enjoy during the waning days of a long Texas summer. Our shoes sink into a lawn so thick it looks like carpet, and evening dew kisses my ankles.

Diane stops us and lets go of my hand. She points up at a second-story window, black shutters jumping out against the palatial white brick house, the biggest house I've spied on Chevy Chase Drive. Inside the lights are off.

'How many bedrooms does this house have?' I whisper, unable to stay silent any longer.

Diane shoots me a look, then rolls her eyes and holds up two hands and six fingers.

I gape, but Diane ignores me. From the pocket of her skirt she pulls out a handful of pebbles. She takes one in her right hand and rolls it up and down her fingers, taking a deep breath. She glances up at the window above us and chews her bottom lip.

I reach over and take the pebble from her.

'Let me,' I say, sure I have better aim. Last spring, Connie taught me how to knock empty beer bottles off the back of Ray Swanson's jalopy with my eyes closed. 'Is that her bedroom window?' I ask. Diane nods, and all I can think is *six bedrooms*.

My tongue firmly pressed in concentration against my teeth, I leap and toss. The pebble makes contact with the glass, but I know it will take more than one to get Betty's attention.

If she's even in there, I think to myself. Suddenly this plan seems completely nuts. But I suppose it's all we have.

Diane hands me the rest of the pebbles, and I keep flinging them, one after another, each pebble hitting Betty Howell's window with a small but distinct *plink*. Finally we run out, and Diane and I can only stand and hold our breath.

Just when I'm about to give up hope, the window lights up

and a small, brown-haired head pops up like a jack-in-the-box. Diane reaches over and grips my hand again, squeezes it tight. I squeeze back.

Above us, there's the sound of a window squeaking open, and the brown-haired head leans out, peering down.

'Diane?' Not a whisper. Not even the sound of surprise. Just a calm, clear voice saying, 'Diane?' Like a teacher taking roll.

'Yes, Betty, it's me!' Diane whispers as loudly as she dares. 'Can you please come down here? Please?'

'Wait one moment,' says Betty, her voice still as calm as you please. 'I'll be right there.'

Betty takes the time to carefully shut the window, and I notice the light turning off inside. How long would it take a person to walk the thousands of miles from that bedroom (*six bedrooms!*) to the front door of a palace? Two full minutes, it turns out. I count the seconds silently in my head as Diane chews on her bottom lip and stares at the perfect hedges surrounding Betty's enormous backyard, trimmed as level as a switchblade.

At the two-minute mark Betty appears around the back corner, and Diane and I jump. She's appeared as silently as a ghost, but she's very much alive, her freckled cheeks pink even in the moonlight. Her dark brown eyes widen, carefully taking us both in. I recognize her from Winkler's, but instead of a sweater set, she's wearing a peach bathrobe tied tight around her, and the ruffled lace collar of her white nightgown

217

is peeking out. I bet it's real lace, too.

'Diane Farris, my God,' she says. 'It's really you.'

'Shh,' Diane says. 'I don't want to get caught.'

Betty shrugs. 'It's my house, Diane. And anyway, Mother and Dad are at the club, Leola is almost certainly asleep in front of the television, and Bobby is on a Boy Scout camping trip. But let's go to the guesthouse. It will probably make us all more comfortable.'

She swishes ahead of us, her brown curls bobbing. Betty Howell sounds more grown-up than any girl I know.

We follow her like baby ducklings around the long, rectangular pool, dodging the lawn chairs, and head for a small white structure at the back of the yard. It's unlocked, because I suppose people in River Oaks are so wealthy that even the burglars are too impressed to steal from them.

Betty's guesthouse is more nicely decorated than my real house, and I sink into a soft forest-green sectional in the living room next to Diane, suddenly shy about my faded jeans and thrift-store blouse and cardigan. Betty takes her place in a chair nearest me and crosses her legs at her ankles. She takes a breath.

'Diane,' she says, and something in Betty's voice – up until now so calm and grown-up – shifts a bit. 'It's . . . nice to see you . . .' She coughs and glances at the carpet. Her voice trails off, uncertain of where to go. I look at Diane, remembering what she told me about Betty's parents not letting her come visit after she came back from Dallas. About Betty being the only one kind enough to at least make a phone call.

Betty and I were best friends.

'It's all right, Betty,' Diane says, her voice firm but cut with sadness. 'Although I suppose you could have said hello to me that night at Winkler's instead of just staring at me.'

Betty flushes, appearing unsettled for the first time since we arrived.

'Well,' she says, 'I did try to make Vickie and Sharon leave you alone. I'm . . . sorry they didn't.' Then she composes herself, regains her earlier smoothness and sophistication, and looks back up at Diane. And at last, it's like she realizes I'm there, too.

'I'm sorry,' she says, 'but I didn't catch your name? I'm Betty Howell, but I'm sure Diane has told you that.'

'I'm Evie Barnes,' I say, doubtful this girl will help us with anything.

'It's nice to meet you, Evie,' Betty says, but her eyes are back on Diane, like she's studying a complicated math problem. I can tell she's taking Diane in, maybe trying to visualize Diane's belly as it was a few months ago. Maybe trying to remember what it was like when she and Diane were best friends. Before the world got turned upside down.

'Evie, do you have a smoke?' Diane asks, breaking the uncomfortable silence at last, and I slip out my pack from my shirt pocket, glad to have something to do with my nervous hands. Betty watches with surprise, then excuses herself briefly to find an ashtray.

'I don't remember you smoking, Diane,' says Betty as Diane lights a Salem.

'I'm guessing you don't remember a lot of things, Betty,' Diane answers, and I'm surprised at how sharp the words are coming from her mouth. Almost immediately she shakes her head, apologizes. 'I'm sorry.'

'It's all right,' Betty answers, dropping her gaze, her cheeks reddening. 'I deserve it, I guess.'

There's a shift in the mood. Betty's polished sophistication is suddenly smudged. And I feel uncomfortable, like I shouldn't be here. Not when there's clearly so much history between Betty and Diane that it would take ages to sort it all out. I try to imagine the two of them before Diane was sent away. What sorts of things did they do for fun? Swipe stuff from Woolworth's? Cut class? Paint each other's eyes thick with dark makeup?

I doubt it.

But it's obvious there is so much left unsaid. So many memories. I feel like a spy in plain sight.

'Listen, Betty, I'm going to get right to the point of why we're here,' says Diane. She stares out through gauzy white window curtains at the Howells' pool, ponders what she's about to unveil. 'What I'm about to say you may not believe. But it's true, and Evie will tell you it's true. And . . . we need your help.' She connects with Betty's gaze, and when she speaks again, her voice is deadly serious. 'Betty, I'm begging you to help us.'

My heart thuds. So much depends on whether this rich girl decides to be nice to us. To me, a girl I'm sure she sees as trash.

Betty's eyes widen, frightened and confused. 'All right, Diane,' she manages. 'I'm listening.'

So Diane begins to carefully tell her story – *our* story – pausing a few times to take a drag of her cigarette or gauge Betty's reaction, which is one of total shock. As Diane explains what happened at Winkler's, what she did to Preston Fowler, how Johnny wasn't to blame, Betty's eyes track from Diane to me, her gaze silently questioning us.

Tell me this isn't true.

I hope Betty realizes my steady gaze is my own echo of Diane's words.

Please believe us, Betty.

When Diane finishes her story, including our plans to run away from Houston and hide until everything is sorted out, she removes the confession from her pocketbook, unfolds it carefully, and hands it to Betty, who takes it with a trembling hand. Her eyes scan Diane's words. My own eyes skim over the words I added at the bottom of the letter only an hour or so ago, a reminder of what I'm willing to risk in order to do the only thing that seems right. Even now, with our future so uncertain, I don't regret them.

Betty looks up, her mouth open.

'If you could give that to your father,' Diane says. 'If you could get him to believe what Evie and I wrote, because it is the truth . . . maybe then they would let Johnny go.'

Something snaps in Betty. She shuts her mouth, tosses the letter on the small table in front of us.

'Johnny,' she says. 'It was always about and for Johnny.' She crosses her arms tight in front of her and scowls, like a little girl about to throw a fit. I sit up, anticipating a fight. My stomach drops. She isn't going to help us.

'Betty, you know I loved him,' Diane protests, wounded. 'You know I *love* him.'

Betty's eyes narrow, and she turns her face toward her former best friend. 'All that boy brought you is heartache. Can't you see that, Diane? Oh, if only you hadn't been so foolish . . .'

Diane gasps at Betty's words, then stabs her cigarette out angrily in the small silver ashtray on the table, her auburn hair swaying with each stab. 'Foolish!' she shouts, her voice matching her expression in its intensity of disbelief. 'Betty, how could you? How could you be so mean? You didn't even come and see me when I . . . when I left.'

Suddenly Betty's eyes are wet with tears, and her face is flushed bright red. When she speaks, her voice shakes, then breaks in pain. 'But, Diane . . . you left me, too,' she says. 'You did! We were best friends, and then all you cared about was Johnny. It was like I didn't exist! Mother and Dad had one of their awful fights, and where were you? With Johnny. Mother told me I was too pudgy and would never find the right sort of boy, and where were you? With Johnny! Even when the president was killed, when everyone was crying and scared and it felt like the world was ending, you were with him. It was like I didn't even matter to you anymore.'

Betty buries her face in her hands, and my mind jumps back to that awful day almost a year ago. How Mama and Grandma and I spent hours in front of the television sobbing, even though Grandma always said she didn't trust President Kennedy because he was a Catholic. And then how Juanita and I whispered and smoked on her porch into the early hours of the morning, trying to imagine how the country could go on without that handsome man in charge.

Diane and I don't move as Betty sobs into her hands. Finally I look over at Diane. She is crying as well. Something about all of it makes my throat ache, too. I can't help it.

'Betty,' Diane says, standing up, walking toward her. 'Betty, I'm . . .' Her voice trails off into a whisper. Diane wraps Betty in her arms. 'Oh . . . I'm sorry. I didn't know.'

I light a cigarette, unsure what else to do with myself. Betty and Diane hold each other for a moment until Betty pulls back and looks Diane in the eyes.

'No, Diane, I'm sorry,' she says. 'I let you down. I was a rotten friend.'

'No, you're right . . . I was the rotten one,' says Diane. 'I got caught up with Johnny. Betty, I do love him, but . . . I didn't stop and think about you. And you had to keep it all a secret, and you did. You never betrayed us and you could have. I'm sorry. I'm so sorry.'

Betty wipes her eyes with her fingers, sniffles hard. She nods. 'It's all right,' she manages. 'It doesn't matter now.'

Diane takes a deep, shaky breath and moves to sit next to me on the couch. 'No, it still matters. But, Betty,' she says, her voice cracking, 'Betty . . . why didn't you . . . why didn't you come see me? Didn't you ever guess how . . . alone I was?'

Betty closes her eyes. 'Oh, Diane,' she manages. 'Diane, I wanted to . . . Mother and Dad. You know how they are. And I never had the guts. I never had whatever it is you have, Diane, that makes you so unafraid.'

Diane tips her head back and offers up a soft laugh. 'Unafraid. Hardly. I've spent the last year practically terrified.'

Betty doesn't respond. At least not with words. She reaches out for Diane, takes her hands in hers. The two girls offer each other shy smiles. I take a slow drag of my cigarette and my eyes fall on Diane's confession on the coffee table, staring at us.

I offer a soft cough, then push Diane's letter just a bit with my fingertips as I move to stub out my smoke.

Betty notices and takes a deep breath, gently lets go of

Diane, and accepts the letter from me.

'I'm going to give this to my father,' she says, her voice firm. 'And I'll explain to him everything the both of you have shared with me tonight. I'll tell him he has to let Johnny go.'

Diane smiles and reaches over to squeeze Betty's hand in gratitude. I wait for my body to sink with relief, but it doesn't. What does this mean for Diane and me? Where will we go? Where will we hide?

But Betty answers my questions for me. 'Listen,' she says, and she begins to change back into the savvy, world-weary young woman who first popped her head out of her bedroom window, 'y'all cannot run off somewhere. Not to Mexico or Oklahoma or anywhere. That's ridiculous and dangerous with no set place to stay, plus it just makes you look suspicious. It's safer to stay put. Find a place to hide, but don't leave town. I know I can convince Dad that what Diane did was only because she had to.' She pauses, then scowls, her eyes darkening. 'The truth is, I remember how Preston Fowler could get when he'd had too much to drink. So could a lot of girls at school, I'll bet.'

'Betty,' Diane says, her eyes widening. 'You went on a few dates with him, didn't you?'

Betty frowns at the memory, then shakes her head like she's trying to get rid of it. 'Yes,' she says. 'He wasn't a gentleman when he'd had his share of alcohol. That much is certain. Of course it didn't help that his parents let him get away with everything he ever did. No one ever set limits on that boy or led him to believe he needed to consider other people. Ever.' At this she looks over at me, holds my gaze in hers.

'Evie, it wasn't right what he did,' she says. 'I'm so sorry that happened to you.'

Something about Betty's voice – the way she makes this declaration with such authority – makes my throat ache again, and I whisper, 'Thank you.'

Betty nods, sure of herself. She gets back to what Diane and I should do next.

'But listen, I'm serious, don't leave town and certainly don't leave the country,' she continues. 'It's too risky. I'd be willing to give you my car, of course, but . . . it's far too dangerous for you two to be running all over creation. Do you have a place you can hide in the meantime?'

Diane glances at me, her bleary, bloodshot eyes searching mine.

'Part of me still feels we should just run away,' she says, her voice starting to break.

I shake my head. 'Betty's right. It's too risky, and it really could make us look worse. I think I know what to do,' I say, an idea building inside me, 'but we need to go see Connie first.'

'Who is Connie?' Betty asks.

Diane exhales, then laughs softly. 'Just you wait and see,' she says.

CHAPTER

20

Betty told Diane she was impressed by how unafraid Diane seemed to be, but in the end she turns out fairly fearless herself. After she convinces us we need to stay in Houston, she drives us back to our neighborhood in her brand-new cherry-red Mustang, by far the nicest car I've ever been in. From the back seat I can imagine her taking in our side of town, her eyes probably widening at how different our modest homes and postage-stamp lawns are compared to the palaces of River Oaks. But she doesn't say anything rude.

'You should take us to our friend Sunny's,' I say. 'Connie and Juanita were going to hang out there tonight, I'm pretty sure.' I give Betty the directions, and soon we're in front of Sunny's two-bedroom house on Leeland Street. The porch light is on. My mind flashes back to Betty's home on Chevy Chase Drive. *Six bedrooms!*

'You should come in, too,' I tell Betty. 'Meet the girls and catch them up on the plan.'

Betty glances at Diane, who nods in agreement, before gazing at Sunny's place. I wonder if she's thinking it's smaller than her guesthouse.

'Are you sure they won't mind meeting me?' she asks, shifting her eyes to the rearview mirror and checking her hair and lipstick.

'It'll be fine,' I say as I scoot out the back seat. But I cross my fingers briefly just in case.

Sunny's mother is working the overnight shift at the hospital, and her drunk stepfather is passed out in his bedroom, but we huddle in Sunny's tiny room for privacy anyway. Sunny locks the door tight with the dead bolt that Connie swiped for her from the hardware store a few years ago. She once told me she started locking it after she caught her creepy stepfather lingering near the bathroom whenever she got out of the shower. He's the main reason none of us girls like hanging out at Sunny's very much.

Connie is pacing with nerves, bouncing and smoking and circling the bed, where Diane and I are sitting with a nervous Betty, whose River Oaks coolness has fizzled completely and transformed into a clear anxiousness. Sunny and Juanita are seated cross-legged on Sunny's rag rug.

'I'm glad y'all weren't so dumb as to try and go to Mexico. What was your plan? Sleep on the beach or something?' Connie asks.

'I know, but we just didn't know what else to do, I guess,'

228

I respond, my cheeks flushing, fully aware now how risky our original plan was.

'I get it, Evie,' she answers, 'but even though I'm glad you didn't try to pull that off, I'm not inclined to trust some tea sipper.' She waits a beat, then eyes Betty, her mouth turning into a scowl.

Betty just glances at Diane and me.

'I trust her, Connie,' I say, peering back at Betty. 'We're right to trust you, aren't we?' I try to make my voice sound hard and in charge like Connie's, but I'm sure I fail miserably.

'You *can* trust me,' Betty says, then looks around the room. 'All of you can. I promise. I know what sort of boy Preston was. I know Diane and Evie are telling me the truth. I swear to you, I'll do whatever I can to help fix this.'

Connie shrugs, bites her bottom lip, and bounces some more.

'We don't have any other ideas,' Sunny offers. 'Let's let Betty try it. And we can hide Diane and Evie in the abandoned house.'

'It's still empty,' Juanita agrees. 'And it would only be for a few days. We could bring them food. The water is still on. It's a good idea, Sunny.'

Sunny puffs with pride, but Connie frowns. 'I don't know. It still seems too risky. If y'all are right and *you*' – at this Connie fires another look at Betty – 'can get your rich daddy to believe her, Johnny will be free and Diane will only get a slap on the wrist for protecting Evie. But it still seems like a big chance to me.'

'I believe in Betty,' Diane insists. She turns and looks at her friend and smiles, grateful. Betty returns the smile, flashing her perfect white society smile.

'Didn't she let you down before?' Connie asks, like Betty's not even sitting in the room with us. 'I mean, she didn't exactly stick by you earlier.'

Diane glances down at her hands, her face strained for a moment, and Betty's smile falls. 'Yes,' she says. 'That's true. But I forgive her.'

'You're a real soft one,' Connie says to Diane, rolling her eyes. Her voice is a mix of annoyance and awe. Betty blushes.

'I think Diane and I should go tonight to the abandoned house,' I say, trying to keep us on track. 'I think it's the best choice.'

'What about your mother, Evie?' Sunny asks. Then she looks at Diane. 'And your aunt?'

Diane scowls. 'My aunt won't even realize I'm gone. Trust me.'

'Your mom'll notice,' Juanita pipes up, eyeing me.

My face stings at the memory of what happened earlier. It seems a lifetime away. I put my hand up to my cheek again, and I can feel my mother's slap. I push the urge to cry down as deep as it will go while I tell the girls what happened. I don't want to break in front of the girls. Not now. I try to act like it doesn't matter.

'Damn,' says Juanita when I finish my story.

'*Your* mother hit you?' Connie says, incredulous. 'That's a first.' Then she mutters a quiet, 'I'm sorry, Evie.'

'Thanks,' I whisper, staring down at Sunny's threadbare bedspread. Maybe Connie is the soft one. But Connie knows what it's like to be hit. She says sometimes it's the only way she can be sure her parents know she exists. A lump in my throat builds, and I take a deep breath, making sure it's really gone before I open my mouth again. 'My mother doesn't want me around right now anyway,' I say, forcing myself to believe it's the truth. 'So I think hiding out with Diane is the best choice.'

Connie waits a beat and we all look to her, even Diane and Betty.

'Okay, fine,' she says at last. 'There's something about this I don't like. But I can't put my finger on it.' She stands up and bounces on her heels again, crosses and uncrosses her arms. 'But all right. Let's do it. We'll gather supplies tonight and get Diane and Evie over there.' She looks at Betty again as she gets up off Sunny's bed and reaches for her black pocketbook. 'Don't mess this up, all right? I want my brother out of jail. He doesn't deserve to be in there.' At this Connie's chin quivers, almost imperceptibly. None of us say anything, and Betty just nods, her dark eyes wide and serious. Connie would hate it if we ever treated her like she might break down and cry.

Sunny unlocks the dead bolt and Diane walks Betty to the front door. She takes one of Betty's hands in hers and gives it a squeeze.

'Betty, thank you,' she says. 'Thank you for everything you're doing for us.'

Betty doesn't let go of Diane's hand. She only looks right into Diane's eyes and furrows her brow, her face serious. 'I promise I'll convince my father Johnny didn't do anything,' she says. 'I know he'll believe me.'

Even though the rest of us are milling around Sunny's living room and Connie is clearly ready to get moving, Diane takes a moment before she leans over and embraces Betty, hugging her tight. She whispers something into Betty's ear, and Betty nods in agreement. I feel like a spy again, like I shouldn't be here. Like none of us should. Juanita and I catch eyes, and Connie and Sunny stare at the floor, but none of us interrupt. We know it wouldn't be right. Finally both girls pull apart, and Betty offers us a quick wave before she heads out Sunny's front door.

CHAPTER

21

'Evie?' Diane calls out to me from her side of the abandoned living room. A fat white candle in between us melts to a disfigured stump.

I peek my face out from under a thin blanket and lean up on one shoulder.

'Yeah?' I whisper. Then I raise my voice to normal volume. After all, Diane and I are the only ones here, and even though it was well past midnight when Connie, Sunny, and Juanita left the two of us on a mess of blankets and pillows taken from their own homes, Diane and I haven't been able to fall asleep. It's not just the hard floors and unheated house, either, although they certainly aren't helping.

'I wish I could drift off,' Diane says.

'So do I,' I answer. 'But my brain won't stop.'

'Neither will mine,' she says. She reaches out and lazily passes a finger through the flame of the candle.

'Don't go so slow,' I say. 'You'll burn yourself.'

'I won't,' says Diane. 'I've done this since I was a kid. It used to drive my mother crazy.' She pauses. 'Maybe that's why I like doing it.' At last she pulls her hand away from the candle flame and lies down on her back. 'I keep wondering what she'll do when my letter hits the papers. Pass out first, I guess. And when she comes to, she'll disown me.'

I picture my mother and grandmother reading the same story. I can only imagine my mother bursting into tears, not passing out. Certainly not cutting me out of her life. A knot of sadness builds in my stomach. I try to ignore it.

'Do you honestly think she would disown you?' I ask.

'Why not?' Diane says, her eyes still trained on the ceiling. 'She practically has anyway. I'm a disaster. A disappointment. That's what she called me, anyway. Before they sent me away to Dallas. And then here.'

Part of me wants to bring up my mother's slap again in solidarity with Diane. But I know it's not the same thing. Not even close. I just tell Diane I'm sorry. She shrugs.

'I'm used to it,' she says. 'My whole life all I've ever been to her is some sort of doll to parade around in the dollhouse of her life.' She pauses. Then she brings her voice to a whisper. 'Evie, I'm scared, though. I don't care what my mother and father think. But what if the police lock me up for what I did to Preston? What if Johnny gets out and I'm put in?' She presses her hands up to her face and then rubs at her temples.

234

'No, Diane,' I answer. 'I won't let them do it. I won't! I'll tell them the truth.'

Diane lowers her hands to her sides and takes a deep, shaky breath. 'I know you will, Evie. I know. I'm just scared, I guess. It's so ridiculous what Betty said to me tonight. When she called me unafraid.' She scoffs at the word.

'I think Betty's right,' I say. 'I do. It took guts to stand up to Preston. But more than that, Diane . . . it took courage to fall in love with Johnny when everyone told you it was wrong. And it took courage to keep on living after everything that's happened to you.'

Diane rolls to her side and looks at me through the soft glow of the candlelight. She manages a smile. I hear her humming softly for a moment, something slow and mournful.

'Evie, you're so wise for fifteen,' she says at last.

I snort. 'Hardly.' But a compliment like that from Diane means almost as much as one from Connie. Maybe more.

'It's true,' she protests. 'But seeing as I'm older, I'm in charge here. And we have to try and go to sleep.' She licks her thumb and forefinger and presses them to the wick of the candle, and a soft sizzle escapes into the air around us.

'Good night, Evie,' she whispers.

'Night, Diane.'

* * *

The next morning is Sunday. We nibble the apples and saltines that Sunny was able to snatch from her house late last night, and I teach Diane how to play Spit with the deck of cards Juanita snagged from her place. In the old composition book she also thought to give us, we doodle and play game after game of MASH and tic-tac-toe. Diane writes out the lyrics to songs by Irma Thomas and the Crystals and Roy Orbison and quizzes me on how well I know them. The two of us sit on the floor, careful to stay out of sight of the windows even though we're desperate to peer out of them. Connie insisted we couldn't even take a peek, and I know she's right.

After our millionth game of Spit, Diane tosses her cards up in the air. 'I'm going crazy!' she cries. 'I can't believe everything that might be happening out there, and we don't know a single bit of it.'

'I know,' I say. 'But the girls will be by here soon. I'm sure of it.'

'It's too early for there to be anything in the papers,' Diane tells me. 'But maybe they'll know something anyway.'

Diane's wristwatch reads almost two o'clock when we hear three light raps on the back door, followed by a pause and three more light raps. Our signal. Diane and I lock eyes. Finally.

'Hey.' Juanita's voice carries from the kitchen. 'It's me. Sorry I couldn't come sooner. I had to make sure the neighbors weren't out to see me sneaking in.'

She's carrying a paper sack of food, including two bologna sandwiches wrapped in wax paper. Diane and I unwrap them and bite into them hungrily. Through bites, Diane asks what the news is.

'Nothing yet,' Juanita says, and Diane's face falls. 'I'm sorry, Diane. It's just too soon. But I'm sure Betty's talked to her father by now. I'm sure we'll hear something any moment.'

Diane nods, then puts the sandwich down in her lap. It seems she's no longer hungry. She leans back on her hands and stares out at nothing. I know her heart is aching.

'I guess I do have some news for Evie,' Juanita says, and I can tell she's hesitating as she picks her words.

'What?' I ask.

She briefly chews her bottom lip. 'Your mom is really upset. She was over at my house at the crack of dawn this morning, begging me to tell her where you are.' She pauses, then adds one more detail. 'She was crying so hard, Evie.'

A wave of nausea rolls through me. I feel the sting of my mother's slap again. I remember the look of hurt and panic in her eyes as I shoved past her. I hear her begging me to tell her what's wrong.

'What did you say?' I ask.

'Nothing,' Juanita answers. 'I told her nothing. But it wasn't easy, Evie. You know your mom loves you.'

I can only nod. Juanita and Diane and I sit in silence for a little while longer. My appetite has disappeared, too. After

Juanita promises to let us know as soon as news breaks, she sneaks out the back door.

I take a deep breath, trying to bury the guilt I feel over what Juanita has just shared. Then I feel Diane's gaze on me.

'You want to play cards or something?' I ask, able to speak at last.

Her soft voice answers, 'You know, my parents haven't visited me once. Not since I moved here. Juanita is right, Evie. Your mother cares.'

I shrug, fighting a lump in my throat.

'Do you want to talk about it?' Diane asks, her voice full of concern.

I light a cigarette. 'Nope,' I answer honestly. Talking is the last thing I feel like doing.

'All right,' Diane says, and she doesn't push it. She just reaches out to collect the cards for another mindless game of Spit.

Monday passes a lot like Sunday did, only I have to occasionally wrestle the image of my crying mom out of my head. I wonder if they've told Cheryl, who already has so many problems of her own, and my guilt surges. As the sun starts to go down and Diane and I are sure we are going to lose our minds from boredom and wondering and nerves, we suddenly hear our signal at the back door. The pause between the three raps is barely a pause, and before we can register what's happening, Connie is in the living room, her face beaming, her smile so big you can see her cracked incisor. In her hands is a copy of the *Houston Chronicle*. She tosses it at us and tackles Diane in a hug, something so un-Connie-like I can't believe it's really happening. The two of them practically fall on the floor.

'Diane,' she says, pulling back, still grinning. 'Diane, it worked. Johnny's getting out!'

Diane, Connie, and I spread the *Chronicle* out on the wooden floor and sprawl out next to it, our eyes trying to take in everything at once.

'It's all over the evening news, too,' Connie says, breathless. 'Look! Your pictures are in here and everything.'

Peering up at us in black and white from the front page is my school picture from ninth grade, my eyes traced in dark liner and my mouth barely cracking a smile. I look scary. Scarier than I thought I did, to be honest. The picture of Diane is one of her in pearls flashing a big, perfect grin at the camera. It doesn't look like a school picture, more like it was taken at some fancy party. Above our photographs is one of the biggest headlines I've ever seen.

MISSING RIVER OAKS DEBUTANTE WANTED FOR QUESTIONING IN EAST SIDE DRIVE-IN SLAYING

And then, in smaller print, *Police Plead with Girls Involved to Come Forward*.

There's a picture of Preston Fowler, too, smirking and handsome. I slide my eyes right over it, trying to ignore his face and the way it knots up my stomach, choosing to focus on the words instead.

Diane and I race through the article while Connie sits cross-legged next to us, bouncing and smoking, careful to stay out of view of the windows. The paper says the police claim to have received 'new information' that makes Diane a suspect in the death of Preston Fowler, but it doesn't mention the letter Diane and I wrote or Betty Howell or what Preston did to me. One part of the article talks about Diane's parents being big, important, rich people, listing all the organizations and guilds and councils they're a part of.

'When's Johnny getting released?' Diane asks, biting her bottom lip, her eyes skimming over the columns of text at lightning speed, trying to take in everything at once.

'Tomorrow,' Connie answers. 'That's what the paper says. The evening news, too.'

Relief washes over Diane's face.

'It worked,' she whispers.

Connie stabs out her cigarette in the empty jar Diane and I are using for butts and looks at Diane. I can tell she's thinking carefully about what she wants to say, something unusual for her.

'Diane,' she says, frowning slightly, 'I . . .' She stops, leans back on her arms, tips her head up at the ceiling. She blinks once, twice, then keeps her eyes shut as she half whispers, 'Thanks for my brother. Thanks for getting him out.'

Diane lowers the part of the paper she's holding, resting it in her lap. Her face softens. 'Oh, Connie, of course. I told you. I loved him. I know you love him, too.'

The silence is broken by our signal at the back door. Three knocks, a pause, and three knocks more. Connie looks up at us, confused. 'I didn't even take the time to tell the other girls I was coming here,' she says.

But it is the other girls, Juanita and Sunny, Sunny clutching a paper sack. Diane and I greet them eagerly.

'Shhh!' Connie says, holding a finger up to her lips. 'No one saw you come in, did they?'

'No,' answers Juanita. 'We waited until it was all clear. We just heard about Johnny on the evening news.'

'I stole whiskey from my crummy stepfather so we could celebrate,' says Sunny gleefully, sneaking a bottle of Old Crow out of the sack. Then her face grows serious. 'And I have information.'

'What?' Connie asks, her momentary softness transformed into toughness and irritation at not being the first to know something important. 'Spill the beans.'

'Well,' says Sunny, taking a sip of Old Crow and wincing before passing it toward Connie, 'Betty Howell called my house.'

'What did she say?' Diane asks almost as soon as the words are out of Sunny's mouth.

'That girl's voice sure is posh,' says Sunny, pausing to press her lips together to make sure her red lipstick is perfectly applied before continuing. 'She actually asked if she was calling the Wilcox residence when I answered the phone.' At this Sunny affects a bad English accent. 'Excuse me, m'lady, but is this the Wilcox residence?'

'So what'd she want?' Connie asks impatiently. She takes a big sip of Old Crow and starts bouncing away.

'She wants Diane to stay hidden for just a little bit longer,' says Sunny.

Diane frowns, furrowing her brow. 'Why?' she protests. 'I want to see Johnny.'

'You read the papers,' I say. 'The police want us both in for questioning.' For a moment I imagine Grandma and Mama reading that article, and my heart quickens. How crushed my mother must be. My grandmother is probably praying for my redemption right now. I try to ignore the images in my mind.

'Yeah,' says Sunny, 'it's that. Betty says she wants more time to explain to her father what happened. More time to convince him of Diane's innocence, because I guess she's worried he isn't buying it. You know, that it was all because Diane was defending Evie.' She takes a deep breath. 'She said she was even gonna try to get a bunch of girls who'd had bad dates with Preston explain to her father what he could be like, so he would be more inclined to believe Diane and Evie. She didn't seem to think she could get any of them to say anything, but she said she was going to try.'

'Really?' Diane says, her eyes bugging out of her head. 'Goodness. I didn't think Betty would do that much for us.' She pauses, recalculates. 'No, that's not true. I guess I did know. That's something Betty would have done back when we were best friends.' She pauses, her gaze drifting off, away from the rest of us.

'And there's more,' says Juanita. 'It's about Johnny's guys.' She hesitates and fumbles with a cigarette. I can tell the news isn't good.

'What about them?' I mutter, thinking of Ray and Butch and Dwight and the other boys we run with, some of them all right but lots of them as rough as they come, always itching for a fight.

'They're mad,' Juanita explains. 'We just ran into a bunch of them at the park.'

'And Ray was griping to me, too, earlier,' Sunny chimes in.

'Mad about what?' I ask, confused. I would think they'd be thrilled the leader of their pack is about to be released.

'C'mon, Evie,' Connie mutters, her fingers gesturing for the bottle of Old Crow to come back around to her. I hand it over. 'They're mad that one of their own took the fall for something he didn't do, when it was a tea sipper who done it.' At this she shakes her head in disagreement with herself. 'I didn't mean that, Diane. About the tea-sipper part. But . . . that's how *they* see it.'

'They were champing at the bit for Diane,' Juanita says, nodding in agreement. 'They blame her for Johnny having to spend time locked up for nothing and probably getting kicked around by the fuzz, too. You know how brutal the cops can be with kids like us.'

'Ray started after me, asking me how much I knew, since Diane had been hanging around with us,' adds Sunny, crossing her arms tight across her chest and scowling. 'He got real mad when I said I didn't know anything. I told him to drop dead.' She smirks at this. 'It sorta felt good, to be honest.'

Diane motions for the whiskey, then takes a small, ladylike sip. 'They have no idea,' she says. 'No idea at all that Johnny and I love each other.'

We all murmur our agreement. None of us has spilled anything about that to anyone.

'We have to come forward eventually,' I say, but the idea of the world outside the walls of this stinky, abandoned house suddenly seems terrifying, even though I've been dying to feel the sun on my face since we got here. Having to see Mama and Grandma, having to deal with Johnny's angry friends. And the police, to top it all off. What if the cops don't believe that Preston was trying to hurt me? What if they think Diane and I were just making it up? Or worse, that I asked for Preston to mess with me? I could see people believing that easy, given what they'd think of a girl like me.

'I know you can't stay here forever,' Juanita says. 'But

maybe you should stay put until Johnny is out and can explain everything to his friends. And to give Betty more time, too.'

'You mean not see Johnny?' Diane asks, stricken. 'He'll be out tomorrow and I can't see him?' Her voice is laced with panic.

'You'll see him soon,' Sunny reassures her.

'Maybe you could bring him here,' Diane says. She bites her bottom lip.

Connie shakes her head emphatically. 'No,' she says. 'That would be too risky. I don't think *Johnny* should even know you're here. The cops know Evie and Diane live in this neighborhood. They're bound to be casing it right now, looking for them. We're risking a lot just being here together. Tomorrow we act normal, go to school, act like we don't know anything. Then we wait for Johnny to explain everything to his friends and for Betty to win her daddy over.'

'It's not exactly normal for you to go to school,' Sunny says, arching an eyebrow. Connie kicks at Sunny's foot with her own, but in a good-natured way.

'That's true,' Connie admits, 'but I'm willing to make a sacrifice for the good of the cause.'

At this we all allow ourselves a giggle, and Diane lays herself out on her back and stares at the ceiling, losing herself in her own thoughts. It's still for a minute. Soon, all I can hear is the rush of the cars on Telephone Road, not far away from us.

'Diane, I've been meaning to ask you, how do you get such

gorgeous skin?' a tipsy Sunny asks at last, peering over at her. 'I mean, I've tried every scrub and wash, and my complexion never looks as lovely as yours. Do you use Pond's?'

Diane gazes over at Sunny with a soft smile. 'Well, a few times a week I get a big bowl of the hottest water I can find, and I put my face over it and a towel over my head. Like a little steam bath for my face, I guess.'

Sunny's eyes open wide at this apparently miraculous revelation. 'Of course,' she says, her voice a reverent whisper. 'Diane, you're an absolute genius.'

Diane starts laughing first, loud and loose. She sits up and keeps laughing, and soon we're all joining her, except for Sunny, who cheerfully protests that such a beauty tip is evidence of a very high IQ.

A good, warm feeling spreads over me, and it's not just the Old Crow. I feel like I could sit here like this forever with my friends.

At last we settle down, and Diane draws her knees up to her chin. She looks around at all of us.

'I want to tell y'all something I've been keeping a secret,' she says, offering me a meaningful glance. I know what Diane is about to share, of course, and there's warmth in my heart, knowing that she feels she can share it.

'My heart can't take much more excitement,' Connie mutters, making light of Diane's comment. She doesn't know what Diane's about to admit, even if I do.

'What is it?' Sunny asks, her expression curious. 'Is it about Johnny?'

Diane crosses her legs, motions for the bottle. After another sip – this time not so ladylike – she says, 'I wanted to tell y'all this because . . . you've become . . . my friends. I know we've only known each other for a little while, barely a week. But until I met all of you, I didn't know if I'd ever have another friend again in my life. Honest.'

I glance at Juanita, whose brow is furrowed and curious. Connie, usually eager to joke, is now staring at Diane suspiciously as Diane reaches up and tugs on a loose strand of auburn hair, takes a deep breath. My heart swells. I know how hard this must be for Diane to say out loud.

'I'm glad you're our friend,' offers Sunny. 'I mean it.'

'Me too,' says Juanita.

'Same here, but get on with it,' says Connie, reaching for a Salem. 'You're killing us.'

Diane glances at me again, maybe looking for a vote of confidence. I try to give it to her with a nod and a smile I hope reads as reassuring. *You can trust them. You can trust us.* Slowly, her voice quieter than normal, Diane unfolds the reason she got sent away to Dallas. She talks about the suffocating home and the boredom and the way she couldn't write a single letter to Johnny to tell him what was happening to her. Her voice is almost a whisper, but it's laced with confidence that comes from telling a story for the second time and from knowing –

247

she has to know – how much the people listening are on her side. Not on her parents' side. And not on the side of a world that tells a girl that just because she got pregnant she has to be hidden away like the worst sort of criminal.

She's among real friends.

Diane speaks, her voice growing louder as she does. More sure of itself. When she finishes, all of us are quiet. I reach out, put my hand on Diane's back. Leave it there for a beat or two.

At last Connie says something. 'There was a girl up in Gainesville who'd been sent away like that,' she tells us, frowning at the memory. 'She was real messed up over it, and when she got back home, she started pulling stupid stunts, getting in trouble with the fuzz. She told me she was sent away because she was sent away, if that makes any sense.' She pauses, glances at Diane and then adds, 'She missed her baby real bad.'

We peer at Diane for her reaction.

'I think I know how she must feel,' she says at last.

'I'm really sorry that happened to you,' says Sunny, and I can see her eyes are glossed over with tears about to spill. 'You didn't deserve that, Diane. No girl does.'

'Nobody stood up for you?' Juanita asks, confused. 'Not even Betty?'

Diane shakes her head. 'No, but she says now she feels sorry for it. I believe her. But at first, no. And it hurt.'

Sunny frowns. 'Well, all I know is that if that ever

happened to one of us, we would stand up for each other, wouldn't we?' She looks around at all of us, ready to take inventory of our answers.

'Of course we would,' says Connie, not giving the rest of us a chance to open our mouths. 'We all would.' Then, a moment later, she says, 'My brother still doesn't know, does he?'

Diane shakes her head slowly, sadly. 'He doesn't.' She takes a deep breath and looks up at all of us, suddenly gripped with a new concern. 'Please, let me be the one to tell him? Okay? Once he's out? I want him to hear it from me.'

We nod, and Connie stares all of us down. 'You heard her,' she says, giving us her best leader-in-charge voice. 'Not a word until she says so.'

I can't help but grin a tiny bit to myself when I think about how just a few days ago Connie wanted nothing to do with Diane Farris. Now she's acting like her fiercest protector. But with Connie, nothing is ever an act. In her own brash and violent way, Connie Treadway is the most sincere girl I know.

'Thanks, all of you,' says Diane. 'But now I need some more of that whiskey. Pass it over.'

CHAPTER

22

It's not long until our cheeks start to burn and everything we say seems silly. The edges of the day blur at last, and we allow ourselves a little bit of an escape. Just us. Friends. Girls against the whole wide world.

Soon the streetlights come on outside, casting their lonely light through the windows. Finally Connie says it's time for her and Sunny and Juanita to cut out.

'Y'all okay in here?' Juanita asks. 'For just a little bit longer?' She hiccups and claps a hand over her mouth, then starts giggling.

'Yes, Juanita,' I say, and I lean into her and give her a hug, and she hugs me back. Soon Sunny is crawling over to me and hugging me, too, and reaching out to pat Diane on the forehead. Even Connie gives in and swings her arm around Sunny for a moment. Part of it feels awkward and new, I guess. We don't really hug all that much.

But part of it feels right, too.

Hugging doesn't make us less tough. Maybe we know that now.

'Sleep tight, sweet Diane,' Sunny says, like she's tucking in a child. 'Thanks for the steam-bath tip for my complexion.' Diane manages to crack a smile from her position on the floor.

'Y'all are a bunch of lightweights,' says Connie, but when she attempts to stand up, she trips over her own feet and falls down again. Everybody laughs, even her, and then we all hush each other just as much.

I wish they wouldn't leave. I wish we could stay here forever, just drinking and smoking and laughing and being together.

Finally they make their way out the back door, moving as quietly as they can under the circumstances. My head is buzzy and swimmy and I'm definitely feeling the Old Crow, but I'm not totally blitzed or anything. Diane still hasn't moved from her position on the floor, so I find myself crouching down to join her, resting my cheek against the cool, well-worn hardwood floor underneath me.

'Diane?' I whisper. 'Are you all right?'

She nods, her eyes still focused on the ceiling. Suddenly she rolls over onto her stomach, reaches out for our matches, strikes one, and lights our candle. She takes a deep, shaky breath.

'There's this part of me that wants to sneak out tomorrow and go see Johnny.'

I feared this was what she was going to tell me. I think I'd guessed the idea had been running through her head from the moment Connie insisted she had to stay put.

'Diane, no,' I say, stubborn. 'You're nuts to try something like that. Absolutely not. It's way too risky.'

Diane frowns, tears welling up in her eyes. 'I know it's reckless. But after all Johnny and I have been through . . . after being separated and realizing how much I really love him, I just . . . I don't know. Maybe it's the wrong idea. But I can't stop thinking about it!' The tears that have been building spill down her cheeks. She sits up and I follow.

'Diane,' I say, 'I'm so sorry. I know how awful all of this must feel.' I haven't experienced the head-over-heels love that Diane clearly has for Johnny, and, to be totally honest, there's a small part of me that's glad I haven't. Diane's pain fills the rooms of this house, threatens to drown her. It's frightening.

As she cries softly into her hands, an idea occurs to me. It's risky, I know. But I think about that night at Winkler's. That evening that feels both minutes and ages ago. I remember Diane's face in the moonlight, her dress splattered with blood. I remember those first moments in her aunt's house on Coyle Street, her sad, tiny oasis of a bedroom even sadder in my memory now that I know the reason Diane was exiled there by her own parents.

'Diane,' I whisper, my heart pounding at the offer I'm about to make. If I say it, I'll do it. I know I will.

'Yes?' she manages, her face buried into her arms.

'Diane, I have an idea,' I say. 'What if I bring Johnny a letter? I could sneak out. I know where his and Connie's house is. You're the one the police are really after, you know. If they catch me – and they won't – I won't rat you out. You know I won't. You could at least let him know you love him. That you want to be with him again as soon as it's safe.'

Diane lifts her face up with a gasp. 'Oh, Evie,' she begins, her voice laced with excitement. Then she frowns, shakes her head. 'No, I can't ask you to do that. It's too much.'

But now that I've made the offer, it's like I can't deny this to Diane. And anyway, I don't want to. She's my friend, and I want to make her happy.

'Diane, please,' I say. 'Let me do it.'

She tucks her hair behind her right ear and studies me. Her cheeks are still pink from the Old Crow, but suddenly we both seem pretty sober.

'Evie, what if the cops catch you? Johnny told me what they do to kids around here when they get hauled in.'

I've heard those stories, too, of getting roughed up and pushed around just because of the neighborhood you come from. I've even seen the evidence a few times, in kids with black eyes and torn T-shirts who got picked up for questioning. I'm sure Johnny's been through all that and worse these past few days. But I shake my head and try to nudge the thoughts away.

'I can do it. At least let me try.' My voice is firm and my

mind is set even if my heart is pounding.

Diane nods, tears sliding down her face. 'Oh, Evie,' she says, embracing me tight. 'You're the best friend ever. In the entire world.'

I can barely breathe she's squeezing me so tight, but I don't care. I just squeeze her right back.

When she lets me go, she immediately reaches for Juanita's old composition book — the one that's held dozens of our games of tic-tac-toe and MASH — and a stubby pencil.

'I'm going to start writing to him right now,' she says, scooting back so she can lean against the wall of the abandoned house. 'I'll have it done by the morning.' Then she looks at me and says, 'You should get some rest.'

A yawn slips out as if on cue. I am tired. As I settle into my makeshift bed, I can hear the quick scratches of Diane's pencil on paper, followed by the occasional squeak of eraser and a long pause. I drift off to the rhythm of it, too exhausted to even dream about what might happen tomorrow.

When I wake up the next morning, Diane is sleeping next to me, her mouth hanging open, a tiny stream of dried saliva down her left cheek. A folded piece of composition paper is tucked partway under her pillow, and I wonder if she'll let me read it.

By the time I get back from the bathroom, Diane is sitting

up, rubbing at her eyes and checking her watch for the time.

'Hey,' she says, stretching.

'Hey, back.'

She takes the letter from near her and hands it to me, her arm outstretched. 'I want you to read it,' she says. 'Since you'll be delivering it.'

'All right,' I say. 'If you're sure. But don't watch me while I read it. It makes me nervous.' Diane complies and looks away.

Johnny,

I don't know where to start. Well, let me start here. I love you. I want you to know that. After all this time, after everything that's happened, I still think of myself as your girl. I know the last time we talked at Winkler's, it was such a disaster. I wish I could have the fall to do over again. I didn't have the words then for what I was going through. But by becoming friends with Evie and your sister (yes, I know it's wild to think about, but yes) and the other girls, I've admitted to myself what happened to me. It's not like I didn't ever think it was real. It was all too real. But it hurt too much to think about it, so I just blocked it out. The reason I was sent away from you. Johnny, I wanted to tell you. I honestly couldn't. But I'm telling you now.

I had a baby. Our baby. Our daughter. I didn't know her long before they took her and gave her to somebody else to raise, but she is the most perfect little girl. I know this must come as such a shock to you, and I know it's strange to learn about it like this, but I hope

255

you'll understand why it's easier for me to tell you this way. If I told you in person, I don't know if I could get out the words without sobbing the entire time. As it is, I'm crying while I write this letter, but at least I can write it.

I still struggle to believe it, but it's true. I had our baby. I found out not long after Christmas, not long after my parents threw you out of the house that one awful night. They never let me out of their sight after that. I was watched constantly. I couldn't even bribe Patty to put a letter to you in the mail. And not long after that I was sent away to Dallas, where I had the baby, and she was taken away. Johnny, if you could have seen her. She was so sweet. Is so sweet. Just like a gumdrop with your dark eyes. I hope she loves music like us. I hope she's wild like you and me. I hope her heart knows joy in this life. And I hope she's allowed to love anyone she wants.

Johnny, when I was with you — when we were together — I felt so free. I felt like I could be myself, or at least start to figure out who that is. We could just be together and talk about anything. Everything. It didn't matter that we were from different worlds. We belonged together. I still remember that night by the beach in Galveston and how you held my hand in yours and what you whispered to me. I want you to know that the answer is yes. It's always been yes.

Everything is so confusing and awful, and I know you've read the papers and know about everything that's happened to me. I'm so sorry that when I showed up at Eastside I was such a wreck about everything that had happened and I didn't know how to be honest with you. But how can I blame myself for that after all that I've been through? I was *just reacting after going through something so terrible, and I know you understand because you always understood me.*

I hope that everything will get resolved, that Betty will get her father to believe that what I did was to protect Evie, and that soon you and I will be together again. I long for that day. I know you do, too.

Johnny, I love you. Always.

Your girl,

Diane

'Diane,' I say, and she turns her gaze to look at me.

'It's perfect,' I tell her. I do wonder what Johnny whispered to Diane on the beach at Galveston, but she doesn't offer the information, and I know it's not my place to ask.

She draws her knees up under her chin, folds into herself. 'Do you think that's all right . . . telling him about the baby like this?' she asks me, her face twisting up in concern. 'Is it rotten of me to spill something like that in a letter?'

'Diane,' I say, folding the paper, 'after everything that's happened to you, I think you have the right to tell him however you want.'

She smiles, grateful, and I slide the letter reverently into my pocket, proud that Diane trusts me as her friend. Proud that I can be the one to be honest with her and help her when she needs someone most.

'Thanks, Evie,' she says.

'Of course.'

Then we sit in quiet for a bit until I gather the courage to ask a question I've been wondering about. Maybe because one day, I'd like to know the answer.

'What's it like to be in love?' I ask. 'I mean, really?'

Diane's smile stretches out slowly and easily, like she couldn't be more thrilled to answer this question and is grateful I've asked it.

'It's . . . wonderful,' she says. 'It's . . . I don't have the words, really. Johnny and I . . .' She traces her finger lazily along the hardwood floor. Then she's still for a moment. 'When you love someone,' she starts again, 'it's like listening to a song you adore. And every single time you listen to it, you hear something new. And you know you'll never get sick of listening to it. Ever. And as soon as it's over, you want to listen to it again so you can know it even better. Until it's just a part of you.' She smiles, blushing. 'Maybe that sounds stupid. I don't know.'

I shake my head. 'It doesn't. It really doesn't.'

Connie told Diane and me that Johnny was set to be released this morning, at least according to the papers, so even though I'm anxious to get my dangerous deed over with, we decide it makes sense to wait until after lunchtime before I sneak out to Connie's house on Mable, just a few blocks away. We sit cross-legged on the floor and occasionally take a careful glance out the windows at the overcast October sky, munch saltines to try and soothe our nervous stomachs, and talk through the plan in between long, anxious seas of silence.

'I'll try to cut through backyards when I go,' I say. 'And when I get to the Treadway house, I'll go in through the back.'

'And Johnny's parents?'

'I'm not worried about them,' I say, shaking my head and lighting a cigarette. 'They're either not home, passed out, or they won't give a damn. I wonder if they're even aware Johnny got hauled in.' I let myself think about my mother and how she never, ever let me and Cheryl spend a day hungry. How she never, ever let us spend a sick, feverish night alone. Connie and Johnny have been fending for themselves for as long as I can remember.

Diane sighs. 'Yes, I know about Johnny's mother and father.' Her voice drops into a sorry whisper. 'I think that's one of the reasons Johnny and I fell in love. We both got cursed with lousy parents. Mine just have more money.' She shrugs.

Then Diane looks up at me again, her green eyes shining. 'Evie,' she says, 'thank you so much. For everything.'

'Of course,' I answer.

A shadow suddenly falls over her face, and she lets out a small gasp. 'But what if he's not even at his house when you get there?' Diane asks.

'If he's not there, I'll search around a bit at some of his regular hangouts,' I say. 'Don't worry, I'll find him.'

259

Diane shakes her head hard. 'No, Evie. That's too much. You can't be running all over the east side. If he's not at the house, just come right back here. Promise?'

'Promise,' I lie. I'm bound and determined to find Johnny. I have to.

Finally, enough hours pass that Diane and I figure it's safe for me to head out. She hugs me tight for good luck, and, after peering as carefully as I can out the windows, I slowly turn the doorknob, holding my breath as I do, and slip out onto the back steps.

It's been two nights since I've been outside the walls of the dilapidated, musty house, and the fresh air feels good on my face and in my lungs. I take a moment to enjoy it before regaining my focus. Two blocks to Elliston and two blocks to Mable. It should only take minutes if I move fast enough.

I scan for anyone out and spy no one. Not even a housewife hanging laundry. I start cutting through yards, thinking only of getting from one house to the next. A scuttle of leaves makes me jump until I realize it's just a stray tabby cat chasing a squirrel or a mouse. Heart thrumming, mouth dry, I have to remind myself to breathe.

Finally, I make it to Connie's place. It's almost as pathetic as the house Diane and I have been hiding in, its back porch cluttered with boxes and rusting junk. We rarely hang out here, and I know it's because Connie – even as tough as she is – is embarrassed by it. By it and by her parents.

Connie is at school, but as I climb the creaky back steps, I say a silent prayer in my mind that Johnny will be home.

Step, *creak*.

Step, *creak*.

Please, please, please let him be home. Please let me catch a break. Just this once. Please.

And then, suddenly, like a hoped-for birthday present or a shiny quarter you discover on the street, there he is at the back door, opening it wide, like he's been expecting me. Johnny Treadway. As handsome and lanky and dark-eyed as ever, with a ripe bruise across his left cheek and a dark red slice across his right eyebrow.

'Evie Barnes?' he says, a confused smile on his face. 'What the hell are you doing here, kid?'

23

In all my years I never thought I'd be here, in the Treadway family living room with Johnny Treadway, smoking cigarettes and sharing secrets.

We ash into a chipped, puke-green plastic ashtray on the table in front of us, Johnny leaning forward in a recliner that's seen better days and me on a tattered sofa with more than a few cigarette burns in it, their perfect circles reminding me of a demented connect-the-dots. So far as I can tell, we're the only ones here.

His dark eyes bore into me with curiosity. He *is* handsome. The kind of handsome that would turn the head of a girl from River Oaks and make her risk it all to be with him. The kind of handsome that makes even the mothers in the neighborhood high-pitched and giggly when he passes by. Normally, he'd make me nervous. But on this strange October afternoon, any nervousness I should be feeling left me the moment Johnny let me inside the house.

I did what I promised Diane I would do. I found her true love for her, and soon, I'll share her words with him.

There's a copy of the morning paper on the table next to the ashtray, and Johnny motions to it. Of course he knows about what Diane's done and her confession – it's everywhere. And he knows from Connie that Diane and I are in hiding.

'She's sworn it's better if I don't know where y'all are, and she's probably right,' he says. 'You know she'd flip out if she saw you here.'

I nod, reaching for another Salem. 'I know. But I promised Diane I'd come and deliver this. She couldn't wait. She wanted to come and see you herself, but I offered to at least do this so she could stay safe.' My heart skips a bit as I slide the letter out from the pocket of my jeans. I'm about to change Johnny's life forever, and he doesn't know it yet.

'I still can't believe Diane did what she did,' he says, his voice a mix of awe and sadness.

'She did it to protect me,' I say, the torn piece of Juanita's composition book clutched in my fingers. I realize they're shaking.

'I know she did,' Johnny says. 'That girl is brave as hell.'

'She is,' I say. Braver than he realizes, even now. 'Here. This is . . . I've read it. It's . . .' I pause, unable to find the right words, then simply say, 'Diane wants you to have it.'

Johnny reaches out, eager for the paper. He opens it, and I freeze to the couch, unable to move even though I think I probably should. I should step away. Or leave entirely. I wish Diane and I had thought this part through.

I watch his eyes scan Diane's perfect script, widen, and reverse course to read her words again. My mouth goes dry, and I try to drag my eyes away from Johnny. I feel like a thief, like I'm stealing a moment from Johnny that he deserves to have alone.

We sit in silence until at last Johnny folds his hands in his lap, Diane's letter still clutched in his fingers, then simply says – in the most heartbreaking voice I can imagine, a voice so heartbroken it cracks, '*Diane.*'

To see tears well up in the eyes of Johnny Treadway seems almost as unreal as the story that just produced them. But what happened to Diane did happen. It *is* real. And so are Johnny's tears.

He sniffs, composing himself, and I look down at my shoes, trying to give him privacy in the only way I can.

'I have to go to her,' he says, breaking the silence. 'I have to go to her now. Tell me where she's hiding.' I whip my eyes up and see him heading for the back door.

My heart starts to race again. This is what Diane wants, after all. But as Johnny moves toward the door, he stops suddenly.

'Wait,' he says out loud. To me or to himself, I'm not sure. 'This is too risky.' He looks at me, ponders the situation. Does a million calculations in his head. Johnny is no kid on the streets. He knows the score.

'Y'all are hiding out somewhere close, aren't you?' he asks, his brow furrowing.

'Yes,' I admit. 'At an abandoned house that Connie found.' I know I'm breaking my code by revealing our location, but this is different. It's not about impressing anyone with blind loyalty or never spilling a secret. It's about helping Diane, and that's what matters most right now.

He sits back down on the recliner, his blue-jeaned legs bouncing, just like his sister's do. He lights another smoke.

'Tonight,' he says. 'I'll go tonight when it's dark. Eight o'clock. It's safer that way. It kills me to wait, but the cops might be tailing me. Just because they released me doesn't mean they don't still suspect I had something to do with what happened. And if they're following me, I'll lead them right to her.' He closes his eyes, rests his head in his hands. 'Oh, Diane,' he mutters to himself. His voice is aching again, and I'm not sure what to do or say.

'Maybe you should stay put here, too,' he says, lifting his eyes toward me. 'Damn. It's too risky for *you* to be out, Evie. Diane should never have sent you. But . . . I'm also glad she did.' He curses in frustration under his breath and leans forward, pressing his forehead into the heel of his hand, his lit cigarette inches from his hair. For a moment, I worry he'll burn some of his hair off. It seems silly to worry about something like that in the face of everything that's happening.

'No, I think I have to leave,' I offer at last. 'Diane will be waiting for me. If I don't come back eventually, she might come out looking for me.'

Johnny's face crumples as he stabs out his second cigarette. 'She would do that. I know she would.' He runs a hand through his hair, the cut on his eyebrow even more visible. It's a mean and angry slice, still red and on fire.

'How'd you get that cut and that bruise?' I ask, wincing.

'How do you think?' he snaps. 'The fuzz when they hauled me in, trying to get me to confess to offing that rich kid.' I pull back a little at the anger in his voice, and he immediately mumbles an apology. 'You didn't deserve that, kid. Sorry. This is all just . . .' He gives up finding the words, and I don't blame him.

'It's okay,' I murmur, but warm tears start to prick my eyes, and I sniff, managing to hold them back. Johnny gives me a sympathetic smile.

'Look, Evie, don't get upset. I'm sorry I snapped. It's going to be okay.' He leans back in the recliner, taking on the position of someone in authority. Someone who isn't afraid. His panic and emotion from moments earlier have leveled off, and he's speaking like the Johnny Treadway I've always known and maybe even feared a little.

'Here's what you need to do,' he says slowly. 'Before you leave, you're going to tell me the address of where you're staying, and then you're going to head back there, careful and sneaky so you don't get seen. Just like how you got here. You're going to go back there and you're going to tell Diane that I'll be there tonight at eight sharp. And you're going to tell her that I miss her, and that soon everything is going to be all right. Tell her that I swear this. That I swear to God. Tell her' – he pauses, looks me dead in the eyes – 'tell her she rules my heart. Those exact words, okay?'

I nod, committing them to memory. Carving them into my mind so Diane can carve them into her heart.

'I'll do it,' I tell Johnny. 'And you and Diane will see each other tonight.' As I stand to go, already nervous about my journey home, Johnny tells me to wait and runs down the hallway to his room. He's gone for a few minutes before he comes back with a folded piece of composition paper.

'Can you give this to her?' Johnny asks. 'And can you tell her it's from me?'

'Sure,' I say.

'And can you not read it?' he asks, his voice suddenly tender, almost shy. 'It's for Diane.'

'I won't read it,' I swear. I can only guess that what's written on it is more private than what he's just asked me to repeat to Diane.

'Thanks, Evie. You're a swell kid.'

I blush. I can't help it. I tell Johnny the address of the abandoned house, and then I slip out the back door and head toward Monroe.

The sprint home feels similar to the trip over. I admit I'm still anxious, but I've got some confidence now. I'm already imagining the delight on Diane's face as I tell her the good news about Johnny.

As I hustle up Elliston and cut over to Monroe, making my way through a backyard, I hear the sound of steps behind me, movement of some kind. I stop in my tracks, my eyes trained on a pile of rusted-out children's toy trucks sitting in the middle of the unkempt grass. Gripping the paper for Diane that Johnny gave me, I turn my head slowly over my left shoulder, frightened of what I'll see. I'm holding my breath.

Nothing. There's nothing there. No one.

I face forward again and start walking quickly, practically jogging, convincing myself it was probably a cat like before. This neighborhood is full of strays, after all. By the time I make it back to our hideout, by the time I hand Diane the paper from Johnny and share the good news, by the time she is hugging me and spilling tears of gratitude, I have very nearly put the moment out of my mind.

After Diane opens the paper and devours Johnny's note, I share his message word for word. When I get to the part about how she rules Johnny's heart, Diane's tear-filled eyes look up from the paper, and her face breaks out into a wide grin.

'He's quoting that Irma Thomas song I played you in the listening booth at the Jive Hive,' she says. 'It was one of our favorites.' Then she turns her focus back to the letter.

Diane rereads Johnny's words more times than I can count, opening up the letter, taking it in, smiling at it like it's Johnny's face itself, folding it up, holding it up to her nose and smelling it, then opening it again. At last she slips it into her skirt pocket.

I don't ask to read it or even what it says. That feels too personal. Diane doesn't offer to tell me anyway. But whatever Johnny's written, it's set Diane's heart to flying.

She offers her thanks, over and over again.

'Evie, you're truly the best friend I've ever had,' she says. 'I mean that.'

It feels good to hear her say it again, and I smile.

'Diane, do you know what's so funny?'

'What?'

'We met ten days ago!'

Diane runs a hand through her auburn hair and laughs. 'It feels like ten years.' Her face grows serious. 'But, I mean, in some ways that's a good thing. Do you understand?'

'Sure,' I answer, opening up the saltines. I slip one out and pick at it. I'm hungry but not. I'm tired but not. I'm a million feelings at once with no shelves to store them on.

'Diane, can I ask you something?' Part of me wants to push my feelings away. Hide them. Ignore them. Ride them out.

But what if, just this time, I let them out? Diane has proved to me it's possible.

'Of course,' she says, holding up the cracked handheld mirror we found in the bathroom. She examines her face and scowls. 'I wish I'd thought to bring makeup and a decent hairbrush. I want to look nice when Johnny and I see each other.'

'You do look nice,' I offer. I wait until Diane sets the mirror down carefully, tilts her head expectantly.

'What is it, Evie? You know you can ask me anything.'

I pick and pick at the saltine until it crumbles into a pile on the floor.

'Will we still be friends after this? I mean, after you and Johnny get back together and the police know you're innocent and all?'

Diane frowns, confused. Then a soft smile spreads out on her face. She stares at me for a moment, quiet.

'Evie, what on earth would make you ask such a thing?'

I shrug and press my fingers into the ruined saltine, making a mess. 'I don't know,' I mutter, unable to look at her. 'You're older than me. You're practically a grown-up after all you've been through. And once Johnny and you are back together . . .' My words drift off, unable to take shape.

'Evie, hey, look at me,' she says. 'You're not some kid. I mean, yes, you're younger than I am, but you don't give yourself enough credit. Don't you know what a special person you are?'

Diane's words confuse me instead of comforting me. What am I but a girl whose own mother is probably terrified of her? A girl whose future feels so tiny and suffocating she doesn't know how to react, so she acts just to feel something, if only briefly?

'How am I special, Diane?' I say, and I hear my voice cracking, surprising me. Diane cries, and so freely. But I'm so scared to let myself sometimes. And yet, here with Diane, I let the tears come.

'Oh, Evie,' Diane says, practically shouting my name in distress. She scoots over across the floor and rests one hand on my right shoulder, shakes it a bit. 'Evie, listen to me! How are you special? My God, you stood up for me! You've risked everything to help me! You're a true friend. Don't you know how rare that is in this world?' A stricken look crosses her face. Her voice drops in volume. 'Or at least, that's been my experience. You're so special, don't you know?'

'Diane, after all you've done for me,' I start. Then I realize how that might come out wrong, but I push through, trying to get the words out no matter how difficult it is for me. Because I know I'll feel better when I speak my heart and mind. 'I'm not saying I've helped you just because I think I owe you, even though I have to tell you . . . there's part of me that feels I won't ever repay you. But what I did . . . it wasn't all that much.'

'Evie,' Diane presses, 'you're the one who got Connie to

give me a chance, aren't you? You were the one who said you'd stand up for me, and you believed me before any other girl did. And in front of Connie, too. And you were the first person I felt I could tell – really tell – about the baby. And you didn't judge me. You just listened. Really listened.' She pauses, holds my gaze with hers. 'You didn't have to do those things, Evie.' She squeezes my shoulder tight. 'Evie, this wasn't all about feeling like you owed me something. You're just a wonderful person is all.'

I sniff and keep crying. 'Thanks, Diane, but . . . I don't know. Everything's been so mixed up and awful. My grandmother thinks I'm going to hell. I miss my big sister, and she's having a hard time. My mother hates me, probably. After the way we left things, I don't think she'll even want me to come home. I'm not a perfect daughter. I don't want the same things she wants for me. I don't really know *what* I want, to be honest. But I do know that I think I should be able to at least have permission to find out for myself what it is.' When I say this last sentence out loud, I realize that it's true. I realize that I've decided I refuse to live my life for someone else no matter what the consequences might be.

Diane lets go of my shoulder and clasps both her hands tightly together, like she's about to pray. 'Evie, I only met your mother that one time, but I can't believe she doesn't want you to come home.' She tucks a loose strand of hair behind her left ear, then presses her hands together again. She squeezes them so tight her knuckles turn white.

'Evie, you *do* have a right to figure out what you want to be. Maybe your mother hasn't realized that just yet, and maybe not everything is perfect in your house. I don't think any house is, probably. But I know what it's like not to be wanted,' she says. 'Not to be wanted by your own folks.' She closes her eyes. Takes a deep breath. Then she opens her eyes again and looks into mine. 'Evie, I bet your mother is worried sick about you. I practically guarantee it.'

I sigh, remembering how Mama came to me with that plate of bacon our last morning together. Begged me to tell her what was going on. I remember our late-night snuggles when I was a little girl, back before my life turned wild. Maybe Diane is right. I want her to be.

I don't say anything, but I dry my face with the cuff of my cardigan. Take a deep breath. Then I lean over and blow on the saltine crumbs until they spill out in every direction like dust. Like I could blow away every unsettled, anxious feeling inside me.

'My mother would flip if she could see me now,' Diane says. 'Her awful daughter turning out just as she'd feared. A criminal in a dump of a hideout.' She waves her arms in the air like a model showing off a new car. Then she manages a rueful laugh. 'I almost wish she could see me now.'

'I'm sorry, Diane,' I say. 'I don't understand how your parents couldn't love you just as you are. You're such a terrific person.'

273

'Thanks, Evie,' she says. 'But I made my peace with all that the day they sent me away to Dallas. Maybe even before then. I knew I wasn't ever going to be anything but a disappointment, so giving up trying to change their minds was sort of freeing, I guess.' She sighs, then lays herself out on her back, staring up at the ceiling. 'God, I wish I could make the clock speed up. I wish it could be eight o'clock right now!'

I think about Johnny heading over here in the dark and then realize I'll be the ultimate third wheel in their reunion.

'I could go hide out in one of the bedrooms,' I say. 'Or maybe you'd rather do that?' I blush just as I say it, and Diane catches me and laughs.

'Wow, Evie, your cheeks are pink!'

'Shut up!' I shout, covering my face with my hands, laughing.

'Don't worry,' Diane says. 'All I want to do with him is talk. Catch up again. Maybe we'll just sit out on the back steps.'

And then what will happen? I wonder. *Then the police will believe our story? Betty will be able to convince her father? Preston's rich, powerful parents will give up trying to blame their son's death on someone?* But I don't say anything to Diane about those unanswered questions. All that matters right now is that she's happy, the happiest I've seen her since we met. Let her have her letter and Johnny and dreams of this evening. Let her have a fairy tale with a happy ending for once. And as Diane and I prepare to pass the time until this evening, I decide I'll even

274

let myself have a happy ending, too. It's not as clear in my mind what mine will look like, but I want to believe in it.

I think maybe Diane has helped me believe in it.

Eight o'clock approaches, and Diane can't stop wriggling with anticipation. She keeps checking herself in the mirror, finger-combing her hair.

'I look awful,' she mutters, alternating between checking her watch and the mirror. As the moment she's been waiting for ticks near, she takes a deep breath, exhales carefully. My stomach is fluttery with nerves just waiting with her.

'All right,' she says, 'I'm going out on the back steps. Would you give me . . .' Then she pauses, and now she's the one who blushes. 'Would you give me a moment alone with him outside? I want our first kiss after all this time to be outside in the autumn air, not inside this musty old dump.' She wrinkles her nose in disapproval.

I can't help but grin. It's the most tea-sipper thing she's ever said to me, but I just nod.

'Sure,' I say. 'I'll stay inside. But be careful. Don't venture too far off the back steps.'

'I won't,' Diane says, and as she walks toward the kitchen to head out the back door, she turns and flashes me a big, beautiful Diane smile. 'Evie, thanks again. For everything.'

'Sure, Diane,' I say, and I smile back.

Leaning up against the living room wall, my knees drawn tight up under my chin, I wait, hearing only the occasional honk of a car on Telephone Road or the angry howl of an alley cat. I imagine Johnny racing up the back steps, taking Diane in his arms. I grin to myself as I envision him kissing her, then smiling when she says she'll be with him forever. I even picture the two of them stumbling back inside the house arm in arm, Johnny thanking me for everything. *You're the best, kid*, I can picture him saying, as my heart swells with pride and love.

And then, suddenly, I hear a scream. Loud, shrill.

Frightened.

I stand up fast, my mouth dry. My brain says, '*Move!*' but I'm stuck in place.

Another scream, even more frightened than the first.

Diane.

Finally my feet catch up with my mind, and I head through the kitchen and toward the back door. I tug it open, not caring at all who might see me.

It takes a moment for my eyes to absorb what I'm seeing.

Standing in a snarling, angry pack in the strip of backyard are Ray Swanson, Dwight Hardaway, Butch Thompson, and a few other boys Johnny runs with. One has a switchblade in his hand. Another, a broken beer bottle. Their faces are one collective angry leer, aimed right at Diane, who's standing feet away, her face stricken, her eyes wild.

I don't see Johnny anywhere.

'What the hell do you want?' I shout, surprised at my sudden bravery. Ray's eyes are beady, red, and cutting right through me. Dwight offers up a mean cackle. These boys are drunk and stupid. But more than that, they're clearly aiming for a fight.

'Well, look who it is,' Ray says, laughing sharply. Almost like he's bored. 'The dumb bitch who's chosen to help out some girl from River Oaks instead of standing up for her own kind.'

Diane keeps searching over her shoulder, looking for Johnny. She's crying hard, her breath coming in sharp, short bursts. She's panicking, I can tell.

'You're drunk, Ray Swanson,' I say. I have to buy time, to stop them from whatever it is they want to do. 'How'd you even know we were here?'

Butch laughs, and my body goes numb. I remember that sound on the way back from the Treadway house. The sound that I convinced myself was a cat.

'You thought you were so sneaky,' he spits out. 'You thought you wouldn't be followed.'

Diane manages to speak between shaky breaths. 'You don't understand,' she says, trying to reason with this pack of boys. 'I love Johnny. I never wanted him to take the fall for something I did. It's why I confessed!'

I take this moment to slip down the back steps and move closer to Diane. For the first time, I wish I had a blade on me.

Ray yelps in amusement at Diane's words. 'You love Johnny! That's a bunch of bull. You wouldn't look at a boy like that twice on the street.'

'He got his ass beat by the fuzz because of something you did,' Dwight adds. 'You let him rot in the cooler for a week.'

Ray advances, followed by the rest of them.

These boys are ready to do anything.

I turn, frantic, my eyes searching our dark neighborhood streets for Johnny, for anyone to help us. I want to cry out.

What happens next happens so fast. The sort of fast that even in this moment I know I'll never be able to remember in full detail. Only in flashes. Only in awful splotches of color and squeals of sound.

Diane is running, blindly. The boys are moving, angry. Like a wave they rush toward Telephone Road, where the bright headlights of traffic pulse past us.

'Leave me alone!' Diane screams, running without thinking.

'Diane, Diane, stop!' I shout.

A honking horn.

A pack of boys.

A gentle, auburn-haired girl whose only crime was believing in love.

The next thing I know, there's a sound so terrifically loud and horrible – a screech of brakes, a sick thud.

Diane is there on the blacktop, a broken body in the yellow glare of the headlights.

Shouts and screams. A man's voice cursing. The sound of a car door slamming.

Blood rushes into my ears. Everything swims in front of me. Bile kicks up inside my mouth, and I puke, right there in the street.

The last thing I remember seeing as I sink into blissful darkness is Johnny Treadway, running up to us, pushing past the crowd, dropping to his knees by his Diane.

He screams so loud in agony I think he might die, too, and take the rest of us with him.

24

A sheet of white fabric stretches out in front of my immediate vision. If I focus, I can see the small, neat stitches in it. There's a metal rail. A hint of disinfectant in the air that reminds me of the city pool in summertime. Bleach.

I'm in a bed somewhere I don't recognize. Whispered voices hover over me, punctuated by the sound of quick footsteps on tile.

I roll from my side onto my back, and my mother rises up into my line of sight like a sunrise. She reaches out to touch my cheek, the feel of her cool, gentle fingers as familiar as my own face. Even though it's been years since I've let her comfort me like this.

'Where am I?' I ask. The dry, thready sound of my own voice frightens me.

'The hospital,' she whispers. 'You fainted, and you hit your head. But you're going to be fine.'

I blink once. Twice. And then the entire memory of

how I ended up in the hospital floods over me like a sudden fever.

The boys. The car. The figure of a girl in the headlights.

'Diane?' I ask. Because I have to know.

The beat before she opens her mouth to answer is all I need to understand the truth.

'Evelyn,' my mother says at last, her own voice cracking.

I shake my head, wince at the pain, and close my eyes.

'I don't want to think about anything,' I manage, and it's like my body understands, because I drift off into an inky, dreamless sleep.

I'm not in the hospital for long. Everything happens *to* me there. I don't have to think or make decisions. I open my mouth for the thermometer and for the watery hospital applesauce and to say no or yes to easy questions from the doctors. 'Are you feeling any new pain in your head?' 'No.' 'Can you sleep?' 'Yes.'

All of it's easy, and I find myself thinking I wouldn't mind staying here forever, not having to think or do. When they roll me out in a wheelchair two days later, the Houston sun makes me squint, and suddenly everything feels real again.

Painfully, awfully real.

Back home Mama and Grandma have fresh sheets on my bed, and someone – probably Grandma – has cleaned and organized my bedroom until I can barely recognize it. Everything is all straight lines and neat, tidy stacks. My Raggedy Ann doll has been moved to my bed, just like back when I was a little girl. As soon as I get home from the hospital, I change into a white cotton nightgown and crawl under the covers, and I bury my nose in Ann's head, breathing in the musty red yarn. My heart swells with gratitude toward Grandma even as my brain has to adjust to the walls of my bedroom. Cheryl's side is as lonely and empty as ever, and I wonder briefly what she knows, but I can't bring myself to ask about that yet.

I keep waking up from sleep thinking I'm back in the abandoned house on Monroe, until my foggy, groggy brain catches up.

Once I call out for Diane until Mama comes in to check on me, and as my mind clears, I realize where I am. I don't cry, though. I just stop calling out and stare out my bedroom window at our tiny backyard.

I don't want to think about Diane.

I don't want to think about anything.

Mama and Grandma hover around me, bringing me trays of food and encouraging me to eat. I try, but everything is absent of taste. I force myself to take exactly three bites of everything to keep them happy. They don't ask me about anything that's happened to me. They don't bring up the awful events of my last night in the house before I ran off with Diane. Every question is about something superficial. Is it too cold? Is it too hot? Am I hungry? Am I sleepy? Every comment is about something unimportant. *It's going to rain today. The Carters got a new Chevrolet. I can't remember where I put my coat.*

Even though the doctors at the hospital said I could get back to 'a normal routine', Mama and Grandma almost seem happy to have me tucked away in bed, easy to find and keep track of. Several days pass and I don't go to school, I don't do chores, I don't do anything. And I like it fine, too. It's almost like the hospital. I can just be a body, numb and quiet. The most I venture anywhere is out to the den, where I watch television nonstop, not laughing at anything funny and not crying at anything sad. Just watching. From *Get the Message* to *Search for Tomorrow* to *The Match Game*, I let the buzzy, fuzzy images wash over me. White noise. Once I stay up so late Mama finds me watching the test pattern, staring at it like it's any other television program.

Cheryl calls me late on the first Sunday evening after that awful night. Everything that's happened in Houston has been splashed all over the state newspapers, I'm sure, even though I've avoided those. Mama must have filled her in on everything, too.

'Baby sister, how are you?' she asks. She sounds so far away, like her worried voice is fighting to get to me through the phone lines.

'I'm all right.'

'I miss you so much,' she says. 'I didn't know you were going through all this.'

'I miss you, too,' I say. I'm so exhausted it hurts to even say these words. I want to ask Cheryl how she's doing, how things are with Dennis. But I can't manage it. Besides, we can't stay on the telephone for very long.

Juanita and Connie and Sunny try to visit that same day. I know because Mama tiptoes into my room to tell me they're at the front door.

'Just tell them not now,' I say, and the flat, blank sound of my voice scares me even more than my thin, sickly voice at the hospital.

Mama opens her mouth like she's going to protest, but then she shuts it and gives me sad eyes before turning around and closing my bedroom door behind her.

A little over a week after I get home from the hospital, two men appear on our front stoop while Mama is at work. Grandma has left the front door open to let in a breeze, and I spy them through the screen door from my spot on the couch.

'Grandma!' I holler, not taking my eyes off these two figures looming in my doorway. My heart starts to race. It's a strange sensation, almost like I'm remembering that I'm still really alive.

They tell Grandma they're police officers, but they're wearing suits. They could be twenty or fifty, I'm not sure. I just know they're cops, and they want to ask me questions.

The way they say all this, I know I can't send them away like I sent away my friends.

Grandma brings coffee out and they arrange themselves awkwardly on our secondhand furniture. I notice the one losing his hair scanning the walls, taking in everything, probably quietly judging our house and us.

'So what do you need to ask my granddaughter?' Grandma says primly. 'She's been unwell, and I don't think you need to be taking up that much time, if you don't mind my saying so.' I shoot Grandma a look of thanks, and she manages a very tight smile. I think she's nervous, too.

'We just wanted to ask Evelyn about the situation involving Diane Farris,' says one of the officers. The one who isn't losing his hair. His eyes are a little warmer, and the way he smiles at me makes me think maybe he has kids at home. 'We're just wrapping up a few things.'

'All right,' Grandma says, 'but please try to keep it brief.' She gazes over the officers' faces as she sits down, her eyes filled with concern.

The officers start slow, asking me about my head injury and how I'm feeling and how long I was in the hospital. They have little notepads and stubby pencils in their hands, but they're not taking any notes. I have a feeling these questions are only being asked to get me used to answering.

'Can you tell us how you came to know Diane Farris?' the balding cop says at last, and he leans forward in his chair, like he's actually interested in what I have to say.

My throat tightens and my heartbeat picks up again.

'We met at Winkler's,' I say. Connie always says never give the cops more than they ask for.

'When?'

'A while back.'

'The night of October tenth?' the not-as-nice cop presses. 'The night she killed Preston Fowler?'

I look down at my hands folded in my lap. I want to disappear.

'Look, Evelyn,' says the smiling cop. 'We already know what happened. We have the written confession with your writing on it, too. We're just trying to fill in the details before we officially close the case.'

Maybe they're pulling a good cop, bad cop routine with me like they do in the movies, but anyway, what does it matter? There's no one left to protect. Diane is gone.

Something inside me cracks, and I feel warm tears start to pool in my eyes, but I blink them back. I remember how easily Diane cried. How she wasn't ever afraid to let her tears out. I admired that so much, but I don't want to cry in front of these cops.

'You're upsetting my granddaughter,' Grandma says, pulling a handkerchief from her pocket and handing it to me. I take it, grateful for her kindness. Surprised, I guess, that she would defend me so strongly. I manage to fight the tears back completely, and a stillness comes over me. Then I remember what the papers said when Diane and I were hiding out. Only that the police wanted to question us. Grandma doesn't know what happened with Preston and me.

'Ma'am, we won't be much longer,' the nice cop says, smiling politely. Then he turns to me. 'Evelyn, in her written confession and in what she shared with Betty Howell, Diane claimed to have killed Preston Fowler because he was hurting another girl, and . . . in an additional note in this confession, you suggested that . . .' At this the cop pauses, thinks, glances at my grandmother. I can tell he's choosing his words.

Grandma gasps.

'Evelyn!' she says.

She's figured it out even before the cop finishes his sentence.

I take a shaky breath and summon all my courage – all the courage Diane promised me I had – and look at the cop directly.

'Preston Fowler tried to attack me that night at Winkler's,' I say, my voice beginning to shake but steady enough. 'Behind the bathroom. He grabbed me and he wouldn't let me go. I fought back, and he just laughed. He told me all he needed was a minute. Those were his exact words, and I'll never forget them. I've never been so scared. Not ever! We struggled, and I passed out, and when I woke up, Diane Farris was there, holding a switchblade. She told me she killed Preston, but she didn't mean to. Honest, she didn't! She was just trying to scare him off to protect me. And she didn't even know me! Not really. I was just a stranger to her, a girl in her English class. And she risked everything to help me.'

Tears are threatening again, but I manage to fight them off and instead point at the nicer cop's notepad in his hands and say, 'So why don't you write *that* down? *That's* what you need to put in your damn notepad. That's what you need to put down to fill in your damn details! I was nobody to Diane, just a girl from the wrong side of town. She could have walked away. But she helped me because she was a good person. A great person. She was my best friend, and I miss her so much!'

And at last I let the tears fall, let them drain from my eyes and slide down my cheeks. Then I bolt up so fast I knock one of the officers' cups of coffee from the table in front of us, and I hear it clatter and break into pieces as I race to my bedroom and slam the door behind me. Collapsing into bed, I sob and sob until I can't cry anymore. I let myself feel – really feel – what's happened to me. To Diane. I sob until everything in my body aches, I sob through my grandmother's knock on the door and her hands rubbing my back and her voice begging me to talk, but I can't. I just sob until I fall asleep.

When I wake up, the sun has fallen but my watch says it's only just past dinnertime. I sit up in bed, groggy and confused. Then the afternoon with the cops comes flooding back. I long for the same numb feeling I had in the hospital. The same numb feeling I've had sitting on our couch watching *As the World Turns* and *Password* and every other mindless soap opera and game show I can find. But every nerve ending is exposed now. My guts are turned inside out.

I feel terrible.

There's a rap at the door.

'Evelyn?'

My mother.

For a moment I consider pretending to be asleep. It would be so easy to keep my mouth closed. My eyes squeezed tight.

'Evelyn, baby. Ladybug. Please don't shut me out.'

But then I give in. Something deep inside tells me it's time.

'Come in.'

Mama sits at the foot of my bed, still dressed in her uniform from the Shamrock. She rubs my feet under the covers and I let her. She gives me a sad look and I match it.

'Grandma called me at work,' she says.

I nod. She doesn't need to say it.

'Sweetheart, why didn't you tell me?' Her voice cracks.

I look down at my hands in my lap.

'I don't know,' I whisper, my heart breaking, splitting in two just like Mama's voice. I find myself crossing my fingers briefly – for what? Luck? Courage? And then I take a deep breath and hear myself say, 'I just . . . didn't. I thought you'd be disappointed in me. Because you want me to get married and be a good girl, and good girls don't get themselves into fixes like I did at Winkler's.'

I briefly hold my breath, ready for any response. But grateful, too, that the words have finally been spoken out loud.

My mother's face falls, and she crawls up close to me, hugs me to her, and I cry into her shoulder for a little while. She cries into mine, too, but mostly she just pets my hair like she did when Cheryl and I were little and would snuggle up with her after her long shifts. I feel my jaw unclench, just a little. I sense my shoulders sinking in relief.

Finally we pull apart and she looks into my eyes, searching them for something. She takes my hands in hers and squeezes them, tight as she can. I don't even mind that it hurts a little.

'Evelyn, what that boy tried to do . . .' At this her words drop off into a whisper. She closes her eyes and takes a breath, then goes on. 'It wasn't your fault. None of it. I hope you know that.'

The girls never said this to me. Of course I knew that's how they felt, too, and Juanita tried to get me to talk about it. But I guess they figured everything was implied. Hearing my mother say it, though? Listening to her voice say those sentences out loud? Something about it feels like the heaviest weight I didn't know I was carrying has slipped off my shoulders.

'I know,' I say. 'I know.'

She pets my hand and pets my hair, like she's afraid if she stops petting me, I'll disappear again. 'Oh, Evelyn, I'm so sorry all that's happened. To you . . . to . . . us.'

I picture my mom on the floor the night I pushed her.

'I'm the one who should be sorry, Mama,' I manage. 'That night I ran away, I . . . didn't mean it. I honestly didn't! I've felt awful about it. I was just so mixed up . . . and . . . scared.'

My mother nods, looks down. 'I'm sorry I slapped you, Evelyn. Never in a million years . . . You know, Grandpa – I know you don't remember him – he used to take a switch to me whenever I acted up. Or if he even thought I was gonna act up. And I always swore I wouldn't hit my own kids if I should ever be lucky enough to have any.'

We sit in silence for a little while. Mama pulls away and opens my bedroom window at the foot of my bed, and a gust of cool evening air draws in. She sits back down next to me. Studies me.

'Evelyn, I want things to be better between us,' she says.

I take Raggedy Ann and pull her into my lap, tug at her yarn hair.

'When you were little, you told me everything,' she continues. 'Lord, sometimes you prattled on so long I wished you'd stop so I could think. Five hundred little details about everything that happened in the cafeteria or in the book you were reading or something some little girl said to you in the schoolyard. And then Cheryl got married and moved out and it was like I couldn't get you to say the alphabet. Why did you stop telling me things?'

I sigh, lean back against the wall behind me. Clutch Ann to my face.

'I don't know the answer,' I mumble. 'I don't know. I just . . .' I draw Ann down to my lap and hug her to me.

'After everything happened with Cheryl, I started thinking . . .' I begin, then stop. Think. Take a breath. Then I let the words spill out. 'I know you've always told us that what matters most is settling down with some boy who'll keep us safe. Some steady guy. Not like our father. I want . . . my life to be good, but isn't there a way for me to have a good life that doesn't just mean finding the right boy? I'm not saying I don't ever want to get married. But what I'm saying is . . . I think I want to be able to figure out what I want. In my own way.'

Mama takes this in, and I can tell she's really listening. But she doesn't say anything. So I keep going, unable to stop, surprising me maybe as much as her.

'I want . . . things to matter. I want to *feel* things. Have adventures. *Live*. I don't want Cheryl's life. I love her, but I don't. It's not that I don't ever want to meet someone or become someone's wife, but I am saying I don't want it like that. It seems if you want to really love and feel and breathe in this neighborhood . . .' At this I stop, thinking of Diane. 'No, it seems like if you want to really love and feel and breathe in this *city*, you're labeled as trash. Or bad. Especially if you're a girl.'

My mother runs a hand through her hair, pushes back at the streaks of gray near her temples.

'Evelyn, I don't know what the heck to say in response to all that!' she says, exhaling. But she says it with a smile on her face and a sound of surrender in her voice. She lets herself laugh, there on the foot of my bed. I can't help it. I smile, too.

'I don't think I expect you to have all the answers,' I say. 'But . . . you *did* ask what was on my mind.' I shrug, all guilty-as-charged. But I manage another grin and my mother smiles back.

Neither one of us says anything for a little while. Another gust of breeze blows through my open window.

'I don't think I have all the answers,' she says. 'I don't. I know I don't. But I'm asking you, please don't shut me out. Please don't forget that I was young, too, once. And not so long ago, really. I just want what's best for you, Ladybug. But maybe I'm going to have to learn what that is.'

'I won't shut you out, Mama,' I say, then drop my voice to a whisper. 'I promise I won't.'

She pats my leg and takes a deep breath, then scoots up next to me.

'Let's just sit here for a bit,' my mother says. 'We don't have to talk or anything. Just sit. Let Grandma think we're still hashing it out. What do you say?' She rolls her head in my direction to look at me, smiles a tired smile.

I nod. 'That sounds fine by me.'

So my mother and I sit there enjoying each other's quiet company, the sounds of nighttime and outdoors floating in through my bedroom window. She yawns and doesn't even cover her mouth. Her stockinged feet rest on top of my well-worn bedspread, and I find myself staring at them, thinking about how those feet must have walked me up and down the hallways of this house a million times when I was just a tiny, crying baby, even when they were bone-tired.

The day after my mother and I make our peace, on a bright and sunny Sunday, I curl up at what's become my usual spot on the couch to watch television. Suddenly there's a knock on our front door, loud enough to be heard over the clatter and splash of Grandma doing the dishes. Mama crosses the living room to answer it, and I find myself hoping it's the girls again, and that they'll try to talk me into leaving the house. I think I might be ready to talk to them, but I wouldn't blame them if they don't ever come back after how I turned them away last time.

But standing on our sagging porch in a cheerful yellow dress the color of freshly whipped butter, a bright smile on her face, is my English teacher, Miss Odeen.

I'm in my pajamas still, and I freeze in shock until at last I think to grab the quilt at the foot of the couch and throw it over myself. I can't speak.

'Hello,' says Miss Odeen, focusing on Mama. 'I'm so sorry

to barge in like this, but I'm Beverly Odeen, Evie — Evelyn's — English teacher over at Eastside? We've missed her so much at school, and I wanted to say hello and see how she's feeling.' She pauses at the end of this little speech and smiles broadly, and my first thought is how strange it is to hear Miss Odeen refer to herself by her first name. Mama runs a hand through her hair in a way that tells me she's trying to put on her company face. Miss Odeen couldn't be much older than Cheryl, but there's something so polished about her, so put together, that I can understand Mama's reaction.

'Miss Odeen, how nice to meet you. I'm Evelyn's mother, Marjorie Barnes,' she says. 'Please do come in.'

'And please call me Beverly,' says Miss Odeen, stepping inside. She glances toward me on the couch. 'Evie, it's so nice to see you.'

I manage a smile and a tiny wave just as Grandma chooses that very moment to come out of the kitchen, dish towel in hand.

'Marjorie, who is it?' she says, then notices Miss Odeen and stops short. 'Oh, hello.'

'This is Beverly Odeen, Mama,' she says. 'Evelyn's English teacher. She just wanted to stop by and check on her.'

'How nice,' Grandma says, clearly taking in all the hallmarks of Miss Odeen's refinement in one quick once-over. The shiny hair, the perfectly applied pink lipstick — enough, but not too much. The elegant posture, like maybe Miss

Odeen took dance classes once. Grandma offers her a cup of coffee and a spot on the recliner, which she accepts carefully, crossing her legs at the ankles. At this moment Mama must realize my situation and takes pity on me.

'Evelyn, why don't you run to your room and get dressed,' she says before turning to Miss Odeen. 'I'm so sorry she's still in her pajamas. She's been through so much, you know. So we've been letting her relax a bit.'

'Of course,' says Miss Odeen, like it's nothing at all.

''Scuse me,' I mumble as I race toward the bedroom, still clutching the quilt for cover. I can feel the heat radiating from my cheeks.

As quickly as I can, I make myself presentable – clean dress, brushed teeth, washed face – before I venture back out, my heart hammering. What on earth am I going to say to my English teacher on a Sunday in my living room, with Mama and Grandma hovering in the kitchen trying to tease out every word we say?

Maybe Miss Odeen can read my mind because when I return, bashful and nervous, she suggests the two of us go sit on the porch.

'It's lovely out there,' she says, standing, her coffee cup clutched in her manicured hand.

'All right,' I say, and I open the front door.

I've been shuffling between my bed and the couch for enough time that to go outside feels strange, and the sun is pretty blinding. We settle into the rusting white metal chairs that stare out at the street, and I can't help but glance toward Juanita's house, hoping she isn't outside to see and wonder about this strange situation. But there's no one.

'Evie, we've missed you in class,' says Miss Odeen before taking a ladylike sip of coffee. 'And I've been worried about you.'

I squirm a little in my seat.

'I'm fine, I guess,' I say.

Miss Odeen nods like I've just said something profound, then gazes off at the house across the street. 'You know, when I was young, I got into some trouble, too.'

I snort. I can't help it. I snort in front of my English teacher.

'You?' I ask. 'I can't picture it.'

Miss Odeen grins and shrugs. 'I know it's hard to believe, but I wasn't always a grown-up, Evie.'

I can't help it. I ask her how old she is.

'I'm twenty-four,' she answers, not pausing. 'I'll be twenty-five in December.'

'Oh,' I say. 'I'm fifteen, but you knew that.'

Miss Odeen smiles broadly.

'I did,' she says. 'And like you, I was also fifteen once. And while I won't go into details, I had a rough go of it for a bit. Quite rough, actually.'

My mind fills in the possibilities. Did Miss Odeen run away? Shove her mother in the hallway of her home?

Lose a dear friend in the glare of headlights?

That last thought hits, and my body numbs for a moment. The loss of Diane is humming in the back of my mind at all times, like a terrible song that's skipping, but every so often the heaviness of her absence really hits me, and I can barely breathe.

'Evie, are you all right?'

I shake my head, feel hot tears coming on. I remember how Diane never apologized for crying, and I don't hide my tears from Miss Odeen.

'Here, Evie,' she says, pulling an embroidered handkerchief from her pocket. 'Take this. You can keep it.'

I reach for the folded piece of cloth, grateful, and dab at my eyes.

'I'm just thinking of Diane,' I say. 'I just . . . I miss her so much, Miss Odeen. It honestly hurts.'

Miss Odeen looks at me, and I think I see her eyes gloss over, too. She swallows once before speaking. 'I know, Evie. I miss her as well.' When she says this, her voice cracks.

'It's almost . . . I mean, I want it to get easier because it hurts so much, but I also worry that if it gets easier, it means I'm forgetting her.' Now that I've said it out loud, the fear feels even more raw. But something about naming it feels right, too.

Miss Odeen nods, then gazes up, like she's collecting her thoughts. At last she says, 'I can promise you that it will get easier, and I can promise you that even when it does, you'll never forget Diane.'

I wrap my fingers around Miss Odeen's handkerchief – it's got strawberries embroidered on the border; it's really too nice to give away – and I try to trust her words. I want them to be true. I need them to be.

After a little while of sitting in a comfortable silence, Miss Odeen asks me when I might be ready to come back to school.

'Yours is the only class that I miss,' I admit. 'I like the people you've taught us about. Like Jerrie Mock and Fannie Lou Hamer.'

'That's flattering, Evie. I hope you're not my only student who feels that way,' she says, smiling, 'but I'd love it if you eventually came back for all your classes, not just mine.'

I shrug. 'I don't know, Miss Odeen. School is just . . . I don't know if it's for me.'

'I understand you feel that way,' she says. 'But school does give you options, Evie.'

I pick at a rusty part of my chair. 'What do you mean?'

'Well, college, perhaps,' she says. 'I think you'd really enjoy it. You may change your mind about that, of course. But I do know having a high school diploma gives you choices.'

'My mother thinks it's the best choice for a young girl to get married and settle down with a nice guy,' I say, before stopping to think back on our conversation and wondering what my mother really thinks now. 'I mean, that's what she's always told me I should do. That's what my sister did.'

Miss Odeen smiles, switches the cross of her legs at the ankles, and pauses. 'There's nothing wrong with getting married,' she says. 'I think I'd like it. One day.'

I wonder if Miss Odeen has a boyfriend, but of course, I'd never ask. I also wonder if Grandma and Mama are peering through the windows behind us, spying. I'm tempted to turn and look, but I don't.

A car rumbles past, and a cardinal flies down, perches on the sidewalk, and pecks at something frantically before flying away. Miss Odeen takes a deep breath, like she has all the time in the world to sit with me. Maybe she does.

'I really can't believe you ever got in trouble when you were younger, Miss Odeen,' I say. 'I truly can't. You're always so . . . put together.' I blush.

Miss Odeen laughs a high, tinkly laugh. 'Tell that to my mother,' she responds, but she doesn't elaborate. Then she says, 'Evie, listen, do you have a study hall?'

'Yes, during sixth period,' I say. Students are supposed to go to the library or the auditorium during that time and, well, study, I suppose. I usually spend it smoking with the girls behind the gymnasium or putting my head down and taking a nap at one of the big library tables.

'Excellent,' says Miss Odeen. 'I don't have a class at that time. I was wondering if I could talk you into being a sort of teaching assistant for me. You know, helping me organize my papers, grade vocabulary quizzes, that sort of thing.'

It's not uncommon for teachers to ask upperclassmen to do this, to be a teacher's aide. But I don't know anyone in my grade who does it, and certainly not anyone in my crowd. I picture sitting in Miss Odeen's bright and organized classroom, stacking papers, sharpening pencils, maybe scrubbing her desks clean. I imagine the two of us talking to each other while we work. I also imagine the other girls and what they might say about this offer, but something tells me they'll understand. Or maybe I just don't mind too much how they'll react.

'I'll think about it,' I say. 'I'll let you know for sure when I'm back at school.'

'Wonderful,' she says. 'I hope that will be soon.'

'It will be,' I say, and I know as I say it that it's true.

'Well,' she says, standing and handing me the coffee cup, 'I should be heading home. Will you please tell your mother and grandmother it was lovely to meet them both?'

'Sure,' I say, taking the cup in hand. There's a bright pink kiss stamped on the side of the white cup. 'Your lipstick is such a pretty color.'

'Thank you,' says Miss Odeen. 'It's Revlon's Cherries in the Snow. It's actually something of a ridiculous name if you think about it too much, especially when you live in Houston, where there's rarely any snow.' She peers at me. 'You don't have your eye makeup on like you normally do.'

'I've been too tired to bother, I guess,' I say. 'My friend

Juanita next door was the one who taught me how to do it.' I feel a prick of guilt that I've pushed my friends away lately, and I glance over at the Barajas house again for a moment, wondering when I'll see Juanita and the others, and how that will ever happen.

'Well, I like your makeup,' she says, heading down the porch steps. 'I don't think I could pull it off, but you can. It's very daring!' I grin, wondering what Grandma might think of Miss Odeen's opinion.

'Miss Odeen,' I say as she reaches the sidewalk. She turns to look at me, smiling softly. 'Thanks so much for coming to visit me.'

'Of course, Evie,' she says. 'Please take care of yourself, and please don't forget about sixth period, all right?'

'I won't forget.'

Later that day while I'm watching television, Juanita and Connie and Sunny appear on my front porch, peering in through the screen door.

'Your mother said you're ready for us,' yells Connie through the screen. 'So we're here.'

Just then, Grandma comes in from the kitchen, and you can tell she's holding her tongue.

'Would you like your friends to come inside and sit?' she asks.

Confused, I stare at my grandmother, then back out onto the porch. A small smile appears on my face, and on hers, too.

'Your mother went next door while you were napping and before she left to run some errands,' she says. 'She told Juanita you wanted to see your friends.'

My smile grows wider, and a warm feeling of happiness floods over me.

'Thanks, Grandma,' I say, getting up off the couch. 'I'll just go outside.'

As I step onto the porch, I suddenly feel shy. 'Hey,' I say. Even though it's only been just over a week, I've gotten used to being alone and inside my own head. I feel a pang remembering the last time my friends came for me and I turned them away. Still, looking at Connie's face and Sunny's face and Juanita's face, my heart swells.

If they're upset about last time, they don't show it. They've waited for me until I was ready.

'Hey, kid,' says Connie, and she punches me gently on the shoulder, smiling wide enough to reveal her cracked incisor. 'We thought maybe you were never going to leave the house again.'

'I thought so, too, for a little bit,' I say, rubbing my shoulder with a small laugh.

'You wanna go sit on my back steps?' asks Juanita. 'Out of sight of old grandma?' She winks.

'Yeah, sounds good,' I say, sensing a lightness in my feet as we start walking. 'I'm crazy for a cigarette, now that I think about it.'

'I'm not sure you should be smoking,' says Sunny with a serious look on her face. 'You were in the hospital.'

'Okay, Mom,' says Connie, sassing Sunny like she does. But then she pauses and studies me, her eyes suddenly clouded with worry. 'I don't know, though. Maybe you

305

shouldn't have one, Evie. Maybe Sunny's right.'

Sunny's eyes go wide at this. 'Does anyone have a pencil? I need to write this date down. The day Connie said I was right. It won't happen again until we're at *least* twenty-five.'

Everyone cuts up and starts laughing as we head toward Juanita's back steps, scoot and sit close to one another, and light up our smokes.

After a while I start. I get the sense the girls are waiting for me to speak anyway. I exhale long and hard and close my eyes for a moment.

'I can't believe she's gone,' I say. 'I mean, gone for good. It doesn't feel real.'

Sunny nods, her pretty blue eyes so sad. Juanita leans over and rests her head on my shoulder. Connie doesn't bounce or move. She just sighs real deep and says, 'I know. I can't believe it, either.'

I'm scared to know the answer, but I ask how Johnny's doing and what else has been happening in the neighborhood.

'Johnny can barely get out of bed he's so damn depressed,' says Connie. 'Not that I blame him.' She pauses and takes a drag of her cigarette. 'It's the first time in my life I ever saw my brother cry, if you want to know the truth.'

I remember that afternoon in the Treadway house after he learned about the baby and read Diane's letter, and I ache for him and the pain he's in. I imagine his eyes filling with tears, and I hope he lets them fall sometimes.

'Connie,' I say, 'I know Johnny has Diane's letter. The one where she told him about the baby? You know about that, right?'

'Yes,' Connie says. 'He let me read it, too. He sleeps with it under his pillow.'

'Gosh, how romantic,' Sunny whispers. 'And how sad.'

'Yeah, it is,' I say, my throat aching with sadness as I speak. 'Listen, I don't know if it will help him to hear this, but he should know . . . those last few hours when Diane was waiting for him . . . she was so excited. She went outside that night because she wanted their first kiss after everything to be under the moon and not inside that creepy house.'

Connie lights another cigarette. 'I'm gonna tell him,' she says, a rare softness in her voice. 'I bet it makes him feel better, don't you think? Or would it make him feel worse? I'm not sure.'

At that we all look at each other, mulling over her questions in our heads.

'I think you should tell him,' says Juanita, her voice strong and clear. 'It will hurt, but in the end, I think he'll be glad to know it.' Sunny nods in agreement.

'I wish the fuzz had at least given him back the letter he wrote her,' Connie adds. 'Diane had it on her when she died. I wonder what happened to it.'

'I wonder what it said,' I respond, trying to imagine what Johnny might have scribbled down in those final moments, unable to know that it would be his last chance to communicate with the girl he loved.

'I don't think he'll ever tell me,' Connie answers. 'Anyway, he shouldn't. It was just for her.'

I think — not for the last time, I'm sure — of the little baby out in the world who's a part of Johnny and a part of Diane. I make a silent wish that maybe one day, somehow, Johnny will get to look into that baby's face and see Diane in it.

'It's so good she got to read that letter,' I say. 'It made her eyes light up when she did.'

'I'll tell Johnny that, too,' Connie says, and our gazes meet for a good long while.

'What about Ray and all those boys?' I ask at last. 'What happened that night after I passed out?' I'm ready to know. All these days that I've spent avoiding the newspaper and the television news broadcasts, and Grandma and Mama have been shielding me from them, but now I'm curious.

The girls trade glances. Finally, Juanita speaks. 'Well, of course we weren't there to see it, but we found out later through the grapevine that Johnny started beating the tar out of all of them until the cops came.'

'As he should have,' mutters Connie.

'And the car that . . .' I can't bring myself to say the words.

'The driver didn't get charged,' Sunny says. 'There's no way he could've stopped in time. It was the boys' fault, but nothing's happening to them because I don't know if they can

308

really prove it. It all got written off as some wild accident.'

'The cops just want to close the whole deal,' I say. 'Now they can say they solved what happened at Winkler's without a lot of fuss.' I tell the girls about the two detectives who came to my house. 'It's all over now in their minds, I guess.' The police may consider this case closed, but I know what's happened the past few weeks has changed me, which means it's far from really over. At least the fuzz never found a way to try and pin what happened to Preston on me or anyone else from the neighborhood.

'I never want to look at Ray Swanson's rotten face again,' says Sunny. 'He can drop dead as far as I'm concerned.'

We smoke for a while until Juanita breaks the silence. 'I wonder . . . if Diane's parents had wanted to do something about it, don't you think they could have? I mean, they're from River Oaks. They know important people. Don't you think they could have gone after Ray and Butch and all those boys if they'd really wanted to?'

I remember my nighttime chats with Diane in the abandoned house, the candle illuminating her face as she talked about being nothing but a disaster and a disappointment to her folks. About being a doll in a dollhouse.

'It's hard to imagine,' I say, 'but maybe they're glad she's out of sight for good now. They don't have to ship her off to an aunt's house or some awful place up in Dallas to hide her from their rich friends.'

Juanita and Sunny nod, but Connie just says, 'It's not that hard to imagine, really.' And after that nobody says anything for a while.

'Evie?' I hear my grandmother's voice from the front of our house. 'Evie, are you hungry for dinner? Your mother will be home soon.'

'In a minute, Grandma!' I shout. Then I look at my girls. My friends. My best friends. One of us is missing, but the rest of us are here. And I'm never going to let them go.

Almost like she's reading my mind, Connie speaks up. 'I want to say – in case there was any question – that Diane was one of us.' She stubs her cigarette out in the dirt. 'I'll never forget her. I swear to God I never will.'

'Same,' says Sunny.

'Same,' says Juanita.

'I swear it, too,' I say, and I stay outside with my friends a little bit longer, leaning into them, not even needing to talk. Not even wanting to. I stay so long that Grandma has to come outside and holler for me twice.

EPILOGUE

Glenwood cemetery is beautiful and green, even in mid-December, covered in oaks and pines and nestled right up against Buffalo Bayou. It's where the rich people of Houston are laid to rest. My best friend Diane Farris didn't have a public funeral. I only found out she was buried at Glenwood in a small family ceremony because that's what it said in the paper. It was Mama who discovered this information, not long after our heart-to-heart. She came and sat on my bed, holding the folded *Houston Post* in her hands as she told me. And then she let me cry into her arms for a long time until her blouse was damp with my tears.

'I'm so sorry, Ladybug,' my mother kept saying, pushing my hair back with her tender hands, like she was trying to brush the pain away. All I could think about was how Diane had never known a mother like mine, and how unfair that was.

I still cry about Diane at least a few nights a week, and sometimes at school, too, in front of Miss Odeen, who always

311

has fresh tissues on her desk when I need them and time to listen to me when I feel like talking. It's almost like now that I let myself cry, it's a faucet I can't turn off. Since Diane died two months ago, the time in between crying spells is growing longer, but Miss Odeen has been right. Just because it's getting a little easier, it doesn't mean that I'm forgetting Diane. Forgetting Diane would be like forgetting my own name. Impossible.

Speaking of Miss Odeen, she still hasn't told me what she did when she was younger. Maybe one day she will. She has plenty of opportunities to tell me now that I'm helping her out in her classroom. Connie and the other girls joke around that I'm turning into a teacher's pet, but they don't give me too hard a time. After all, they're still my best friends, even if I don't cut class as often as I used to.

It helps to have Cheryl home. About a month after Diane died, she surprised us by showing up at our front door with a stuffed suitcase and her dark brown hair cut shorter than I'd ever seen it. I reached out with a squeal and hugged her right there on our porch.

'I told Dennis I need some time to think,' she said to us when at last I let her out of my arms. Mama opened her mouth, glanced at me, and then shut it. After a moment she answered, 'You can have all the time you need.'

Now Cheryl spends her days working the cash register at Samperi's and thinking about taking classes at the

University of Houston. She's also started reading a new book called *The Feminine Mystique* that looks boring to me, but I guess she finds it interesting. She's always underlining parts of it with a pencil.

Her first night back home, having Cheryl back in our shared bedroom made me the happiest I'd been since I lost Diane. When it was time to go to sleep, she crawled under the covers with me.

'I'm so glad to be here,' she said as she got under the blankets. I didn't even care that her feet were ice cold.

'I'm so glad you're back,' I answered, snuggling closer. She still smelled of Noxzema like she always did at bedtime, and this comforted me so much.

'Do you want to know something shocking?' she asked.

Of course, I told her yes.

'Grandma was the one who sent me the money for the bus ticket home,' Cheryl admitted, her whispers tickling my ear. 'She sent it in the mail with a note that said just in case. But don't tell Mama, all right?'

My eyebrows popped in surprise, but then I smiled, pleased with this development.

'I honestly think maybe Mama would understand,' I told her.

'Things have changed around here, huh,' Cheryl said. It was a comment more than a question.

'They sure have,' I said, and we ended up staying awake

until two in the morning talking about all of it, our voices weaving together like they'd missed each other, too.

The day I finally decide I'm ready to visit Diane's grave, I take the city bus to Washington Avenue. I tell my mother I'm going, but I don't tell any of the girls. Maybe one day they'll want to come out here with me. In fact, I know they will. Connie especially.

But this time is just for me.

There's a small caretaker's cottage planted among the enormous trees and the angel statues and the winding paths in between large oaks and carefully maintained hedges. I go inside, and when I tell the kindly-looking older caretaker I'm looking for Diane Farris's grave, he tilts his head and looks at me through rheumy eyes, then offers me a soft, sad smile. We head outside and he points me in the right direction. I walk, aware of my own breathing, each exhale painting a cloud in the air ahead of me. Wanting to never make it to my destination but at the same time knowing I must get there eventually.

And suddenly there it is. Diane's grave.

The headstone is modest and plain, but I think Diane would like it that way. *Would have liked* it that way. I wince at the revision of the sentence in my head. Then I study the words carved into the white marble laced with gray.

Diane Amelia Farris
1948–1964
Beloved Daughter

I feel my fists clenching, my nails digging into my palms. *Beloved daughter*. How dare Diane's parents put such a lie on this stone that will be here for as long as the earth turns? They kept their lies up until the very end, I guess.

Beloved friend! I think to myself. That's what it should say. That's the truth. *Beloved friend.*

The air is cool and fresh around me, but suddenly I'm warm and light-headed. I start to sink to my knees, then collapse in front of the headstone into dirt covered in patches of new grass. I feel sobs begin to build from my gut, from the deepest possible place, and soon they come heaving out of my throat, unstoppable. Full-throated cries, harder tears than I've ever shed.

Diane, the girl who saved my life. Diane, the girl whose baby will never know her. Diane, the girl who believed in love above anything else.

Diane, the girl I'll never see again, except for maybe, hopefully, in my dreams.

I don't know how long I cry, but my tears eventually lessen enough that I can hear the sound of footsteps behind me, twigs cracking. I jump and look around.

It's Betty Howell, dressed sharp in a pink sweater set

and gray skirt and carrying a bouquet of red geraniums. I exhale shakily.

'Evie,' Betty says, taking an uncertain step forward. 'I'm sorry, did I startle you?'

I wipe at my nose with the back of my sleeve, not even caring how it looks. Betty reaches into her pocketbook and hands me a white handkerchief edged in pink. I stand up and take it.

'No, it's all right,' I say, sniffling and dabbing at my face.

Betty leans over and rests her pocketbook and flowers in the dirt, then takes a few steps forward to stand next to me. She stares at Diane's headstone, her face expressionless.

'Damn it,' she says at last.

At this I glance over at her, and our eyes meet.

'I know,' I say. 'It's rotten what they put.'

'It's rotten, but I'm not surprised,' says Betty, glancing down at the gravestone again and frowning. 'And they didn't let anyone come to the service. They wanted to keep her hidden until the very end, I guess.'

We stand there in silence, and I think about Diane under our feet, her teenage body wrapped up in the cool, hard earth, stopped still forever at sixteen and Betty and me still breathing and moving and growing up. And I think about what Grandma says about Jesus and heaven and good souls going to their reward, and I want to believe that this is true for Diane, because she was a good soul. I want to believe that somewhere unknown, she is gliding among the clouds, golden light trailing from her fingertips. But I don't know how much I can believe this. How much I can take comfort in this. I don't have faith in the same way Grandma does, I guess. But I believe in my friendship with Diane, and that feels like its own kind of conviction.

I glance over at Betty. Silent tears start slipping down her face, so I offer her back her handkerchief, but she just shakes her head. She doesn't even try to stop the tears. Just lets them race down her apple cheeks, running into the corners of her mouth and dripping down her jawline.

'It's my fault,' she whispers. 'I shouldn't have told her to stay hidden like I did. It's my fault.'

'No,' I say, turning toward Betty, my voice urgent. 'No, Betty, you can't think like that. You can't.' I grab her hands, not caring if she might find it odd. But she must not because she grips mine back just as tight. 'Betty, I know how you feel,' I continue. 'Because I've felt that way, too. I still do sometimes. I've cursed myself so many times for not being more careful when I went to talk to Johnny that day. If that boy hadn't overheard. If he hadn't followed me back to the hideout. If I'd never gone to the bathroom that night at Winkler's. If, if, if. But, Betty, the truth is we were only trying to do the right thing. The right thing for Diane. You loved her. And so did I. And that will always be true. No matter what happened and no matter what will happen. It will *always* be true.'

Betty nods, still crying. I barely know this girl, I realize, but something makes me reach out and embrace her tight, until I can feel her wet face pressing into my neck. Something makes me want to tell her it's all right to cry and keep crying.

The something that makes me do it, the something that makes me hold her and reassure her, is Diane.

And Connie.

And Juanita.

And Sunny.

The something that makes me do it is friendship. Because Betty is a girl who wanted to help another girl out of a fix and was willing to do whatever she could to do it.

So that means Betty is my friend, too.

I hold Betty until she stops crying. Then she pulls back and lets go of my hands.

'You know,' she says, sniffling, her face flushed and her mascara smeared, 'I'm so sad but I'm angry, too. I'm angry because Diane wasn't allowed to just . . . be. I'm angry because Diane didn't deserve this, but she's not the only one.' Her red cheeks redden some more. 'Evie, I'm so tired of living in a world where a girl is seen as dirty because she loves someone. Because she gets in trouble. Because she doesn't look perfect or do every little thing *perfectly* or because she wants something different. Because she isn't always *good*.' At that last word she scowls and balls up her hand into a little fist, shaking it for emphasis.

I nod, and then something occurs to me.

'Bad girls never say die,' I tell Betty.

'What?' she asks, confused.

'It's something my friend Connie said once,' I explain. 'You met Connie that night you drove Diane and me back to our neighborhood. This world wants girls to be good all the time, whatever that means, but I don't care about that. I don't care if they call us bad, because bad girls never say die. They never give in. Let them call us bad. I don't care anymore.' Something in my voice surprises me. Whatever it is, I like the sound of it.

Betty looks at me, then nods in quiet agreement. She turns and fetches the red geraniums and rests them gently in front of Diane's grave, leaning them just so, so they cover up the lie of *Beloved Daughter*. Her fingers lightly trace the top of the gravestone, and then she pulls her hand back. We stand together quietly for a moment.

'I like what Connie said,' Betty says at last.

'I do, too,' I say.

'I wouldn't mind seeing Connie again one day.'

Betty and I catch eyes again and I smile at her.

'Something tells me she'd like that,' I tell her. 'I know she would.'

The December sun streams through the tops of the oak trees that surround us. A light breeze blows by, tickling the backs of our legs. I hear a skittering in a nearby bush. Maybe a lizard or a rabbit.

Diane is in our hearts, and Betty and I are here, alive and awake. We will stand at our friend's grave for a while longer yet, and when we leave, we'll leave together.

RESOURCES

For more information about Fannie Lou Hamer, Jerrie Mock, Betty Friedan, and other 'bad girls' from history, please visit the National Women's History Museum, a virtual museum. womenshistory.org

If reading this story brought up issues or concerns for you, below are some resources that may be helpful. They are available twenty-four hours a day, seven days a week, both by phone and online. You are not alone.

If you are in immediate danger, please call 9-9-9.

If you or someone you know has been sexually assaulted:
Rape Crisis England & Wales
0808 802 9999
https://rapecrisis.org.uk/
Rape Crisis Network Europe

Find help in your country at: rcne.com/contact/countries/
Or internationally at: rcne.com/links/sources-of-help-for-
survivors/

For domestic violence:
Refuge's National Domestic Abuse Helpline (England)
0808 2000 247
nationaldahelpline.org.uk

Hot Peach Pages (international directory)
hotpeachpages.net/index.html

Men's Advice Line
0808 8010327
mensadviceline.org.uk

For child abuse:
Childline
0800 1111
childline.org.uk

For free crisis support:
Text SHOUT to 85258
giveusashout.org

For teen pregnancy:
Family Lives
0808 800 2222
familylives.org.uk/advice/your-family/parenting/where-
can-young-parents-go-for-support/

ACKNOWLEDGEMENTS

This book would not be possible without a group of generous men and women who gave of their time as they recalled their teenage years growing up in Houston. Our conversations in their homes and over lunch were some of my favorite parts of writing this novel. Many thanks to Sheila Harrison, Kay Waddell Laycock, Anne Sloan, Anna Wirt, Juan Lira, Marilyn and George Frank, Linda and Bob Cook, Biff and Frances Reed, James H. Ford Jr and Doris E. Thomas Ford, and the wonderful ladies of Clayton Homes – Juanita Vallejo, Eloise Chavez Buenrosgro, Virginia Arce, and Martha Castro. Linda Cook deserves a special thanks for the many emails she answered! And Doris Sanders was kind enough to read an early draft and offer thoughts, too.

A million thanks to the wonderful academics and Houston history buffs who were so generous with their time in providing information on everything from school integration to maternity homes to music. I learned more about Houston and the early

1960s than I could ever fit into one novel, so I'll have to write another one someday. Thank you to Lisa Gray, Kirk Farris, Carlos Calbillo, James Schafer, PhD, Roger Wood, PhD, Kristen Contos Krueger, PhD, and Alex LaRotta, PhD.

Tyina L. Steptoe, PhD, was a tremendous resource, and her book *Houston Bound: Culture and Color in a Jim Crow City* is a must-read for any proud Houstonian.

Many thanks to the lovely librarians at the Houston Metropolitan Research Center, part of the Houston Public Library system. Many thanks to Debbie Harwell, PhD, for our wonderful talk and the many issues of the outstanding *Houston History* magazine, plus her detailed memories of the city bus in the early sixties!

To my dear friend Kate Jacobs, who was instrumental in helping birth this book. You always believe in me even when I don't. You don't know how much that means to me!

To my lovely editor, Kate Meltzer. Thank you for your patience and guidance as we helped shape this book together. *Especially* the patience.

To everyone at Macmillan who helps me get my words out into the world, especially Johanna Kirby Allen, Mary Van Akin, and the entire team at MCPG. You are still making my childhood dreams come true.

To my amazing agent, Kerry Sparks, who can walk and talk on the phone like no one I have ever met in my life – a million thanks. You and everyone else at Levine Greenberg Rostan always make me feel so cared for.

Thank you to those good folks who help me on the business side of things, including Nancy Tellez, Dave Roach, Andy Smith, and Belinda Rey.

Many thanks to Jeff Zentner and L. Scott Sherman for their help in answering several questions about the legal process and criminal justice system in Texas in the early 1960s.

To my friends at Blue Willow Bookshop, I adore you. To my book community, both here in Houston and all over the world, I appreciate you. We may write and read in solitude, but we survive publishing via frantic phone calls and texts. You know who you are.

To my first family in Virginia and California, thank you! To my second family at Bellaire High School, thank you! I am Cardinal Proud.

This book was written to the music of several artists past and present, but most regularly to the sounds of Elyse Weinberg (thank you, Mike Higgins) and Alvvays (thank you, Jeff Waller – and thanks also for the maps!).

Last but never least, a million thanks to the man who has been making me laugh for twenty years, the 'ruler of my heart', my husband, Kevin. I needed the laughs for this one especially, and you never failed to provide. Texas-sized love to you and Elliott forever.

Discover more by

JENNIFER MATHIEU

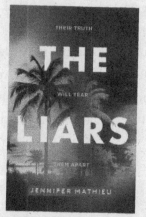